M000195610

Unleashing Echoes

UNLEASHING ECHOES (RECONSTRUCTIONIST 3)
Copyright © 2017 Meghan Ciana Doidge
Published by Old Man in the CrossWalk Productions 2017
Salt Spring Island, BC, Canada
www.oldmaninthecrosswalk.com

All rights reserved under International and Pan-American Copyright
Conventions. No part of this book may be produced in any form or by
any electronic or mechanical means, including information storage and
retrieval systems, without permission in writing from the author, except
by reviewer, who may quote brief passages in a review.

This is a work of fiction. All names, characters, places, objects, and
incidents herein are the products of the author's imagination or are used
fictitiously. Any resemblance to actual things, events, locales, or persons
living or dead is entirely coincidental.

Library and Archives Canada
Doidge, Meghan Ciana, 1973—
Unleashing Echoes/Meghan Ciana Doidge—PAPERBACK EDITION

Cover design by Damonza.com

ISBN 978-1-927850-63-3

Unleashing Echoes

MEGHAN CIANA DOIDGE

SPILL THE TEA
2023

Published by Old Man in the CrossWalk Productions
Salt Spring Island, BC, Canada

Author's Note

Unleashing Echoes is the third book in the Reconstructionist series, which is set in the same universe as the Dowser and Oracle series.

While it is not necessary to read all three series, *in order to avoid spoilers* the ideal reading order is as follows:

Cupcakes, Trinkets, and Other Deadly Magic (Dowser 1)
Trinkets, Treasures, and Other Bloody Magic (Dowser 2)
Treasures, Demons, and Other Black Magic (Dowser 3)
I See Me (Oracle 1)
Shadows, Maps, and Other Ancient Magic (Dowser 4)
Maps, Artifacts, and Other Arcane Magic (Dowser 5)
I See You (Oracle 2)
Artifacts, Dragons, and Other Lethal Magic (Dowser 6)
I See Us (Oracle 3)
The Graveyard Kiss (Reconstructionist 0.5)
Catching Echoes (Reconstructionist 1)
Dawn Bytes (Reconstructionist 1.5)
Tangled Echoes (Reconstructionist 2)
An Uncut Key (Reconstructionist 2.5)
Unleashing Echoes (Reconstructionist 3)

Other books in the Dowser series to follow.

More information can be found at:
www.madebymeghan.ca/novels

For Michael
With you, the echoes of the past haunt a little less.

For twelve years, I had managed to separate my personal life from my professional life, becoming one of the best reconstructionists in the world—and proving to myself that I could do so on my own merits.

Then I'd been forced into contact with my family, reuniting with someone I thought I'd lost forever, and rescuing my best friend. Now I had to savor what little time I had left before the contract with the Conclave came due and my future was wrenched from my control.

Except there was one last case to solve.

One last set of puzzle pieces to collect, then assemble again.

But this time, I would have to be the investigator and the executioner. Whether I wanted to be or not.

Because it seemed as though the future wouldn't be allowed to finally unfold until the past had its way.

Chapter One

The moment that Jasper reclaimed the manor... the moment he regained control of the magic embedded in the Fairchild estate, I fell to my knees in the produce section of a Whole Foods in Chicago. Losing hold of the lemon I'd been about to add to my basket, I gasped as the magical connection was ripped from me—torn from what felt like my very soul, my very essence.

Then, with a wash of brownie magic, rough-skinned fingers I couldn't see brushed my arms, and a disembodied voice whispered, "I'm sorry."

"Lark," I murmured, struggling to focus through the aching emptiness radiating out through my chest and into my limbs.

"You must come." The brownie's hushed request was woeful.

Lark had pledged herself to me after I'd claimed the Fairchild estate magic almost four months before, in a rash attempt to free Jasmine and Declan from the clutches of three vampires. Even as I struggled to regain my equilibrium, I felt a moment of honest surprise that it had taken

Jasper so long to wrestle control of the ancestral magic back. Though I didn't doubt that it had taken some terrible feat to break the connection, anchored as it was to the power of three—namely Jasmine, Declan, and me.

That same manner of dreadful magic had most likely been responsible for my uncle getting out of his wheelchair. He'd been walking when I saw him in Litchfield, for the first time in more than twelve years. But I'd chosen—selfishly perhaps—to once again walk away from Connecticut and everything it represented only a day after rescuing Jasmine. And I had no plans to return, despite my aunt Rose's repeated attempts to woo me back into the Fairchild coven.

The energy of the brownie's magic lingered around me for the space of a single breath. Then I was alone.

Once again, I was disconnected from the magic of the Fairchild coven. Severed from the power that was my ancestral right to wield.

I should have felt relieved of the burden, of the obligation. Instead, I knelt on gray-stained wood flooring and felt … bereft.

Weak.

Incomplete.

Missing.

A low pulse of frenetic energy nearby informed me that Jasmine was running back through the grocery store toward me. I'd left her drooling over the candy bars and chips a couple of aisles away. I could feel her magic and her panic before she cleared the towering display of organic Royal Gala apples, then slid to a stop as she spotted me.

Her dark golden curls tumbled across her shoulders. She was pale, frantic. Her bright-blue eyes were wide with tension and simmering with her witch magic. The vivid and unusual power display was likely a residual of whatever effect Jasper's reclaiming the estate was having on her—on us—since I'd inadvertently bound her and Declan, along with myself, to the estate's magic.

Jasper. Our uncle. The bane of my existence. Reaching out once again and playing with my life, as easily as the wind stirred the leaves in the apple orchard that had once been a haven from my childhood.

Perhaps I shouldn't have walked away so readily. But there was no place for me in Litchfield. Nothing but constant reminders of an abusive childhood, despite us holding the ancestral ties to the magic of the Fairchild estate. The coven was corrupt from within, and I had no ability to forgive and forget. Honestly, I hadn't wanted the responsibility of confronting our elders, purging the corruption and destroying the coven in the process.

Jasmine took another step toward me. Her expression twisted with despair, reacting to whatever she saw on my own face. Reacting to a decision I hadn't even made yet. But Lark wouldn't have asked me to return to the manor if it wasn't crucial.

"You aren't his keeper, Wisteria," she said. She meant Jasper.

"If not me, then who?" I whispered, placing my palms flat on the floor and pushing myself to my feet.

Jasmine's phone buzzed.

Glancing around and hoping I hadn't drawn any awkward attention from the few patrons quietly grocery shopping alongside me, I smoothed the fabric of my fitted, dark-navy, stretch-linen dress, making sure the subtle black lacework appliqué that ran from the center neck to the hem wasn't oddly twisted.

Jasmine pulled her phone out of the pocket of her figure-hugging brown suede jacket, answering the call but not taking her gaze from me. "She's here."

Declan. He would have felt the severing of the connection to the estate magic, as Jasmine had.

Ignoring the way my heart rate momentarily ramped up at the thought of Jasmine's brother calling out of concern for me, I checked to make sure my white-to-teal-blue gradient silk scarf was still draped around my neck, artfully tucked underneath my open Burberry heritage navy-blue trench coat.

"We're on a job in Chicago," Jasmine said, still eyeing me as she spoke to her brother. "A missing girl."

Turning away from her conversation, I collected the items that had spilled from my basket—two bananas, an orange, and the lemon I'd lost hold of. We'd been shopping for light breakfast items for the following morning, filling the hour between our flights and the meeting that had brought us to Chicago. Well, along with snacks for Jasmine, though she appeared to have left her basket elsewhere.

"You know I can't stop her," Jasmine said crossly. "But duty will keep her in Chicago. For now."

I contemplated the apples. Jasmine was partly correct. Duty did drive me. Duty to my job as a reconstructionist for the witches' Convocation. But despite my resolve and resistance, I understood that Lark's plea was going to force me back to Connecticut once again.

Because of Jasper. Because of whatever malicious spell he'd cast to reject the brownies' dominion over Fairchild Manor. Whatever magic had let him tear through the familial ties I'd grounded in my own, Declan's, and Jasmine's magic.

Because investigating terrible deeds was our job. My duty.

Even if it meant facing our family again. Even if it meant facing our own ingrained fears and nightmares.

Unfortunately for me, those were one and the same.

"It's time," I said to Jasmine, heedless of whatever Declan was saying to her. "We're just hypocrites otherwise. Investigating the crimes of Adepts not powerful enough to hide from us, from the Convocation. But ignoring those crimes committed by our own coven."

"A child is missing—"

"And we'll find her," I said, interrupting the beginning of my cousin's protest. "Then we'll go and collect enough evidence to bring Jasper to a tribunal. We'll depose him. Properly."

Jasmine stared at me, utterly aghast.

I placed two apples in my basket.

Declan shouted something through the speaker on Jasmine's phone. I didn't catch his words, just the furious intonation.

Jasmine snapped her mouth shut, then spoke into the phone rather than to me. "If you want to stop her, then get your ass over here." Then she ended the call, hanging up on Declan.

"No one in the family is clean," she said to me. "None of them are without some tarnish. Are you prepared to head the coven?"

I shook my head. "Rose will. Officially, as she does now. And the coven magic will naturally settle on her."

Jasmine snorted. "If you rip down the facade, she'll be the first conspirator to be condemned."

I closed the space between us, gently placing my hand on Jasmine's arm. She shuddered at the touch of my magic.

"It's time," I said quietly. "You don't ever have to be in the same room as him. But it's time."

"Just tear it all down, hey?" Her voice cracked with emotion. "Just expose all our darkness? Invite the world to witness our wounds?"

"Yes. It's time to move forward." I dropped my hand. I crossed through the produce section, adding seedless red grapes to my basket, then moving toward an open-front refrigerator that held freshly blended juices.

Jasmine trailed after me.

I couldn't carry the pain any longer—mine, Jasmine's or Declan's.

I had almost lost myself, almost allowed myself to be consumed within my own reconstruction of my happiest childhood memory in order to flee that pain. We were all lost within it even now, clinging to each other—though none of us stood on solid ground.

Jasper wasn't a monster. He was just a man. Flawed and depraved, yes. Insurmountable, no.

So though I felt like sobbing at the devastating loss of the magic that had just been torn from me, I would move forward. I would force the three of us into the future. I had no other choice, really.

It was time to put an end to the feud with Jasper. And it would be better to do so before Kett was compelled to demand my acceptance of the conditions of the contract with the Conclave. Time-sensitive stipulations, which required my lifeblood but would gift me with immortality and invulnerability.

It would be better to defeat Jasper as a witch, on witch terms, and within the bounds of Convocation law.

Because after I was a vampire?

Well, depending on how the transformation affected me, I expected it was going to be much better for the health of the coven if I never set foot in Connecticut again.

And I wanted my vengeance cold and calculated. After all, that was exactly how Jasper had ruined our childhoods. He deserved the same in return.

A violent, terrifying death would be too simple for him. And too easy for the coven to cover up—as they had already covered up the mental and sexual abuse our uncle skillfully inflicted on Jasmine, Declan, and me under the guise of training the next generation of Fairchild witches.

No, I didn't want Jasper's blood. I wanted to strip away everything that gave his life meaning and worth. And I'd do it all aboveboard.

Then we'd finally be even.

But first I had a job to do, and a missing girl to find.

The Camerons lived among a block of brownstones on South Slate Street, only five minutes from the downtown core of Chicago. A series of interconnected parks that created a narrow but well-maintained green space between the shore of Lake Michigan and the metropolis was within walking distance. Well, it would have been walking distance if I'd changed into my work flats, and if a flash thunderstorm hadn't overshadowed the mild, sunny afternoon moments after we'd climbed into a taxi with our groceries.

Whether it was specific to the month of May or not, the weather in Chicago most definitely lived up to its capricious reputation. The thunderstorm passed so quickly that the downpour ceased during our dash from the side street where we'd asked the cabbie to drop us. By the time Jasmine and I jogged up the steps to the Camerons' black-painted front door, we'd stopped cursing our lack of umbrellas.

Jasmine had formally requested my services through the Convocation for the investigation, which she'd been assigned the day before. We'd flown in from different locations, meeting at the airport. Though she was currently living with me in Seattle, my best friend had been on another job in New York.

The Chicago case centered around a nine-year-old witch, Ruby Cameron. She was missing. And to make matters even more sinister, her mother, Coral, swore that her child didn't exist.

It was just after four o'clock as Jasmine reached for the brass knocker on the front door. Having been told that the Camerons wouldn't be available to talk to us until late afternoon had given us the time to have our bags dropped at the hotel, and for our Whole Foods stop. I remembered to take a step back, angling myself slightly behind my cousin—I wasn't the lead investigator—moments before a sandy-haired man in his midthirties opened the door.

He took one look at us, and relief flooded through his entire body. "Thank God," he said. "I've been…worried you weren't coming…that you wouldn't get here soon enough."

"I'm Jasmine Fairchild," my cousin said. "This is Wisteria Fairchild. She specializes in reconstructions."

"Thank you. Thank you." The man thrust out his hand as he spoke, but then at the last minute, he curled his fingers back from the offered handshake. His smile faltered as he glanced back and forth between us. "I'm…Jon Cameron. Jonquil. It's a shade of yellow. But I go by…Jon…"

Jasmine smiled. "We're here from the Convocation, Jon. Not to hurt you. Or your family."

Jon straightened his shoulders, looking embarrassed. "Of course…not. I just…it's been a weird weekend, and I wasn't certain…about…" He trailed off awkwardly.

"Shall we come in?"

"Yes. Um…" He stepped back to allow us entry into the townhouse. "But if we could have a moment, please. Before we involve my sister, Coral."

An open but practically empty closet was tucked into a niche on the left side of the tight entranceway. I closed and latched the front door behind me, then quickly tucked our brown-paper grocery bags inside the closet and hung up my soaked trench coat, carefully allowing space between it and the single coat already hanging there. Jasmine unbuttoned her jacket but didn't remove it.

A steep, narrow staircase led almost directly from the front door to the second level. Given what we'd seen of the building, it seemed likely that there were at least three floors above us and one below. Jon hustled past the stairs, though, turning right into a living room that overlooked the busy street. Jasmine and I followed.

"Tea?" Jon asked, wringing his hands. He paused behind the long, low couch facing a retrofitted gas fireplace.

"Perhaps later," Jasmine said. "I've read the transcript of the conversation you had with your coven leader."

"Well," he said, flustered again as he circled the couch but didn't sit down. "Not my coven leader. I mean, I'm a Cameron, but I'm not a practicing witch. Coral is ... was ... "

The Camerons were one of the founding families of the Convocation, along with the Godfreys and the Fairchilds. They actively held one of the thirteen seats. But those members who resided in Chicago, and in North America in general, were distant relatives to the main branch of Camerons, whose estate was based in Scotland.

"I actually wasn't sure of the protocol," Jon said. "I thought I should call the police, but Coral's mental state was ... " He reached up and adjusted a picture on the mantel, showing a cherub-faced, ginger-haired child sitting in a swing. "Ruby ... taken a few months ago."

Oddly, the photograph seemed to be the only personal item set out in the room. I glanced through a doorway to our left, catching a glimpse of the kitchen at the back of the house.

"How long has Ruby been missing?" Jasmine asked. She would have been issued a report when she was assigned the case, but reconfirming details was always the best way to begin a conversation with a potential witness.

"She hasn't hurt her. Coral, I mean," Jon said in a rush. "Please. You mustn't think she's concealing anything.

Ruby is her life. She's...she's not doing well, but I don't think she's hurt her."

"Jon," I said quietly. "We'll figure it out."

He nodded, swallowing hard. "I know...I know what a reconstructionist is." Then he inhaled, gathering his thoughts. "Ruby has been missing since December, as best as I can guess. I've been out of the country. I returned two days ago, and..." He swept his hand to indicate the tidy room. "No Ruby. And Coral doesn't remember she had a daughter. The very mention of it agitates her. She keeps...keeps..." He clawed his fingers and gestured frantically, then dropped his hand. "I can't talk to her about it."

Jasmine glanced at me.

I nodded grimly. Though another Adept could have been involved in Ruby's disappearance, the worst-case scenario was that the child wasn't missing at all. That her mother, Coral, had murdered her, either accidentally or in some sort of bid for power. And that she was now claiming amnesia when confronted by her brother. Though how or why a witch proficient in herbology—the growing of flowers and plants for magical purposes—would resort to black magic, I had no idea. According to the information Jasmine had quickly put together, there was nothing obvious in Coral's background that would indicate a propensity toward violent or disruptive magic.

Outward appearances were often contrived, though. The Fairchilds understood that better than most.

"She would never hurt Ruby," Jon whispered again, as if picking up on my train of thought. "She lost her partner, Bob, three years ago to cancer, and the only way she got through it was devoting herself to Ruby. That included moving to Chicago last year to be closer to the coven when Ruby showed signs of being magically proficient. Coral has even been homeschooling her."

"Which is why no one else noticed Ruby was missing?" Jasmine asked.

Jon shook his head. "They were supposed to go to our parents' for the holidays, but Coral begged off, citing the recent move and her new business. She bought into a nursery, and with her skills, it's flourishing...and...why would anyone else ask? They've only missed two coven meetings and haven't made any other friends yet."

"Where are your parents based?" I asked.

He glanced uneasily from Jasmine to me. "New Hampshire."

I nodded. If his parents were practicing witches, they were under the jurisdiction of the Fairchild coven.

"We should speak to Coral, Jon," Jasmine said.

"Do...um...are either of you a telepath...or a reader?"

"No. But we'll tackle that when we figure more out, okay?"

He nodded. "I'll go get her. She, um...she's not going to be happy that you're here. That I involved the Convocation. She, ah...she's accused me of planting things...toys...pictures." He touched the photo on the mantel again, angling it to face the doorway to the front hall.

"And when you ask her why the toys were here before you returned?" I asked.

"She gets agitated."

"Okay," Jasmine said. "Maybe some tea would be a good idea."

Jon's face brightened. "Yes, of course. Tea. Coral grows twelve different varieties of mint. And I have some sugar cookies." He hustled out of the room.

Quickly but carefully, I lowered the personal shields I normally kept tightly layered in place, circling the living room with my witch senses open to any residual energy. Then I retraced my steps out into the hall and the entranceway.

"Magic?" Jasmine asked, pitching her voice low.

I shook my head, stepping back into the living room. The house wasn't even warded. If we had just entered the domain of a burgeoning black witch, she wasn't worried about hiding anything. Though I knew I would need to check the basement and the backyard in order to fully assess whether or not Coral had sacrificed her child in some bloody ritual. Most witches preferred to be connected to the earth when wielding their magic—but that didn't mean the child couldn't have been murdered in a completely different location.

My gaze fell on the picture of the ginger-haired nine-year-old on the mantel. My chest tightened at the thought of finding evidence of her death. "It's better to know," I murmured, speaking more to myself than my cousin.

"It is," Jasmine said, grimly agreeing with me without the need for any explanation. But then, we shared the same childhood.

Investigating a missing child with an expectation of her having been murdered was a miserable prospect for us—but not a shocking one.

A woman appeared in the doorway leading to the hall. She was tall and dreadfully skinny. Her short-bobbed hair hung limply around her face, a shade darker than her daughter's in the picture on the mantel. Her clothing was at least two sizes too large, as if she'd suddenly lost a lot of weight she really couldn't afford to lose in the first place. As if she was sick.

Or... fighting off a malignant spell.

I glanced over at Jasmine, whose gaze was glued to the woman. She nodded shallowly, seemingly coming to the same conclusion as I had with a single glance.

Stepping forward, Jasmine offered her hand to the woman. "Hello, I'm—"

"A witch. I know." Coral crossed her arms, her sleeves riding up with the motion. Both of her wrists and forearms were wrapped with a thick, white bandage over gauze. "I don't know what Jon has told you."

"And why would he lie?" Jasmine asked softly.

Coral pursed her lips, then shook her head vehemently.

"Will you at least let me check you for spells?" I asked.

"Fine." Coral crossed into the room, sitting stiffly on the arm of an overstuffed chair that sat perpendicular to the couch.

I closed the space between us, carefully keeping myself in her line of sight. Then I opened my perpetually locked-down witch senses to her quiet, gentle magic. The tenor of that magic, holding no traces of malignancy, instantly informed me that Coral was in no way responsible for anything nefarious that might have happened to her daughter.

I glanced over at Jasmine. "I don't sense any foreign magic."

"I could have told you that," Coral snapped.

Jasmine pulled out her phone, thumbing the screen for a moment before she turned it toward the witch. "You registered Ruby's birth with the Convocation. August 14, 2007."

"No," Coral said, shaking her head too quickly again. "No. No." She started scratching her arms, worrying the edges of the bandages—an action that obviously and heart-wrenchingly spoke of self-harm. Given her behavior, it seemed likely that Coral was punishing herself for something she couldn't remember, but that she subconsciously blamed herself for nonetheless. Her missing daughter.

"It's okay, Coral," I said. "It's all right. We'll sort it out. We'll help you sort it out."

Coral met my gaze intensely. "I know something is wrong. Something is terribly, terribly wrong!"

"We're going to figure it out," Jasmine said. But she stopped short of touching the witch on her shoulder. Adepts didn't voluntarily touch each other. Not easily, at least. And the last thing Jasmine or I wanted to do was to provoke Coral in any way. Even a witch who practiced herbology could lash out with wild magic unintentionally.

Jon hustled into the living room, carrying a tray laden with a green teapot, mismatched mugs, and a plate of cookies. Glancing worriedly at his sister, he quickly placed the tray on the low coffee table in front of the fireplace.

"Please." Coral gasped for air as if suddenly pained. "Please."

Jon crossed around Jasmine, laying his hand on Coral's shoulder. His sister settled under his touch so quickly that I assumed he must be wielding some sort of soothing magic, but so subtle that I wasn't sensitive enough to pick it up.

Coral turned her hollow gaze to the photo of Ruby on the mantel. Even completely untrained in any sort of psychology or mind magic, I could see that the witch was slowly going mad denying the existence of her daughter.

"May I have permission to walk the house and grounds?" I asked. "I'll need to look for residual magic. Anything that wouldn't naturally be in the house. Perception or persuasion spells. Masking charms and the like."

Coral didn't respond.

Jon nodded stiffly, then crossed to the coffee table to pour a cup of tea.

Jasmine followed me out into the hall, texting.

"Are you requesting a reader?" I pitched my voice low as I watched Jon through the doorway. He was trying to coax Coral into drinking the tea.

Jasmine nodded. "The local coven doesn't have one. The Convocation is going to send us a specialist."

"I'm certain Coral hasn't had anything to do with whatever happened to Ruby," I said, though I knew I was basing my determination on instinct rather than rational reasoning. "I know it's been months, but if she was capable of black magic, I'm certain it would leave a taint. And if it was an accident, then why the amnesia act and the self-harm? Did you double-check Jon's itinerary?"

"Yep. He's on the up and up. Out of town on business for the last six months. Numerous verifications. Rare antiquities, the nonmagical kind. The family runs a business out of New Hampshire."

"That's good."

"Yeah. I'd hate for it to be the brother." Jasmine looked up from her phone to meet my gaze. "Not that it would stop me from ripping his heart out."

"Investigating, you mean. Gathering evidence for a tribunal."

"Yeah," she said, turning back into the living room. "Sure."

Uneasy, I watched her for a moment as she settled on the couch with her back to me, snagging a cookie from the plate and updating Jon in a low murmur. I wasn't certain it was a good idea for Jasmine to be investigating incidents involving young children. But turning down a case without cause could have damaged her reputation. And even though we bore the Fairchild surname, it was our individual reputations that actually paid the bills.

I turned to the stairs, then slowly moved up through the house. Looking for any residual magic that might yield a reconstruction.

Jasmine was still healing after being badly bitten by the vampires that had kidnapped her in January. Working through this case would help her regain a sense of control. And finding Ruby alive would be an even better balm to her bruised soul.

I kept that positive thought in the front of my mind as I opened the door into a tiny bedroom swathed in purple and pink. The air in the otherwise tidy room was stale, and the bureau, brass bed frame, and empty shelving was covered in a thin layer of dust. The closet doors weren't fully closed—revealing that it was stuffed full of the clothing, books, and toys that must once have filled the room. I kept firm hold of my resolve, casting my senses out for any residual magic.

Alive or dead, we would find Ruby Cameron. No one magical was capable of concealing their crimes from my reconstructions. And though I didn't know much about the human psyche, Coral's mental state made it more than clear that an Adept was involved in Ruby's disappearance.

Someone had targeted a widowed mother in a new city without friends or family. They'd taken a nine-year-old prodigy witch from her home, drastically altering her mother's memory. But they most certainly weren't going to get away with it. Not if it was within my power to do something about it.

Chapter Two

A text message from Jasmine pinged through on my phone just as I finished checking the master bedroom on the top floor. It was perfectly tidy but sparsely and impersonally furnished.

>*Meet me in the backyard.*

I headed swiftly downstairs. I hadn't had a chance to check the kitchen or the basement for residual magic, but whatever Jasmine had discovered certainly took precedence. The house had an empty, almost sterile, feel to it—maybe partly owing to Coral and Ruby's relatively recent move, but more likely due to the missing child. It also didn't contain any residual magic intense enough to manifest as a reconstruction. If Coral Cameron was a practicing witch, she didn't wield her craft in the house as far as I could tell.

I grabbed my coat from the closet at the base of the stairs, then headed back through the house toward the kitchen, where I assumed I would find an exterior door to the yard. I glanced into the living room as I passed the open doorway. Perched on the couch, Jon was holding Coral's hand and murmuring quietly to her. He looked up and caught my eye, giving me a stiff nod.

I smiled back reassuringly—or at least as reassuringly as I was capable of being while searching for clues that would lead me to a missing child. Continuing along the short hall, I came into the U-shaped kitchen. The tile, countertops, and appliances looked as though they hadn't been updated since the early nineties. Beyond the far counter, a round pinewood table was tucked into a tiny windowed eating area. An empty patio stood just beyond sliding-glass doors to the left of the table.

Sliding open the door, I stuck my head out, looking for Jasmine. A set of wooden stairs led down into a tiny fenced backyard featuring a lawn maybe eight feet across. The space was crammed into the footprint of the property, next to the short drive that led to a partially aboveground garage beneath the kitchen. A private alley abutted the property, with a gated entrance a couple of houses down, off the side street.

One level below me, my cousin was pacing the length of the back fence while peering at her phone. She looked up, beckoning as I slid the door closed behind me. "We need a circle."

I slipped on my trench coat and descended steps of silvered wood to join my cousin. Though the air still felt damp from the thunderstorm that had just passed, it wasn't currently raining. "You found residual?"

She shook her head. "They're transporting the reader."

"What? Here? Outside? What about the basement?"

Jasmine glanced up at the neighboring townhouses, both of which had a clear view of the backyard from their rear windows. "The neighbors appear to be at work or at school. The basement is actually the extremely tiny garage, which is concrete on all sides and barely holds the car currently parked in it. Can you set up your candles?"

I nodded, obligingly pulling a white pillar candle from the huge bag I carried with me everywhere, whether or not I was working a case. "Where is the reader coming from?"

"The Academy."

"They're sending a student?"

"They're sending the best they have on hand. No one is happy about a baby witch going missing...or whatever else has happened." As before, Jasmine's tone was dark. "They just need an active circle."

I dutifully paced a circle in the center of the wet lawn, which was composed of more weeds than grass. A few scraggly red and yellow tulips next to the fence had lost most of their petals, possibly during the thunderstorm. It occurred to me that they had bloomed and died without Ruby Cameron having ever seen them.

I shook off the morbid thought, pressing the grass down again as I circled a second time. Placing my candles at the east, south, and west points, I paused at the northern edge with my green pillar candle still in hand. Jasmine remained glued to her phone.

"Pearl Godfrey sent me to London a few years ago the same way," I said, crouching to set the final candle in the grass. Green for earth. As a witch and a Virgo, I almost always closed my circles near the earth-element candle. "At least the Academy has the necessary number of witches to cast on their end. Pearl drained her magic sending me. Usually, it takes a full coven. Thirteen witches, minimum."

Jasmine's jaw dropped. "Pearl Godfrey transported you to London? On her own?"

"From her home territory. Which the Godfreys have held since there was such a thing for immigrants to hold in the Pacific Northwest. And my magic is receptive to the spell."

Jasmine was still staring at me. "But on her own. She could have...botched it. She could have hurt you."

I laughed lightly. "I doubt it. It might not have worked, but it's not like I would have dropped into the middle of the Arctic."

"That's exactly what could have happened!"

I snorted at Jasmine's exaggeration. Then I leaned down to snap my fingers over the wick of the green candle. Magic sparked. And as the earth candle caught, the three other pillars flared, instilling the circle with the touch of my magic.

I still didn't cast carelessly, but calling forth simple spells had become almost effortless for me since I'd bonded with the Fairchild estate magic. Such spells had always been within my ability, truth be told, so Jasper reclaiming the manor for himself wouldn't affect them. I'd just been out of practice—by choice—focusing all my efforts on being an excellent reconstructionist. And though I was still careful to not contaminate residual energy when collecting magic for a case, it was necessary for me to imbue my magic into a dormant circle such as the one I was currently constructing. It would give the Academy witches an anchor point for their transportation spell.

Stepping back from the circle I'd paced, I raised my palms, gathering the magic that had been left in my wake as I placed and lit the candles. Then, with a tiny push of my will, I closed the empty circle. It was ready to be utilized.

I glanced over to Jasmine, who had stepped back from the magic I was commanding in order to protect her phone. I had a habit of eroding technology unintentionally ... and shorting it out completely intentionally on occasion. My best friend nodded to me without looking up from texting.

I looked up and around at the neighbors' houses again. The fence was tall enough to block most of what was about to transpire from the back alley, but not from the houses on either side.

"Did you place distraction spells?" I asked Jasmine.

"Oh, shoot." She dug in her satchel while she dashed around the circle, toward the back gate opening onto the alley.

I frowned at her retreating back. Jasmine wasn't usually so easily distracted while on a case. Perhaps having the magic of the estate ripped from her had affected her more than it had me. Or it might have added to her current emotional vulnerability. Another loss. Another wound inflicted by our uncle Jasper.

I stepped up beside an anemic-looking cedar tree that might have been intended as the start of a hedge when it was first planted. From there, tucked into the corner of the yard and somewhat shielded from Jasmine's view, I retrieved my phone from my bag and texted Declan. A rare but not completely unusual form of communication between myself and Jasmine's brother. We'd been in tentative contact since we'd all gone back to work, leaving the manor—if not its magic—to Jasper, and Connecticut in general to our family.

Would you call Jasmine again? She's ... off.

Intense magic bloomed inside the circle, pressing against its edges. I quickly shoved my phone in my bag, taking another step back to bring me up against the fence.

Jasmine swore viciously from somewhere in the alley. Likely because she hadn't had time to place all the distraction spells.

A vibrant cloud of blue-and-white-streaked magic filled the circle, then a darker outline of three figures appeared within it.

"Impressive," I murmured, completely awed by the strength of the spell. I could feel it involuntarily, even beyond the barrier of my circle and my own personal shields.

Jasmine jogged back through the gate into the yard, slowing to smooth her suede jacket.

The cloud of magic cleared within the circle, settling down and into the trio standing shoulder to shoulder.

A woman in her early twenties with lavender-dyed hair cast her gaze around the circle, curling her lip. "Four feet wide? You couldn't have spared us a little more space?"

"I...well..." My gaze skipped over the sneering witch to take in the other two within the circle. "We didn't expect...three..."

Standing in the middle, short enough that she had to practically peek over her companions' shoulders, the reader was unmistakable. Her eyes were pale blue, practically white. She was covered head to toe, wearing a light beige raw-silk dress, elbow-length white-beaded knit gloves, and low-heeled boots of supple brown leather. Even at a glance, I felt certain that every item she wore was hand-made—likely indicating that she was so sensitive, she had to know the people who made her clothing so as to not be overwhelmed by any imprint they left behind. So sensitive that she couldn't touch anyone or anything with her bare skin.

The third figure was dressed in shades of charcoal, including a turtleneck, tightly woven slacks, and gloves. A long blade was strapped to her right thigh. Without lowering my personal shields, I had no idea what type of magic the tall, exceedingly slim, olive-skinned Adept wielded. I also wasn't entirely sure whether I was guessing correctly that she was a woman.

The lavender-haired witch glanced between Jasmine and me, widening her sneer. "You'd think Fairchilds would know better." Then she reached forward and ripped through my circle with no effort at all.

A sharp pain shot through my head. I couldn't stop myself from pressing my fingertips to my temple, exposing my platinum white-picket-fence bracelet on my wrist.

The reader gasped. "Lavender! That's just rude." She had a broad American accent.

The witch had no identifiable accent. Though by the way she'd torn through my circle as if doing so was a display of power, not simply childish petulance, it seemed likely that she'd been raised with money and the status that came with it. As Jasmine and I had been. But the sight of my bracelet—to which her gaze was now glued—and all the magic it held had wiped the sneer from her face.

"I'm Nevada," the reader said. "This is Shadow." She indicated the dark-clothed androgynous figure to her left. "And Lavender, you've met."

"Jasmine. Lead investigator. Tech." My cousin offered up her name cordially enough, but her hand was buried deeply within her bag. It was an easy guess that she was clutching one of the offensive spells Declan had crafted for her when we'd faced off against Yale and his brood in Litchfield. Her gaze was riveted to Lavender.

The purple-haired witch tapped her foot, impatiently waiting for me to identify myself. She was wearing wickedly pointed shoes that were just a shade darker than her hair.

I swallowed an involuntary smile.

Lavender followed my gaze to her feet, frowning. And when she lifted her eyes to meet mine, the balance of power had shifted between us. In my favor.

They were practically children. Though I had no doubt that the reader was powerful enough to do her job.

I stepped forward, offering my right hand to the witch. "Wisteria Fairchild, reconstructionist."

Lavender hesitated, eyeing my bracelet. Then she stiffened her shoulders and grasped my hand. Because Adepts rarely voluntarily touched each other, my offering my hand was almost impolite—if an Adept refused the gesture, it would make them appear weak.

The witch dropped my hand almost immediately.

Ignoring her, I offered my hand to the reader next, who barely topped five feet. She met my gaze with delight, eagerly reaching forward.

"Nevada," Lavender snapped.

Ignoring the witch's caution, the reader grasped my hand, stepping toward me and gazing up into my eyes. Even through her gloves, her magic instantly brushed me, curling around my outstretched arm, then reaching up to tickle my senses. I'd never felt anything like it. But if she gleaned any insight from our contact, I had no idea what it might be.

She smiled widely, revealing slightly crooked eye teeth. Then she breathed my name as if we were old friends who hadn't seen each other in decades. "Wisteria Fairchild."

I smiled politely. "We are well met, Nevada."

The reader nodded, reluctantly releasing her hold on my hand, then looking toward Jasmine hopefully. It was an easy guess that she rarely came into contact with anyone—or at least with anyone willing to touch her.

Jasmine glanced at me uneasily.

I smiled reassuringly.

My cousin stepped forward to clasp hands with Nevada.

As she did, I offered my hand to Shadow, who simply inclined her head respectfully in response.

"Shall we move on?" Lavender asked. Her tone was slightly more professional. "The distraction spells won't stop anyone from looking through the windows."

Jasmine stuck her chin out, but withheld whatever retort she wanted to level at the witch.

It was a safe bet that Lavender, who pointedly hadn't offered up her last name even though she knew ours, belonged to one of the main families of the Convocation. Her prejudice upon meeting us was too marked for it to be otherwise. No one liked a Fairchild witch. Unless, of course, they needed something done that took as much guile as it did magical power.

Though the lavender-haired witch didn't appear to be lacking in the power department. Based on what I could still feel of it, the transportation spell that had brought her and the others to Chicago was of her own casting. Hers alone.

Given the obvious sensitivity of the reader and the power level of the witch, it was an equally easy guess that Shadow's role within the trio was that of a bodyguard. It was also likely that the three of them had trained together, forming a set team based around Nevada. Evidently, the Academy had sent us a young team, but also a highly valued resource.

"We believe that Coral Cameron's mind has been tampered with," Jasmine said, turning toward the steps that led to the kitchen patio.

"We'll assess that," Lavender said pertly.

Shadow gestured for me to follow the others as they climbed the back stairs and entered the house.

I nodded politely, but the skin between my shoulder blades crawled for every moment that she was behind me. I still had no idea what type of Adept Shadow was, and that unnerved me. From the bodyguard role that I perceived for her, paired with a slim-but-tall stature that didn't indicate any obvious strength, I might have guessed she was a vampire.

Except I knew vampires. And Shadow wasn't one. Vampires didn't attend the Academy. And vampires weren't trusted to protect powerful readers.

But the trio and whatever magic they wielded beyond telepathy wasn't any of my business. My business was finding Ruby Cameron. And I fervently hoped that Nevada was capable of catching a glimpse of the child in Coral's mind. Otherwise, we didn't have any leads.

As Jasmine, Lavender, Nevada, and I approached the living room, but before any of us could step in, Shadow slipped past us in the hall. Crossing through to the front windows that looked onto the main street, she scanned the block, then drew the drapes, prowling back through the room.

I hovered in the doorway as Jasmine, Nevada, and Lavender entered. With Coral still perched on the armchair and Jon on the couch, the room was too tiny for all of us to cram into it.

Moving swiftly, Shadow exited the living room without a word, checking the locks on the front door, then moving past me to slip up the stairs and explore the rest of the house.

Coral locked her dull-blue gaze on Nevada as the reader stepped up to the back of the couch. The witch's expression was intensely desperate.

In the process of standing and perhaps intending to greet the newcomers, Jon stumbled back a few steps as the living room was invaded by Adepts. He almost tripped over the coffee table as he pressed back against the mantel. Ruby's picture sat just above his left shoulder. And in that moment, I realized that the photo must have been placed on the mantel by Jon himself. Coral had confined every other bit of evidence that she had a daughter to the pink and purple room on the second floor.

Jon's eyes darted between each of the Adepts arrayed before him, settling his concerned gaze on me—as if he found me the most comforting presence out of everyone, which bore thinking about. Between Jasmine and I, he should have been looking to my cousin for assurances.

I smiled. But since I had no idea what was about to happen, I couldn't offer him any platitudes.

"This is the reader who I told you the Academy was going to send to help Coral," Jasmine said. "Nevada, this is Coral and her brother, Jon." She didn't bother introducing Lavender. A deliberate snub that wasn't particularly professional. But it was Jasmine's investigation, so she set the tone.

And since the lavender-haired witch's juvenile power play had already given me a headache—literally—I understood where Jasmine's irritation was coming from.

"Is that Ruby?" Nevada gestured toward the picture on the mantel without looking away from Coral.

When his sister didn't answer, Jon nodded, then forced himself to speak. "Um, yes. Yes."

"How recent is the picture?" Lavender asked.

"Um, recent. Within six months. I...I took it the last time I saw Ruby...and Coral. In New Hampshire."

"Hi, Coral," the reader said. "I'm Nevada."

"Hi, Nevada," Coral replied dreamily, as if she might already be partly caught in the reader's thrall. Though as far as I'd seen, Nevada hadn't touched her, and I couldn't feel any magic shifting between them.

"You didn't secure the front of the house," Lavender said snottily to Jasmine.

"It wasn't necessary," Jasmine said.

"It is now." The purple-haired witch pressed her hand against the curtained front windows, then clucked her tongue. "No wards? Really?" She glanced at Jon disparagingly.

He shifted, uncomfortable and wretched. Already blaming himself for a situation that had been entirely beyond his control.

Magic bloomed underneath Lavender's hand, slipping up across the front walls. I wasn't certain which spell she'd cast without the benefit of a circle. But I also wasn't about to question a witch who was obviously still trying to show off her magical prowess to Fairchild witches who outranked her, both as investigators and within the established pecking order of the Convocation families.

"The Camerons don't practice their craft here," I said coolly. I couldn't have cared less about whatever dominance games the junior witch thought she had to play.

Lavender snorted. "No wonder the girl got snatched."

"Excuse me?" Jasmine growled, rounding on the witch with her arms held stiffly at her sides. "We're here to ascertain what happened to Ruby, not to disparage her family."

Lavender flicked her gaze to me, but then had the sense to look back at Jasmine warily.

"Thank you, Lavender," Nevada said, before either Jasmine or I could take the inconsiderate witch to task any further. "You may leave if you're uncomfortable. Neither Wisteria, Jasmine, Jon, or Coral are going to hurt me."

Lavender looked momentarily chagrined. Then she crossed her arms and eyed us all smugly. "I doubt they could get within reach of you, reader."

"None of us are that stupid," Jasmine said snidely, heavily implying that Lavender was the only idiot in the room.

"May I take your hand, Coral?" Nevada asked, stripping off her knit gloves as she kneeled before the muddled witch.

Coral nodded. Her eyes were wide, trusting.

"Um," Jon said. "Um, wait."

"It's okay, Jon," Nevada said. "I won't hurt her. We want to figure out what happened to Ruby, yes?"

Jon nodded, tears edging his eyes.

Nevada lifted her hand, inviting Coral to touch her.

The witch's hand floated up. Then she settled it down onto the reader's open palm, gasping with awe.

"I'm here," Nevada said. Her eyes were glowing a soft, silvery white. "I'm here in the room with you. Do you see me, Coral?"

The witch nodded, then spoke. "I do. I see you."

"I'm also in your head. You can feel me there. But I'm not going to hurt you. All right?"

"All right," Coral echoed, whispering.

"Show me Ruby," Nevada asked. "Show me your baby girl."

Coral's eyes filled with tears. Her face collapsed into an expression of utter misery and she started shaking.

Jon darted forward. But before his fingers could make contact with his sister's shoulder, Shadow was in the room, grabbing his wrist. I hadn't even seen her return to the main floor or slip past me in the doorway. Her hold looked light, but Jon cried out at her sudden appearance.

"It's best to not touch her right now," Lavender said. Her tone was kinder than at any point since she'd set foot in the backyard.

Shadow let Jon go, stepping back to join me in the doorway.

Jon nodded in acceptance of their caution, but he continued to hover behind his distraught sister.

"Coral?" Nevada asked. "When was the last time you saw Ruby?"

Coral shook her head violently, gripping Nevada's forearm with her other hand. Speechless in her desperation.

"I've never seen this sort of block before." Nevada's tone was remote.

My heart pinched.

"A spell?" Jasmine asked. "A geas? A vow?"

Nevada shook her head. "No. Her thought pathways are blocked…wait…there."

Coral jerked upright, crying out.

"He took my baby! He took my baby! He took her…"

Her voice quieted, but she kept repeating herself. Whispering the phrase over and over again as she rocked back and forth.

"We'll find her," Jasmine said fiercely, stepping up behind Nevada. "We'll find Ruby, Coral."

My cousin glanced in my direction, but then looked away before I could read her expression.

"Can you see who took her?" I asked.

Nevada shook her head. "Not yet. The block is pretty solid, but I see…cracks." The glow of her eyes intensified.

"He took Ruby," Coral said insistently.

"Yes," Nevada said. "He took her."

Coral exhaled intensely, relief softening her posture.

"Where, Coral?" Nevada asked gently, tilting her head slightly. "Where was the last time you saw Ruby?"

Coral opened her mouth to respond, then stopped as if her voice had been stolen from her. She moaned, fighting to speak past whatever was consuming her words.

My heart pinched again. Then, unable to continue watching Coral's painful struggle while I had no opportunity to help her, I looked away. I focused instead on Jasmine, whose gaze was glued to Coral and Nevada intently. My cousin's features were sharper than usual. She'd lost weight. Living under the same roof as we had been the past four months, I clearly hadn't noticed the day-to-day change in her. But standing across the room now in unfamiliar surroundings, I could see the hollows underneath her eyes and cheekbones.

"It's okay. It's okay," Nevada murmured soothingly to Coral. Then, with a twist of a smile, she turned to look at me, reaching out her other hand. "Reconstructionist, I've got a location, I think. A starting point, at least."

Not even pausing to question why she was addressing me rather than Jasmine, the lead investigator, I pushed off the doorframe, reaching my hand toward her. I was desperate to get out of the room, to be useful.

Nevada's fingers brushed against mine, transferring a hint of her magic. The image of a set of swings, a large blue plastic slide, and green-painted benches bloomed in my mind. "A park," I said. "Playground."

Jasmine applied her fingers to her phone while I looked at Jon questioningly.

He shrugged. "I'm sorry. I don't know the area well."

"There are three parks within walking distance," Jasmine said, retrieving her brown suede jacket off the arm of the couch. Fixated on Coral and Nevada, I hadn't seen her take it off. "We'll look for residual magic. Will you be all right here?"

"Why wouldn't we?" Lavender asked snarkily.

"I was talking to Jon and Coral," Jasmine said. "You know, because of your delightful presence."

Lavender looked disconcerted. Apparently, the witch was unaware of how off-putting she was. Or maybe this was just the way she reacted to Fairchild witches.

"We'll be fine," Jon said stiffly. "Just find Ruby, please."

"I'm going to need some more time with Coral," Nevada said. "I think I can remove the block on her mind. It's brutish, without any sense of finesse. But it would be helpful if I first understood how it got there. What kind of Adept affected her this way."

"We'll text as soon as we know anything," I said, buttoning up my trench coat.

Nevada rewarded me with a smile. "I know you will, Wisteria. Would you like Shadow to accompany you?"

"We'll be fine," Jasmine said, eyeing Lavender. "Fairchild witches don't need bodyguards."

Shadow stiffened beside me. It was a subtle shift in energy, but Jasmine's cutting words—though directed at Lavender—had hit home on an unintended target.

"It would be an honor," I said, speaking first to Shadow, then to Nevada. "But with the passage of time since the incident, I don't believe we are in any danger. Thank you."

Jasmine frowned. But then she followed me out into the hall and through the front door without a word.

Chapter Three

A brisk wind rushed us the second we hit the rain-slick front walk. Gray clouds were rolling by overhead, possibly heralding another thunderstorm, but it wasn't raining. Yet. Shivering, Jasmine tugged a massive brown knit cowl out of her satchel and twined it around her neck. She glanced at the map app on her phone, then turned left at the sidewalk. I followed, opening my witch senses in the hope of picking up any obvious residual magic around us.

"Way to back me in there," Jasmine muttered, speaking into the cowl that covered her chin, neck, and most of her shoulders. Her dark-blond curls fanned out over its bulk in a wide, unruly mane.

I glanced at her, but she didn't meet my eye. "They are young," I said mildly.

"Nothing ruffles you," Jasmine said, though without heat.

A bright ping emanated from within the depths of my bag. I'd almost forgotten about having texted Declan with my concern about Jasmine's state of mind. I retrieved my phone from the bag's inner pocket.

Jasmine leaned across, reading the name of the sender before I'd even had a chance to see the screen.

"Declan," she said. "I thought it might be Kett."

I opened my messages app, reading the text.

>*I'm on my way.*

"He knows where we are?" I asked. Then I remembered that Jasmine had mentioned we were in Chicago when she'd been on the phone with him in Whole Foods. I'd still been reeling from having my connection to the Fairchild estate magic torn asunder.

Jasmine nodded without comment.

I texted back.

Thank you.

Then I slipped my phone back into my bag before I tried to address the other half of Jasmine's comment. Assuming she was going to let me. "I haven't heard from Kett—"

"Never mind," Jasmine interrupted, as she had every other time I'd mentioned the executioner of the Conclave since she'd been kidnapped. "It doesn't matter. Not right now."

"I know the contract weighs on you."

"On me? You're the one whose name is on it."

My concern deepening into a heavy ache that stretched across my upper chest, I brushed my fingers across the back of her hand.

She shook her head, waving her hand offishly. "I'm fine. I'm fine. Don't look at me like that. I'm fine."

"I know you are. But I still feel a bit hollow. Since before, in the grocery store."

Jasmine looked relieved at my admission. "Yes. That's it. I'm fine. It's just all that." She glanced at her phone, then up at the street corner we were approaching. "Left here."

I obligingly followed her around the corner, once again wondering if I should push her to address the subject of Kett and the contract with the Conclave. A contract that condemned me to death, then immortality—but only if I survived the transition. Only if my magic and my physical body accepted the transformation. It wasn't yet clear to me what would happen to my soul in the process of becoming a vampire. And I wasn't actually certain I believed in such things, at least not in a religious sense.

But I knew that all living things released an energy when they passed—because I'd felt it when I held our brownie, Bluebell, as she died. And what was magic if it wasn't the energy that fueled us? So perhaps it was our souls?

As best as I could figure it, Kett was proposing to replace, or at least to supplement, my energy with his own. As directed by the Conclave, in conjunction with my uncle Jasper when he'd tied me unwillingly to the contract in the first place. But did that process release my soul—the very energy that fueled me, that fueled my magic? Or did it absorb it into the transformation?

I wasn't certain anyone could answer that question definitively, but I still had a little less than four months before the deadline. And by unspoken agreement, Kett seemed content to wait until the last minute to fulfill the terms. Namely, imbuing me with half his power and remaking me as one of the undead.

So that gave me more time with Jasmine. Even as it gave Kett more time before... well, at least a century of some sort of mentorship, from the way he had described it. A century to guide me through being a vampire. A drinker of blood. One of the immortal—possibly damned—few.

The curve of a metal fence painted light blue ran along the edge of a green space, coming into view before I figured out how to broach the touchy subject with Jasmine a second time.

"Cotton Tail Park," she said.

The park took up about half a city block, ringed by a series of what appeared to be walk-up apartment buildings, and surrounded by deciduous trees in the process of leafing out. I caught a glimpse of a large orange structure, which I assumed was a playhouse. Various paths radiated out from a central ring of green, trimmed grass. Green-painted benches, matching the image that Nevada had planted in my mind back in the living room of the townhouse, were scattered throughout the park.

"Do you see swings?" I asked. "Or a blue slide?"

Jasmine lifted her hand, pointing toward a structure to our left that was mostly hidden by the trees. "I think that's a slide."

I glanced both ways, then jogged across the empty street to the sidewalk beyond. Pausing at the entrance to the park, I eyed the slide that Jasmine had pointed out. "That could be it," I said. "Maybe the reader showed it to me from a different angle?"

"Do you feel any magic?" Jasmine asked. "Leading to or from the path?"

"Not yet." Stepping onto the path, I slowly scanned what I could see of the park, now that it wasn't mostly blocked by trees. "No magic nearby. Though I should check the swings before we try one of the other parks. The image is so drilled into my brain, I doubt I'll ever forget it."

Jasmine laughed. "Yeah, I'm not sure about the body-guard and the witch, but the reader is damn scary. You think she's one of those types that could, you know, snap and turn us all into her brain-dead army? I always thought that level of power was folklore, or a fairy tale."

"I think she's off-the-charts sensitive, given her hand-made clothing." I crossed the trimmed grass, managing to not twist an ankle in the sand as I circled the play structure with the slide. I finally spotted the swing set on the far side of the park.

Continuing on until I was a few feet away from the swings, I turned back to eye the slide from that new angle. Then I looked at Jasmine grimly. "As long as the other parks aren't duplicates of this one, then this is it."

Not picking up any immediate residual, I paced the edge of the play area, approaching the swings from the other direction. I caught a hint of something faint by the second swing from the left. Hunkering down near the far side of the apparatus, I lined up my view of the slide through the loop created by the chains and the bright-blue wooden seat of the swing.

Other than the greenery, the view matched the image the reader had shown me.

I sighed harshly. No matter that I wanted to find Ruby, I wasn't looking forward to reconstructing whatever had occurred at this spot last December.

"You've got something?" Jasmine asked quietly.

I nodded. Still crouched, I glanced around the park and the surrounding neighborhood, which wasn't exactly quiet—and which I was fairly certain was about to get even busier in the hours between the end of work and dinnertime. "We're going to need a perimeter. Do you have something in your bag?"

Jasmine nodded, already digging through her brown leather satchel.

"We can keep it tight." I straightened up, shifting to one side to grab a fallen branch. "And quick. Just in case this is nothing and we need to go to the next park."

I began drawing a circle in the sand, just encompassing the swing set.

"I brought enough to do them all if needed," Jasmine said.

As I passed her, she stepped inside the circle, placing a smooth white stone in the groove I'd left behind in the wet sand. It appeared to have a rune carved on it, most likely rechargeable by the witch who had spelled it. And pricey.

Unless... I almost opened my mouth to ask if Jasmine was using spells she'd gotten from Copper—the witch that Declan was currently cohabiting with. But then I completed the circle in the sand, and I kept the question to myself. I never would have asked any other lead investigator about the magic at her disposal. It wasn't my business.

I pulled out my four pillar candles, pacing a smaller circle just wide enough to include the two middle swings in my reconstruction. I could move the inner circle within the outer one if it became necessary.

Magic spiraled around me as Jasmine triggered a barrier spell designed to hide us from sight. Passersby who knew that the park contained a swing set would still be able to see it, but they wouldn't see Jasmine and me, or the magic we were casting. It was risky to use a single barrier spell on its own, though, which was why Jasmine paced along the inner edge of the larger circle a second time, setting out two more premade spells. Directed toward the paths that converged on the swing set, those would distract anyone who entered this area of the park. As long as they couldn't see through or sense magic.

I was still placing my candles when a mother and her son approached the playground, walking hand in hand. The three-year-old boy was all smiles and awkward steps as he trundled off the path, through the grass, and then into the sand. He tugged at his mother's hand emphatically when she paused by the slide, intending to make a beeline for the swings.

Jasmine straightened up from applying the second distraction spell, watching the mother and son. I could sense her readying some sort of explanation for our activities in case the spells failed. Though with me fiddling around with candles, it was going to be pretty difficult to convince anyone that we weren't performing some sort of witchcraft in a children's park.

A half-dozen feet away, the mother suddenly hesitated. A frown creased her brow. Then one hand pulled her phone out of her pocket, checking the screen. The boy tugged at her other hand.

"Mom! Swings."

"Sorry, Ethan. I was wrong about the time." She started to turn around, heading back the way they'd come.

The boy's face crumpled, reddening. "But they get to play!" He lifted his hand, pointing at Jasmine with tears welling in his large brown eyes. Apparently, he had no trouble seeing through the magic of the barrier, and wasn't at all affected by the distraction spell like his mother was. Magic had possibly skipped a generation in his family. Or he might not have been blood related to his mother, or simply took after his father. Whatever the case, he was a fledgling Adept of some sort.

"Ethan," his mother said, "I'm sorry. But we're going to be late for dinner." Despite her son's insistence, the compulsion of the distraction spell made her tug lightly at the boy's arm.

His lower lip quivered as he turned away, looking mournfully back over his shoulder at us.

Jasmine waved to him.

He offered her a halfhearted wave back. Then, dropping his chin to his chest, he toddled onto the path and out of the park toward the sidewalk, his now-harried mother at his side.

"She's going to be confused when they get to their next destination early," I said.

Jasmine sighed. "Yeah, ruining a kid's day. Top of my list of things to do."

I crouched to light the candles, beginning with green for earth, but my attention was drawn to Jasmine as she stuffed her hands into her jacket pockets. She was still standing with her back to me, looking out at the park.

"Stop watching me so closely, Betty-Sue," she whispered, hunching her shoulders forward. "You know I'm okay. I'm with you."

I dropped my gaze, lighting the candle with a snap of my fingers. Magic flashed through the inner circle, lighting the other three candles. And, with a light mental push, my reconstruction spell sealed into place around the residual I'd felt on the swing.

I straightened, raising my palms toward the energy contained within the circle. "There isn't much here," I murmured, coaxing the residual forward, then directing it to reform.

The light within the circle shifted, marking the reconstruction as closer to evening but still not after sunset. A late-afternoon day shrouded with heavier cloud cover, perhaps. It was difficult to tell without widening the reconstruction.

Coral appeared before me, sitting on a swing. I quickly stepped to the side so I could see her profile. She was staring straight ahead. Her face was etched by terror and streaked with tears.

Despite my continual resolve to be as professional as possible, a heavy dread seeped into my stomach. "I have Coral," I said.

Jasmine turned to press her hand against the side of my circle, tapping into the reconstruction effortlessly. I didn't need to compensate for the addition of my best friend's magic. I knew the tenor of it as well as I knew my own.

Red-streaked energy blurred the reconstruction. For a moment, I thought I'd lost my grasp on the residual. Then a ruddy-haired male set a ginger-haired girl into the swing next to Coral.

Jasmine swore viciously, slamming her fist against my circle. The accompanying thrust of anger-induced magic momentarily dispersed the reconstruction.

I didn't hear her exact words. Every bit of me was focused on keeping the collection running, and on watching the man visible within it.

No. Not a man.

A vampire.

Specifically, Yale.

Yale was kidnapping Ruby Cameron.

A pulse of adrenaline ran down my spine, weakening my knees and souring my stomach. I squeezed my eyes shut, forcing myself to breathe deeply while I attempted to assess the situation as quickly and rationally as I could. Had I contaminated the reconstruction somehow? Had I influenced the residual with the concern for Jasmine that had been building up in me for almost four months, muddying the magic? Was that even possible? And if so, why would my concern have manifested as Yale? Why not Valko, the vampire that had actually ravaged my cousin?

Because Valko was dead? And Yale was alive?

I felt the magic within the circle ebb, then dissipate.

"He let him go," Jasmine said tonelessly. "The asshole let him go."

I opened my eyes.

My best friend was staring straight ahead, but without really seeing anything in front of her. She lifted her arms, wrapping her hands around her neck as if attempting to cover bite marks that had healed months before. "Kett let him go," she whispered, completely lost in whatever was going on in her mind.

"Jasmine," I snapped, harsher than I'd intended in my worry over her mental state.

She flinched. Then she dropped her hands from her neck, looking guilty.

"Ruby was taken in December," I said, the words rushed as I pieced together the timeline. "Kett took Yale to London in January."

Relief softened Jasmine's face. Then she looked chagrined. "Sorry. I...jumped to conclusions."

"Plus, I'm worried I screwed the collection up somehow."

"You? Screwed up a spell you can call forth in your sleep?"

I nodded, distracted as I felt the reconstruction beneath my hands, waiting to be replayed. "I'm going to play it again before I collect it. Hopefully with sound."

Without waiting for Jasmine to respond, and before I could spend any more time thinking about the ramifications of what I had just potentially discovered in the playground, I triggered the reconstruction.

Within my circle, Yale was crouched before Coral, who was sitting on the swing. The pale-skinned, ruddy-haired vampire was reaching up to touch the witch's cheek. Ruby, sitting in the swing next to her mother, was clutching Coral's arm. Mother and daughter both wore heavier wool jackets and cable-knit hats. Matching mittens hung from Ruby's sleeves, connected through the arms of her jacket by a string.

I held the image still for a moment, absorbing the visual. The skiff of snow on the ground. The clothing everyone was wearing. The tears streaking Coral's cheeks.

The bite mark on her neck that wept with blood.

"He's trying to compel her," I said.

"Wipe her mind, more like." Jasmine's voice was hollow. "And he was successful."

"She fought," I said. I felt the need to defend the witch who had lost her daughter to a vampire, in a playground only blocks from her home.

I stirred the magic of the reconstruction underneath my hands, looking for something, anything, that felt superimposed or false within it.

"You didn't screw it up, Wisteria. Play it out. Then we need to make some calls."

I loosened my hold on the reconstruction.

"There is no Ruby," Yale said. His Welsh accent was sweet and lyrical. "You have no daughter, Coral Cameron."

"Mom?" Ruby cried, shaking her mother.

Coral was staring deep into Yale's eyes, as if oblivious to Ruby's pleas. Except for the constant stream of tears running down her cheeks, dripping into the red plaid scarf looped around her neck.

"You hear me, Coral," Yale said, ignoring Ruby. "You have no daughter. Say it."

Coral opened her mouth. Then she clenched her teeth in a fierce grimace.

"You have no daughter," Yale said again, more forcefully. "Say it, Coral. There is no Ruby."

"Asshole," Jasmine said, snarling. "I'm going to stake the bastard myself."

Coral mumbled something under her breath.

"Mom!" Ruby cried, aghast.

"Say it again, Coral." Yale spoke softly, as if he might be whispering sweet nothings to a lover. "I have no daughter."

"I have no daughter..." Coral whispered. She choked on the words as though they'd been torn from her throat. From her very soul.

Yale chuckled, completely satisfied with himself. Then he shifted forward onto the balls of his feet, licking Coral's neck.

"Mom!" Ruby cried, gripping her mother's arm and shaking her like a rag doll. "Mom!"

Magic streaked through the reconstruction. Yale and Ruby disappeared.

Coral sat on the swing, sightlessly staring out at the playground. The bite mark on her neck was slowly fading. By the time she got home that day, there wouldn't have been any evidence of the attack.

I imagined her wandering to the townhouse, visualizing her barely making it in the door, falling asleep on the couch. Then waking up, confused. Picking up the toys and the pictures of a copper-haired girl, shutting them away in the pink and purple bedroom.

Then...nothing. Coral had stopped eating. And she'd started hurting herself.

The magic in the circle dissipated.

I almost stumbled, shocked out of the scene I'd been visualizing. The heartbreaking aftermath of Yale's terrible deed.

"We need to get this to the reader," I said, grounding myself in the present and the next logical steps in the investigation.

"We need to contact Kett," Jasmine said.

"Of course." I allowed the circle to fall dormant while retrieving two oyster-shell cubes from my bag. "But did you hear Yale's repetitive use of names? He's brainwashed Coral. And before anything else, Nevada needs to know." I placed the first cube in the center of my circle, directly underneath the swing where Coral had been sitting. "She said she didn't recognize the magic used on Coral. So she hasn't dealt with vampire ensnarement before. Or whatever that was. Did you know they could do that? Wipe out long-term memory?"

Jasmine didn't answer.

Crouching next to the cube so that I could channel the reconstruction into it, I glanced up at her. She wasn't listening to me at all. She'd pulled out her phone and started texting.

"Jasmine!" I snapped sharply. "Not while you're in a circle."

She froze, her thumb hovering over the screen.

"And not next to a reconstruction." Magic delighted in frying electronics—especially my magic.

Jasmine grimaced as she shoved her phone in her pocket. "Fine. Just be quick about it."

I touched my fingers to the edges of the cube, capturing the reconstruction within it. Then, taking my time as Jasmine paced the edge of my circle, I duplicated the magic into a second cube. One for the reader and one for us.

"Fine!" Jasmine unexpectedly shouted, throwing her hands up in the air as if we'd been having an argument. "You text him! It's better coming from you, anyway. He'll think I'm playing games."

I tucked the cubes into my bag, then snuffed out my candles without responding—mostly because I wasn't certain what Jasmine needed me to say in order to soothe her. She seemed fixated on Kett, rather than Yale.

My cousin scrubbed her foot across the line I'd etched in the sand, breaking the outer circle. Then, still not offering any clarification about her outburst, she collected her premade spells. Even if they weren't reusable or rechargeable, as I had guessed, it was sloppy to leave such things behind.

Waiting for the wax to harden before I packed my candles away, I crisscrossed through the playground area, looking for any other residual magic. But even following the path along which I expected Yale must have taken Ruby, I found nothing. Vampires didn't exude their magic the same way other Adepts did, but I was hoping that by moving as swiftly as he did, Yale might have left a trace.

Jasmine intercepted me as I crossed back to collect my candles, throwing her arm around my shoulders and pressing her face into my neck.

"I'm sorry," she whispered, her voice muffled by my silk scarf. "I'm just hungry."

I rubbed her back soothingly. "We'll get some food at the hotel."

"After we drop the reconstruction off," she said, assuring me that she was actively straightening out her priorities.

"I'll text Kett in the taxi," I said.

Jasmine stepped back from our embrace, nodding.

"And hey, bonus. You've already done all the background work on the perpetrator. So tracking his movements last December is going to be simple. Especially because we know he was in Chicago."

Jasmine smiled, the expression edged in anger and full of anticipated vengeance. But at least it was a smile.

Returning to Coral Cameron's house, Jasmine and I found the reader and her cohorts still huddled together in the living room, trying to help the brainwashed witch while Jon made another pot of tea in the kitchen.

"Vampire," I said. I pulled the reconstruction out of my bag and handed it to Nevada.

Lavender scoffed. "Capable of this level of damage? I seriously doubt it."

Jasmine and I ignored the witch. Despite my own private concerns with the collection, Lavender was now being beyond moronic, especially when presented with a reconstruction from a witch with my reputation.

The reader set the softly glowing cube down on the coffee table, glancing at her two companions expectantly. Shadow and the purple-haired witch settled down beside her, focusing on watching the scene I'd collected in the park without further ridiculous comments. Evidently, they didn't require my assistance to trigger the reconstruction.

"Coral needs to be admitted to the Academy hospital for treatment," Nevada said. Her voice was remote as she watched Ruby Cameron's kidnapping play out in her mind's eye.

"I'll make arrangements," Jasmine said, pulling out her phone.

"Already done." Lavender straightened as she stepped away from the cube. If the short but heart-wrenching scene collected within it had affected the witch, she certainly wasn't betraying any emotion to that effect.

"That wasn't your place." Jasmine narrowed her eyes at the junior witch. "Was it?"

Lavender squared her shoulders. "It's my team."

"Yet I'm the lead investigator," Jasmine said.

Nevada looked up from the cube, shaking her head with disbelief. "The combination of his venom and whatever mind magic he wields is like using a blunt knife to slice a tomato."

Jon appeared in the doorway to the kitchen, wringing his hands in a tea towel.

Jasmine immediately turned her attention to him. "I'll send in a report to the Convocation, but I can tell you that the vampire's name is Yale. We have a lead on his current whereabouts."

Jon sighed with relief.

Lavender snorted, muttering under her breath, "That's something, at least."

On our quick dash back from the park, Jasmine and I had decided we wouldn't go into details about our connection to Yale. Wary of creating a larger incident between the Convocation and the Conclave, we needed to contact Kett first. Almost as important, though, revealing what we knew of Yale would force us to address the fact that we hadn't reported Jasmine's kidnapping—and my subsequently destroying two vampires, even if involuntarily—to the Convocation. But since that information couldn't be used to cure Coral's condition or to solve Ruby's kidnapping, we would keep it to ourselves for the moment.

As lead investigator, Jasmine called the shots and made the reports. But she was under no obligation to reveal outside information to a junior specialist team.

Jasmine took a few minutes to exchange contact information with Jon, promising to keep him updated regarding the investigation. While she did, Lavender—who I had decided was far too powerful for either her age or her disposition—chalked a simple circle in the living room. Then she transported the four of them—herself, Coral, Nevada, and Shadow, who still hadn't spoken a word—back to the Academy.

With the case barely uncovered and nowhere close to being solved, none of us bothered with thanks or goodbyes.

Leaving Jon alone in his sister's house, Jasmine called a cab. She was already glued to her laptop before it arrived, combing through the information she'd gathered on Yale when she was actively tracking him in January.

Settled into the cab and on the way to the hotel, I pulled out my phone and tried to formulate a text to Kett. Since I'd last seen him in the ballroom at Fairchild Manor, we'd only exchanged occasional texts. Surrounded by buildings of varying heights and representing multiple eras of architecture, I scanned through our previous messages as the cab negotiated Chicago's impressively slow crawl of rush-hour traffic. I hadn't heard from the vampire in three days, when he had texted to randomly ask me if I wore so much navy because it was my favorite color. I replied that I liked blue in general. And he had dropped the conversation.

Not exactly a life-altering exchange. And now I was getting him involved in witch business. Again. It wasn't that I didn't want to see Kett, but the executioner's involvement was a double-edged sword. For Jasmine. And possibly Declan.

Only a block from the hotel, which I belatedly realized we could have walked to from Coral's house, I settled on how to word the text.

We're in Chicago on an investigation for the Convocation. I have reconstructed the scene of a nine-year-old witch being taken from her mother, whose mind has been severely damaged by the kidnapper.

I hit send, wanting to separate my thoughts ... and my accusations.

The child was abducted by Yale. Last December. Her whereabouts, or whether or not she is still alive, are currently unknown.

I sent the second message, then paused. Too many other things needed to be addressed, quickly and without overt emotion. I settled on asking a simple question.

Are you in London?

If Kett was in London, I was hopeful that he would be able to go to Yale, drink his blood, and discover what had happened to Ruby. Assuming that the executioner's brand of telepathy could pinpoint a specific event or time. During my sketchy Academy training on vampires, I'd been taught that their ability to read their victims' minds was often referred to as 'blood truth.' And I had witnessed secondhand Kett's ability to access Nigel Farris's memories, before he allowed the beleaguered vampire to sacrifice his immortality to help complete Benjamin Garrick's transformation.

But I also knew that not all vampires wielded the same magic—or even similar magic, beyond being immortal and needing to consume blood for sustenance. And though Kett had seen Nigel's maker—Yale—in his blood truth, he hadn't picked up that Nigel had been turned into a vampire unwillingly. Or at least that was what he claimed.

Whatever the case might have been, Kett would know why I was asking for his location, so there was no point in needless elaboration.

Jasmine shifted her gaze from the computer in her lap to my phone, reading the texts on my screen. She nodded. "You don't think he'll bring him, do you?"

"I hope not."

The hotel came into sight on our far right—a breathtaking monolith of brick and sandstone, replete with columns, relief sculpture, and other classical details. The cab driver slowly forced his way through the crawling traffic toward the guest drop-off area underneath a burgundy-and-gold metal marquee that bore the logo of the Chicago Hilton.

Jasmine hit a key on her computer with vehement satisfaction, then closed her laptop to peer up at the hotel through my side window. "Beaux-Arts architecture," she said smugly. "And, now that the Conclave will be footing the bill, I just upgraded our suite. Two bedrooms with a parlor, overlooking Grant Park and Lake Michigan."

Shaking my head, I laughed under my breath at her audacity. The hotel was gorgeous, though.

My phone vibrated in my hand, reminding me that I shouldn't have been holding onto it. I tapped the screen to read the incoming text.

>*I'm not in London. But even if I were, it wouldn't matter. Yale is difficult to compel.*

"Damn," Jasmine muttered, reading the text at the same time as me.

>*I'm nine hours away.*

We're staying at the Hilton Chicago.

>*Text me if Jasmine finds anything that directs you out of the city.*

I angled the phone toward my cousin.

She snorted, but it was a pleased sound. The executioner of the Conclave might not have thought that Jasmine had the power or the temperament to be remade into a vampire, but he still valued her investigative skills.

The cab inched along, finally stopping before a front entrance dominated by gold-tinted metal and glass. A doorman leaped forward to open my door, while Jasmine handed her credit card and a ten-dollar bill to the cabbie.

"Tap?" the cab asked.

Jasmine leaned forward, intrigued. "You have that ability remotely now?"

"New machine," the cabbie said, eagerly showing off his technology.

I gathered the grocery bags, climbing out of the taxi before I accidentally shorted out any of those electronics.

"Do you have other bags, miss? Or more parcels?" the doorman asked.

I smiled politely. "We had our suitcases dropped off earlier."

"Ah, yes. I'll have them directed to your room. What name are you registered under?"

"Fairchild. Jasmine Fairchild."

He twisted away, crossing purposefully back through the entrance while another doorman held the door open for me.

By the doorman's 'parcel' comment, I gathered that it looked as if I'd been shopping, rather than reconstructing the kidnapping of a young witch. The smooth French twist and simply tailored clothing I favored probably gave the wrong impression, and for a brief moment, I felt like correcting his assumption. Instead, I settled my overly large bag over my shoulder, turning to Jasmine as she climbed out of the cab behind me.

"We already know where Yale was in January," I said, not elaborating that the ruddy-haired vampire's whereabouts included kidnapping Jasmine. "Had you been tracking him for long before that?"

"Not long." Jasmine twisted her lips sourly. "It was the hotel charge in Litchfield that really drew my attention."

"Which is what he wanted," I said, rehashing the events that we'd been too wrapped up in to fully address at the time. "Because they certainly weren't staying there."

Jasmine nodded ruefully, seemingly open to having the discussion, though she'd been reticent to talk about any of it. I hadn't wanted to push and possibly force her to relive the trauma. But now doing so had suddenly become an unfortunate necessity.

"So you must have gotten their attention somehow before that. Something you did? Or an inquiry you made when you were hunting down Nigel's maker for Kett?"

Jasmine shook her head doubtfully as we wandered toward the door that the second doorman was still holding open for us. The pressed exterior concrete gave way to luxuriously thick carpet as we crossed through the grand entranceway of the hotel.

"You were in New York in December, before spending Christmas in Mexico with Declan... and Copper?" I stumbled over the witch's name. Though I hadn't met or even spoken to Declan's love interest.

Jasmine side-eyed me with a smirk. She hadn't bothered putting her laptop in her leather satchel, simply tucking it underneath her arm. It wasn't likely to be closed long enough to justify packing it away.

"Yep."

"With Kett."

She nodded, but her steps slowed as we approached a bank of elevators. She echoed me thoughtfully. "With Kett."

Following the prompts of the discreet signage indicating the route to our check-in, I pressed the up button to call an elevator.

"The rogue vampires were tracking the executioner of the Conclave," Jasmine hissed triumphantly. "It wasn't about me or Nigel at all."

"That makes more sense," I said, thoughtfully. "If Jasper had been involved in your abduction, then I might have thought differently."

The elevator doors slid open and we stepped in. I selected the lobby level. Despite the upgrade that Jasmine had done online, we still needed to pick up room keys.

"Yale must have seen me with Kett in New York," Jasmine said. "Though I'm not sure how, or where or when. It's not like we left the hotel...much..."

She trailed off as if just realizing she shouldn't be proclaiming how much time she'd spent in hotel rooms with Kett. At least not to me.

"Well," I said wryly. "You had to check in...and out, at least."

She laughed. "Right. It's just that a part of me had been thinking all this time that I'd screwed up, that I'd alerted Yale to my investigation somehow. Anyway, it doesn't matter. The asshole isn't going to get away a second time."

"Well, let's confirm he was in Chicago before we start sharpening the silver stakes."

Jasmine turned to me. "Wisteria, you didn't screw up the reconstruction."

"Actually, I'm more worried about what the hell it all means if I didn't screw up."

"That's what we're here to find out." Jasmine flashed a grin my way, then practically skipped out of the elevator before the doors had even finished sliding open.

I followed at a slower pace. It was hard to feel light-hearted under the weight of all the possibilities of what could have happened to Ruby Cameron, whether we figured it out or not. If Yale had killed the girl, the executioner of the Conclave would end his immortal existence and present his head to the Convocation. Or risk setting back the fragile understanding the vampires held with the rest of the Adept, maybe by hundreds of years. Though they were immortal, vampires were few in number. If other Adepts banded together to end their existence, they'd easily be wiped off the face of the earth in a matter of weeks. Quicker if the guardian dragons got involved.

But if Yale didn't kill Ruby, then where was she? There'd been no sign of her in the caretaker's cottage at Fairchild Manor, where Yale and the others had been squatting in the cellar. Lark had cleaned it all out after the vampires were gone. So Yale had kidnapped the girl sometime in December, but hadn't brought her to Litchfield with him in January. And with the vampire confined to London—perhaps even imprisoned by the Conclave, as best as I understood his current situation—who was looking after the kidnapped child?

Jasmine was turning away from the guest services desk with two keycards in hand before I'd finished crossing into the reception area. Grinning saucily, presumably due to the room upgrade she'd requested, she scampered past me, directing me toward a second bank of elevators that led to the guest rooms.

I picked up my pace, snagging one of the keys from her. "I'm sure the restaurant here is fantastic—"

"Yep," she interrupted cheerily. "Classic American fare at the 720 South Bar and Grill. Luckily, they'll send up room service."

I just nodded. Getting Jasmine to take a long enough break from an investigation to eat in an actual restaurant was always a fruitless cause. Not that I minded. I'd miss the atmosphere, but Ruby Cameron needed to be found. The sooner the better.

The two-bedroom suite was classically decorated in beiges and browns, with generous crown molding and baseboards throughout. Highly polished, dark-stained hardwood flooring laid in a herringbone pattern led in from the entrance, past a long bar and through into a seating area filled with scoop-backed leather chairs and wood-framed windows that boasted a one-hundred-and-eighty-degree view of Grant Park and Lake Michigan. Unfortunately, the view was obscured by torrential rain. Again.

After I forced Jasmine to pick something from the room service menu, but before the food actually arrived, I set the reconstruction I'd collected in the playground on the glass-topped coffee table. Perched on the edge of the midcentury modern gray-fabric couch, I watched and re-watched the painful scene I'd collected within the cube, looking for clues.

Unfortunately, vampires didn't emanate magic or leave as much residual in their wake as most Adepts did. As such, what I'd reconstructed and viewed in the playground was exactly what I'd captured in the cube. No hints of other magic at play. No hidden layers that needed to be investigated. Just Yale ravaging Coral's mind and snatching Ruby, over and over again.

Jasmine had overtaken the desk in the parlor area across from the bar, plugging in a multitude of devices to charge. Some of them, I had no idea what they were or did.

"Aha!" she shouted abruptly. "The asshole was in Chicago." She slapped her hand on the desk, then shook it as though she'd hurt herself. "Parking charge. On his Visa." Her fingers flew across the keys of her laptop. "Just a second... I'm seeing if I can access the... yep. Here it is..." She slumped back in her seat, then met my gaze. "The bastard paid for parking two blocks from the goddamn playground."

I nodded, though the idea of Yale stuffing Ruby in a car and driving off pained me. "It would have been an inopportune time to get towed. You know, when you're kidnapping a child."

Jasmine exhaled shakily, getting up and crossing to the bar area to grab a complimentary bottle of water and ransack the treats.

"Did he rent a car?" I wanted to get my mind back on the case, and not perpetually stuck on the image of a terrified ginger-haired child witch in the clutches of an evil vampire.

Jasmine shook her head.

"But they rented in Litchfield?"

She nodded, then chugged half the bottle of water.

"So... stolen car? Or he owns a vehicle, but didn't want to bring it into Connecticut? Any other charges in Chicago?" I cast my mind back to the receipts Kett had investigated when we'd been tracking Jasmine. Things that would be unusual for a vampire to purchase. "Grocery stores? Restaurants? Takeout? Any indications that he was feeding Ruby?"

"He withdrew cash. Couple of thousand dollars. Same day. I'll keep digging, just... give me a minute. I just need a ... minute ... " Jasmine's voice broke as she turned back to liberate a candy bar from among the snack bar offerings.

My heart twisted in my chest. Jasmine's pain was, as always, my own. It was just unusual for her to be so ... emotionally wrought.

A knock sounded at the door.

"Room service," I said, too brightly. "Perfect timing."

Kneeling by the coffee table, we watched as night fell across the expansive lake. Jasmine nibbled on a burger mounded with aged cheddar, lettuce, tomato, and pickles on a brioche bun, and served with sweet-potato fries. I savored a smoked chicken flatbread layered with Mornay sauce, gouda, and pear, and sprinkled with toasted pecans.

While we ate, Jasmine opened all the notes she had compiled on Yale, then read through them out loud. Other than the parking receipt and the cash withdrawal, nothing else she'd found had indicated where Yale might have gone in Chicago. Or where he was in the weeks between his kidnapping Ruby, then kidnapping Jasmine in Connecticut.

"What about his brood?" I asked. "They're dead now, but they weren't then."

Jasmine grunted noncommittally. "I have profiles compiled on each of them, but not a lot of data. First names, most likely false, and observations. But I didn't take it any further after you and Kett had your grisly way with them." The word 'grisly' was accompanied by a wide, viciously pleased grin. "I'll see what I can do."

I didn't dispute my best friend's version of the events that led to me inadvertently destroying two of Yale's brood, Mania and Amaya. I'd used the magic of my white-picket-fence bracelet—which I had impetuously named Vampire's Bane—amplified through the wild energy called forth from the Fairchild estate. It had reduced the two vampires to ash, after Kett beheaded Valko. Yale had managed to avoid the immolation, though I'd ejected him from the estate. Kett had captured him afterward, taking him to London.

Still, I wasn't the one who'd been imprisoned and forcefully fed on for three days. If Jasmine felt that vengeance had been exacted purposely on my part, then I hoped it helped her work through her memories of terror and confusion. Kett's taking of Valko's head had certainly been done at Jasmine's behest. And that had indeed been grisly.

I was slightly surprised that Jasmine hadn't filled the files she'd started for Valko, Amaya, and Mania, as well as Yale's nameless maker, after she'd been kidnapped. Given her psychological makeup, I would have thought that owning her kidnappers and her rapist after the fact—at least on a digital level—would have given her a sense of power over them.

I hadn't thought to suggest that, though. Perhaps because I'd wanted to believe Jasmine's insistence that she was all right, that she'd been seeing an empathic counselor routinely through the Convocation. Though it was likely that she'd been doing okay, at least engaged in the process of healing—right up to the moment she'd been handed the investigation of a kidnapped nine-year-old witch.

Perched over my plate, I cut another wedge from my flatbread, chewing the cheese-smothered smoked chicken thoughtfully as I ruminated out loud. "August 14."

"Declan's birthday," Jasmine said without looking up from her laptop.

I set down my fork, taking a sip of the red wine Jasmine had selected from the generous collection of bottles underneath the bar. "Ruby's birthday. You said Coral registered her birth with the Convocation."

Jasmine glanced over at me, then shrugged. "So they're both Leos. People share birthdays."

"True."

She bowed her head over her keyboard, multiple windows open across her screen. I had no idea how she kept track of what information she was inputting where.

I reached over and pushed her plate closer to her. She smiled, obligingly dipping a sweet-potato fry in garlic mayo.

"Why would Yale kidnap a young witch?" I asked. "He spends years avoiding the notice of the executioner of the Conclave, carefully cultivating his shiver from willing Adepts."

"Or unwilling," Jasmine interjected.

"Or possibly unwilling," I conceded. "But a nine-year-old couldn't be remade, could she? Besides the fact that Kett indicated turning a child was against Conclave edict, would Ruby's magic be mature enough to accept or assist in the transformation? And if she could be turned, to what end?"

"Ask Kett."

I thought about texting the executioner, but then decided the question could wait until I saw him. "I know the particulars aren't important to finding Ruby as quickly as possible, but it bothers me. Yes, Yale likes to play games. But kidnapping a witch is only going to draw the Convocation's notice, then eventually Kett's attention."

"Eventually," Jasmine said wryly.

And suddenly we weren't talking about Ruby anymore. My stomach squelched. "He showed up within hours, Jasmine."

"After you called."

"He probably would have noticed you were missing earlier…" I trailed off, frowning as I realized I was defending Kett's actions and motivations. I really didn't know him well enough to be doing so.

Jasmine eyed me, twisting her lips in a smile. "I get it. He's not omniscient."

"Thank God."

She laughed.

"How does Yale make money?" I asked, turning the subject back to the investigation. Not that either of us were any less emotional about a missing child, but Ruby's kidnapping was something we could hopefully solve instead of simply enduring. As we endured our childhoods, our family. As Jasmine endured having been kidnapped and assaulted by Valko. "I mean, he had money, right? He has money?"

"Not anymore," Jasmine said nastily. "I donated it all. Well, all of it that I found. He's the type to have gold stashed in a few different places."

I couldn't help but grin. Jasmine might not be able to rip a vampire's head off, but she could seriously screw up someone's life with only a few keystrokes.

Taking another sip of wine and allowing the rich, earthy nectar to roll across my tongue, I hesitated to broach the idea that had been planted in my mind months before. "Kett implied that ... well, we were arguing ... so maybe he brought up Jasper as a distraction ... "

Jasmine narrowed her eyes at me. "But he implied that our uncle was involved in my kidnapping."

"He implied the possibility."

"Of course he did. Because then he wouldn't be solely to blame."

"I'm just thinking that we now know Yale kidnapped two witches. But why? You were leverage against Kett. And maybe some sort of revenge on Jasper's part. But why take Ruby? Why take a nine-year-old?"

"Yale boasted about adding you to his menagerie. Maybe he wanted another witch? Maybe that Mania bitch was driving him nuts."

I shook my head. "That was just because I leveraged being Kett's chosen child against him in order to make him back off. In the kitchen of the cottage, when I was trying to buy you and Declan time to get to the manor. I don't think it was an actual offer, much less a plan."

"You think he took Ruby for someone. You think he makes money kidnapping kids?"

"Or maybe doing anything nefarious for a price. I don't know. But I hope so. Because then there's a chance she's still alive."

Jasmine nodded sadly. "I'll look into the family and closer into Yale's finances. If it's work for hire, then Yale was probably hired by someone who knew Coral and Ruby. Otherwise, it's too much of a coincidence, and therefore potentially untraceable. Her father's dead, so that leaves the grandparents on either side."

"Jon was out of the country."

"Yeah," Jasmine said hollowly. "Good alibi."

Silence fell between us. Pontificating without enough information to back up our suppositions was exhausting, though the two-hour time difference between Seattle and Chicago wasn't helping. I forced myself off the floor, cleaning up our dishes and stashing the tray in the hall. Then I wandered into the bedroom to unpack and iron an outfit for the next day. All of my busy work was comfortingly accompanied by Jasmine's fingers clicking away on the keyboard, and by the sound of her voice as she murmured to herself.

After I brushed my hair out of its twist, then brushed my teeth, I curled up on a scoop-backed leather chair next to the window, tucking my legs underneath me and gazing out at the quarter moon hovering over the otherwise dark lake. Another thunderstorm had passed while we'd eaten.

I didn't know Chicago well, even though I'd been to the city a few times on Convocation business. Despite the fact that Coral and Ruby were Camerons, the Chicago coven wasn't comprised of members from the founding three families. A mixture of witches called the city home, with most of those drawn to the metropolis for work rather than magic. But whether or not Coral and Ruby were in contact with the main branch of the family, Mauve, the head of the Cameron coven, wasn't going to be pleased that a vampire had kidnapped a witch child of her bloodline. That was something I needed to tell Kett—though I wasn't sure when it had suddenly become my job to act as a buffer between the Convocation and the Conclave. It wasn't a burden I would have taken on voluntarily.

It was bad enough that the Fairchild elders had been all huffy, demanding retribution for Jasmine's kidnapping. Not that I'd had to deal with the fallout. As always, Jasmine had managed our parents, though she'd refused both Dahlia and Rose when they asked her to stay in Litchfield. She showed up at my doorstep in Seattle instead, with two obscenely large suitcases and three boxes.

She hadn't unpacked those boxes yet. They occupied the corner next to the Pilates apparatus in my second bedroom, perhaps indicating that her stay was temporary. Which worried me. But I didn't ask.

Our past had been blown wide open, and we had returned from a confrontation with our family alive—though not unscathed. But I still didn't want to chance saying the wrong thing at the wrong time.

I didn't want to chance Jasmine leaving.

Chapter Four

A knock on the hotel door woke me from a light doze. I'd fallen asleep on the couch, with my head propped in the crook of my arm and my legs comfortably curled around Jasmine.

She was up and moving before I'd fully opened my eyes. It was dark. A single standing lamp at the far edge of the couch was the only light, with deep shadows spreading beyond it throughout the room. I hadn't drawn the curtains, but I couldn't determine the weather over the wide, dark lake.

"What time is it?" I murmured sleepily to Jasmine's retreating back.

"Almost midnight." She sauntered over and opened the door, revealing her brother.

My breath caught in my throat—just as it had when I'd laid eyes on him for the first time in over twelve years the previous January. I'd been expecting Kett. Though I should have realized the vampire probably wouldn't have knocked.

Over six feet tall and broad shouldered, Declan filled the doorway. Light from the hotel corridor spilled into the room from behind him. I blinked rapidly, forcing my eyes to focus in the sudden brightness. No one would ever call Jasmine's half-brother handsome. Arresting, perhaps, but there was nothing beguiling about Declan Benoit. Swathed in black leather and with his golden-hazel eyes hidden behind gray-tinted glasses, he was intimidating and forbidden.

To me, at least. But I'd broken Declan's heart many years ago, and though he might eventually forgive me, he would never let me forget.

"Took you long enough," Jasmine groused.

Declan grunted, pressed a kiss to his sister's forehead, then stomped into the suite, tossing a large leather duffle bag onto the floor of the closet immediately inside the door.

"I had something to take care of," he said obliquely. "Before I could leave."

"Oh, yeah? What was that?"

Declan didn't answer, turning his gaze on me as he removed his glasses.

Jasmine gave his duffle a slight kick. "And what is that? Your entire wardrobe?"

I shifted off the couch as Declan continued to ignore his sister, prowling the length of the room toward me. He skirted the coffee table, towering over me without a word. Then he leaned forward slightly. I touched his shoulder as I pressed a polite kiss to his stubbled cheek. He didn't reciprocate.

The bond between us was healing, but still tenuous.

"You look tired," he murmured. "Have you found the girl?"

I shook my head, forcing myself to drop my hand. I could feel his warmth even through his jacket.

He pivoted away, eyeing Jasmine questioningly.

"Yale," she said, grabbing her laptop, then settling into a chair opposite the couch.

"Yale?" Declan glanced back at me, incredulous.

I nodded, gesturing toward the oyster-shell cube on the coffee table, swirling with blue-and-red-streaked magic. "I collected a reconstruction implicating him."

I retreated to the far side of the couch, curling my legs up and leaving the remainder of its length vacant.

Declan narrowed his eyes at the cube, his expression grim. "I thought your vampire had him under control."

"Best as we can figure," Jasmine said, "this happened in December."

Declan scowled. "So the vamp is on his way."

"I'm tracking Yale's movements, putting together a pattern." Jasmine's attention was already back on her laptop. "But yeah, we're also waiting on Kett."

Declan grumbled something as he shucked off his ankle-length, pockmarked black leather jacket. Then he reached for the room service menu.

I was feeling completely useless, as I almost always did whenever I participated in an investigation. At least at a level beyond collecting reconstructions, or presenting my findings to a lead investigator or at a tribunal. So I allowed my gaze to rest on Declan as he ordered food and got settled into the suite.

Soon, I expected that he'd be demanding to talk about Jasper reclaiming the estate magic. Though perhaps he was pleased to have been relieved of a burden he hadn't asked for. Soon, he'd be digging into our investigation of Ruby Cameron. And soon, there wouldn't be any impromptu meetings in random cities. Not for me, at least.

Not after I became a vampire.

So I would enjoy this brief moment of peace, allowing my heart to celebrate having the two people I loved most in the world in the same room with me. Just being, just existing in the same space as Jasmine and Declan was the only thing I'd ever really wanted. The only dream I'd ever had for my future.

It was also the only thing I couldn't ever have.

I cupped my left hand over the white-picket-fence bracelet on my right wrist, feeling the magical artifact's intense power ebb and flow underneath my fingers. A whisper of my own magic emanated from the two tiny reconstruction cubes I'd hidden among the bracelet's platinum house, fence, and tree charms. Two collections that contained precious glimpses of Jasmine and Declan, from before Jasper had ruined our future to the extent that we lost the chance to be together. We lost the possibility of our childhood dream of being Betty-Sue, Betty-Lou, and Bubba.

But whether I was a vampire or not, Jasmine and Declan would always be mine to love. And they'd have each other when I was no longer...me. Or at least the me that was my current incarnation. Keeping them safe from Jasper and loving them from afar would be enough.

So I would savor this moment in time. This breath of regular life. I'd keep it tightly in my heart. And I would continue to endure everything else.

Cool fingertips brushed lightly against my lips, abruptly waking me from a dreamless sleep.

I opened my eyes, seeing only the ceiling of the dark hotel room bathed in the dim blue glow from the digital clock on the side table. I could hear Jasmine's soft breathing beside me. She'd climbed into bed with me about an hour after Declan ate, practically falling unconscious the moment she laid her head on the pillow. Ignoring the empty second bedroom, Declan had taken the bed next to ours.

The air about me shifted as fingers brushed across my right hand, lingering for a moment too long on my bracelet. Far too long for him to be touching a magical artifact I'd boldly named Vampire's Bane.

"Kett," I whispered.

He appeared beside me. The vampire was just a pale smudge looming over me, but I could tell he was smiling.

I glanced toward the curtained windows, keeping my voice pitched low. "What time is it?"

"Almost sunrise." His breath brushed across my neck and right shoulder. "I was getting bored of watching you sleep."

Those words would have terrified another witch. A far more intelligent witch. They would have sent her reaching for defensive magic, if not screaming from the room.

And rightfully so.

Except Kett was flirting. His version of flirting, at least. He'd broken into our hotel room and was attempting to flirt with me while Jasmine and Declan slumbered nearby.

Because what woman wouldn't want to know she was being watched by an ancient vampire while she slept?

Of course, I was the one who'd called him.

Something tickled my exposed arm, then moved up to my shoulder, pooling in a soft cloud of fabric on my neck. My teal pashmina, judging by feel, at least. I couldn't see the actual color in the dark.

I shifted up in the bed as carefully as I could without disturbing Jasmine. Kett swathed my shoulders in the pashmina. Wearing only a navy silk shift that had bunched around my upper thighs as I slept, I freed my legs from the covers and sat on the edge of the bed.

Reaching out for the vampire in the dark, my hand settled blindly on his shoulder as he crouched before my legs. I assumed he was wearing dark colors, because I glimpsed only the pale blur of his face in the darkness before me as he moved.

He stroked the sole of my right foot with cool fingers, causing me to curl my toes. And suddenly I was holding my breath, even more aware of Jasmine and Declan sleeping only a few feet away. What had begun as a stealth mission to relieve Kett's boredom had shifted into something forbidden. Something sexy.

The vampire slipped what felt like one of my hand-knit socks over the toes he'd caressed. He tugged the sock onto my foot, then ran his fingers up the back of my calf and behind my knee.

Warmth pooled in my belly.

I forced myself to breathe.

Kett switched his attention to my left foot, running his fingers underneath in the same slow caress. Then he slid on my second sock. And in doing so, he let me know that he wanted me to join him, perhaps even go for a walk, without speaking a word. Seducing me in the process with his casual, intimate touches.

Still crouched before me, he glanced up. Even with the glow coming off the clock, I couldn't see his expression, if he even had one. My heart rate ramped up, fear mixing with desire. But nonetheless, I lifted my right hand, touching his temple, then running my fingers through his surprisingly soft, silky hair.

He turned his face with my movement, brushing his lips against my wrist beside my bracelet.

"Get in the bed, vampire," Jasmine hissed suddenly. Her voice was cuttingly loud against the cocoon of silence and soft touches that had encased Kett and me. "Or get out of the damn room and let the rest of us sleep."

Declan shot out of the bed beside ours, landing solidly on his feet. Vibrant-blue magic flared, outlining glowing runes that appeared to be suspended in midair.

Apparently, Declan slept with his carved wooden blasting rod. Fully charged.

Kett shifted away from the bed, as if to deliberately draw Declan's attention. Otherwise, I wouldn't have been able to see him move.

Magic ignited, directed at the vampire. And without even thinking, I reached toward the blast, calling forth a shield spell effortlessly. My defensive magic sprang forward from my hands, twisting in the air in front of Kett just in time for whatever spell Declan had amplified with his blasting rod to slam against it.

Magic exploded, sending shards of blue light in all directions.

I took a deep breath, coaxing my hastily manifested shield to encompass Declan's casting, then absorb it harmlessly. Which I could really only do that effortlessly because I knew the tenor of Declan's magic as intimately as I did.

Only a moment had passed.

That was the second time Declan had tried to slaughter the executioner on first sight.

Jasmine flicked on the bedside lamp, momentarily blinding me. "What the hell, Declan?" she shouted.

Blinking, I brought the room into focus again.

Declan was wearing nothing but tight black boxers, displaying glorious miles of naturally tanned, sculpted skin. He stood facing off against the pale-skinned, white-blond vampire, more slightly built in a charcoal cashmere sweater and dark-washed jeans.

Both men were staring at me. Declan was scowling, which was completely normal. Kett with what might have been a hint of a smug smile.

Jasmine was kneeling in the center of the bed, beside and slightly behind me. "You could have set the room on fire," she snarled at Declan.

Her brother lowered his blasting rod, looking utterly taken aback. "He's the one who was creeping around the room!"

"Did you think he was going to knock? And do you sleep with that thing?" she asked, referring to the rod.

"So what if I do?"

Jasmine raised her hands, palms facing forward. "No judgement. I'm just not sure who you thought was going to attack the three of us."

Declan looked pointedly in Kett's direction.

The vampire offered him a saucy smile.

I had to stifle a laugh.

"Unbelievable," Declan said. Then he turned and crawled back into bed.

"Yes, go away now. Some of us didn't take a nap." Jasmine turned off the light, burrowing back underneath the covers.

I stood up, leaning back in the dark to pull the covers up on my side of the bed. Jasmine reached out and wrapped her hand around mine. "It's cold in here without you, Betty-Sue."

I squeezed her hand, but she raised her voice, interrupting me before I could respond.

"Bring the vampire to bed when you come back," she said. "He's fun."

Declan cursed, muffled by his pillow.

I laughed softly as I turned away from the bed. Kett slipped a hand underneath my elbow, guiding me out of the room into the main section of the suite.

Softly shutting the door to the bedroom behind us, I crossed to and flicked on the standing lamp beside the couch. The curtains stood open and a hint of light was blooming across the lake. The reconstruction I'd collected in the park glowed faintly from the coffee table, sitting next to Jasmine's open laptop.

"Bored watching me sleep, hey?" I arched an eyebrow at Kett. "Before or after you went through Jasmine's notes?"

He inclined his head. "The tech witch hasn't changed her password."

"Oh, well. That's practically an invitation."

He chuckled softly, crossing to gaze out at the predawn light along the water.

I curled up on the couch, playing briefly with my bracelet and waiting to see where Kett wanted to start the conversation. I didn't mind letting him lead. I found that his questions, along with his rare answers, often gave me a different perspective on things. I watched the magic swirl within my reconstruction as a comfortable silence fell between us. Blue witch magic—my magic, paired with residual from Coral's attempt to free herself from Yale's ensnarement—swirled within slashes of the deep, dreadful red that marked the vampire's power.

"Have you found the girl?" Kett asked, not turning from the window.

"No."

"Will you play the reconstruction for me?"

I shifted forward toward the coffee table, but the vampire settled beside me with the glowing cube in hand before I got my foot to the floor. I managed to not flinch, but only because I was still in the haze of trying to wake up without a liberal application of coffee.

Kett held the reconstruction aloft on his fingertips before us. I settled back on the couch, then deliberately leaned toward him, allowing my shoulder to rest lightly against his in an attempt to initiate intimacy. He relaxed back onto the couch and into the physical contact, acknowledging my awkward attempt to bond without question. Still, it was similar to leaning against a chilly concrete wall. Or, given Kett's complexion, perhaps marble was a more apt comparison.

"So playing reconstructions still stymies you," I said teasingly.

"Witch magic doesn't come at my behest," he said, more seriously than I'd anticipated. "I can feel magic, sometimes even see it. For instance, this cube glows. And I'm naturally resistant to most spells and charms. But I cannot cast."

He didn't sound mournful or regretful, but I felt inconsiderate all the same. "I apologize for the intrusive question," I said. "I was trying to be playful. I'm not … I don't have a lot of practice at … this … "

"I understood. However, I'm simply attempting to communicate more clearly. As requested."

I laughed. Then I quieted as I recalled how the magic we'd called forth had whirled around us as we danced in the ballroom at Fairchild Park, just before I'd made the request for more clarity in our conversations.

"Will it be the same for me?" I forced myself to focus on the present. "When you remake me? Will I be able to cast? To create reconstructions?"

"I don't know."

When he didn't elaborate, I glanced his way with a smile. "That must be difficult to admit."

He flashed me a grin that looked almost involuntary. "I believe there is a good chance you will be able to retain some of your abilities … but you will likely need to relearn most of them. To adapt to casting with your new … form. Few vampires have the patience to focus on such things when they are fledglings. And when the transformation takes full hold of them, they find they have lost the abilities. But it is likely that it will not be so … all-consuming for you."

"The bloodlust, you mean?" Though my stomach twisted with nervous anticipation, I was pleased that my voice was steady.

He nodded almost imperceptibly. "The need to hunt. The desire to consume. Almost as if the act of doing so might fill the ... emptiness that comes with the loss of your humanity." He paused as if remembering something. Then he whispered, "That was how it was for me. A fruitless endeavor. I have not personally guided another fledgling through their transformation, but I have discovered that the process might be different for you. My maker was young."

"While you're absolutely ancient," I said, trying to inject some lightness back into our conversation. Continually focusing on a future filled only with dark prospects was draining. I preferred the present, and the idea—whether false or not—that I controlled my thoughts and actions in the moment.

A smile ghosted across Kett's face. But then he shifted his steady gaze to the cube, lifting it slightly. "My grandsire is ... intrigued with the newest addition to his shiver."

"Yale."

"Indeed. A former amplifier."

An amplifier. An Adept with the ability to amplify or augment another's power, though such Adepts usually had no ability to wield other magic themselves. That explained the silver or white halo I'd spotted in the reconstructions of the ruddy-haired vampire. "Which makes him extra valuable." I couldn't contain the anger that tainted my words.

"For his blood at least."

I glanced at Kett. "But not for his ability to make multiple vampires?"

"What good are weak fledglings?"

"They could control themselves."

"Yale controlled them."

"What do you mean by 'for his blood,' then?"

"My grandsire has...maintained his position for so long because he is the most powerful among us."

"More powerful than you?"

"He possesses certain gifts that I do not."

"Like the one he passed to your maker?"

"And others."

I glanced away from the reconstruction Kett still held aloft, studying his profile for a moment. His lips curled into an amused smile, but he didn't look away from the cube. Everything was some sort of test with the executioner...or a lesson.

"He can absorb the powers of other vampires, other Adepts, by drinking their blood," I said. It was just a guess. But last January, within the maelstrom of magic I'd called forth at Fairchild Manor, Kett had bitten me, drunk my blood, then walked away untouched through magic that had immolated two other vampires. "As you do."

"Sometimes the effects are temporary with the blood of other Adepts. I couldn't wield a witch's magic, even if I drained her."

"But with vampires?"

"I have accumulated much during the course of my time as the executioner of the Conclave."

"Valko wasn't worth draining," I whispered, echoing Kett's disdain after he'd severed the rogue vampire's head. "But others have been."

He nodded slightly.

I swallowed, feeling a bit heady—though not as aghast as I should have been. For a witch who strove to walk in the light, at least.

"Your grandsire is...milking Yale?" I couldn't help feeling a bit vindicated at the thought of Yale being continually drained against his will.

"Fitting," Kett said, darkly echoing my thoughts. "Considering what he allowed Valko to do to Jasmine."

Pleased by the sentiment, I settled my hand on the vampire's knee, leaning sideways to brush a light kiss against his chiseled cheek.

"I wouldn't be too pleased about it," he said, ruining the moment. "That is why we'll be avoiding London as much as possible. My grandsire fears to drink from me, after Peru. But when I take you as my child, that reluctance will likely be negated. For both of us."

Ignoring the chill that ran up my spine at Kett's use of the word 'us' and what that might mean, I asked, "What happened in Peru?"

"I drank from a dragon."

"A dragon?" I echoed stupidly. I wondered how he had managed to find and catch such a creature, and why he wanted to drink its blood in the first place. Then, shocked, I realized what he was talking about. "A guardian?"

"No. A rogue trapped in fledgling form. Powerful enough to distract us from our treasure hunt, but not so powerful that ingesting her blood destroyed me." His tone turned thoughtful. "Not that I knew as much at the time. And I did vomit a fair amount. All over Jade."

"And..." I struggled to follow the sequence of events he was piecing together for me. "Your ability to survive such...consumption concerns your grandsire?"

"Yes."

"But I thought he...I thought power was important to him." And before Kett could answer me, a pertinent piece of our pending future clicked into place for me. "Is that why he forced you into the contract with Jasper...with me?"

"No." He brushed his fingers across my hand, which still rested on his knee. "The contract was inked before Peru."

He touched my bracelet lightly. The artifact fascinated him, though I wasn't sure whether that was more for its ability to harm him—and other vampires—or because it had been created by Jade Godfrey. Perhaps that was the same reason he went treasure hunting with the dowser as well. It seemed an unlikely friendship. But I understood the bond that formed when you almost died for another person. As I had for Jasmine and Declan, and they for me. As Jade and Kett had for each other.

"I'm sure the dowser was pleased that you survived," I said, feeling the need to acknowledge his confession but not wanting to offer empty platitudes.

Kett laughed the way he did when he was thinking of Jade. And for the first time, the sound made me wistful.

"Will we be friends?" I asked. "With the dowser?"

"I hope so," he said earnestly. "Though I'm uncertain as to how she will react when she sees you at my side."

"You haven't mentioned … me … us?"

He shook his head slightly. "She will not be pleased that I've … taken your life. There might not be any latitude in her moral code for that infraction."

My stomach hollowed. Not because Jade and I were any great friends, but because of what Kett was possibly being forced to give up. The vampire, as far as I could tell, didn't have many people he loved. Perhaps even fewer than I did.

"Kett … "

"It's no matter that time won't fix, reconstructionist. As with all things." And with his use of my title rather than my name, he erected a barrier of cool detachment between us.

I shifted my shoulder from his and removed my hand from his knee, reaching for the reconstruction still at his fingertips. Allowing the transition from intimate conversation to professional interaction without hesitation.

I was better at keeping myself distant, after all. It was easier for me. Effortless, even. And some barriers weren't meant to be breached.

"When I first called the magic forward," I said, easily falling into my professional patter, "I thought I'd made a mistake somehow. But I've examined the reconstruction multiple times. I don't believe it's been compromised."

"You thought you impressed your own magic into the scene? Doubtful."

"Jasmine said the same." I rested my fingers on the edge of the cube, carefully not touching Kett. "It's … disturbing."

"I shall survive the viewing."

He was trying to be playful again, but I shook my head. "No. I simply meant that I won't watch it again. I … I … have gleaned all I can."

Kett was silent for a moment. Then he simply said, "Show me."

I nodded, then triggered the reconstruction, allowing the magic to flow so that Kett could view it in his mind's eye.

I shifted back on the couch, folding my legs underneath me. Suddenly cold, I found myself wishing I was tucked into bed between Jasmine and Declan. The vampire didn't seem to generate any heat, so he wasn't helpful in that regard. But I shoved the childish thought away. A girl was missing, and that trumped any chill I might have.

I glanced out the window. The rising sun was brighter across the lake, lightening it from the eastern horizon.

"Again," Kett said.

I brushed my fingers across the cube, triggering the scene once more and trying to not run a memorized version of its events in my mind at the same time. The kidnapping in the park would undoubtedly be lodged in my memory for as long as I lived. Though perhaps that was something I would lose when I was remade in the vampire's arms. When

I was as cold as he was. But the thought filled me with sudden sorrow. Ruby and Coral deserved every ache of my distress and all my stifled tears.

Kett was watching me, not the reconstruction.

I shook my head, negating my tumultuous emotions and ready to move forward.

The vampire nodded as if sensing my transition. "I suggest you look for more missing children."

My chest hollowed. "More?" I asked.

"If he was feeding from them," Kett said grimly, "there will be more."

I stood up, clutching my pashmina shawl around my shoulders and pacing across the ever-brightening room. I was unable to absorb the implications of Kett's assessment and stay seated. "You're saying it's a ... predilection?"

"I'm saying he might be addicted to witch blood. Or to taking the life essence of a child, specifically."

I pressed my hand to my chest, trying and failing to fight the terror that the idea of Yale kidnapping more children evoked.

Kett continued despite my obvious distress. His tone was completely dispassionate, though he held himself stiffly. "He had surrounded himself with adult children, which would seem to be at odds with a predilection ... as you call it."

I steadied myself on one of the room's barrel-backed armchairs. I breathed deeply, then met Kett's silvered gaze. "Tell me he dies for this. If he's ... killed her. Ruby. If he's hunting children."

"I'll destroy him myself," Kett said darkly. "Killing children is outlawed. And has been for many centuries."

"Yeah," I said nastily. "I imagine the Adept wouldn't take too kindly to their children being hunted."

"Indeed," Kett said coolly.

I closed my eyes, aware that my anger toward Kett was unfounded. And completely unprofessional.

Suddenly beside me, he laid his hand on the back of my neck. His cool touch calmed me further.

"Or perhaps I shall take you, Wisteria." His breath brushed across my neck and ear. "Infuse you with the power in my blood, and let you wreak vengeance on Yale yourself."

I opened my eyes.

He brushed his fingertips across my cheek, then settled his hand on my shoulder. The red of his magic was flecked within the silvery-blue of his eyes. He dropped his gaze to my neck, as if he might be watching my pulse.

My heart rate slowed even further. I turned my head toward him, deliberately brushing my lips against his ear. "Promise."

His fingers flexed, momentarily crushing my collarbone, then instantly releasing. "Always."

"Good."

Thus fortified, I stepped away from the embrace, crossing into the bedroom to wake Jasmine. I couldn't look for other missing children without her. And I certainly couldn't wait for her to wake up on her own. I could, however, order her an omelet with extra cheese to soothe her distemper.

Jasmine turned her head toward me as I entered the room, as if she might have been lying awake, staring at the ceiling. Or listening to Declan snore softly. Even with the drapes drawn, the room had brightened enough for me to see her pensive expression.

"What does he think?" she asked, keeping her voice hushed.

"That there might be more missing children."

"Goddamn it." She flipped back the covers, swinging her legs off the bed. But before she stood, she reached back for her pillow, then used it to beat Declan across the back.

Her brother was sprawled across the second bed with the sheet up only to his waist. Leaving inches upon inches of tanned skin to ogle. Or for me to ogle, at least. Apparently, he'd done something to annoy his sister.

He only grunted in response to the pillow beating. So Jasmine stood and pummeled him with the down-filled weapon a while longer.

"What?" he asked blearily.

"We're getting up." Jasmine hit him a few more times for good measure.

"Good for you."

"And you are going to get us some coffee."

"Order it from room service."

"Oh no, buddy. If I'm up, you're up. And being useful. Wisteria likes good coffee."

I interjected. "I'm sure the hotel's blend is—"

Jasmine held up her hand to silence me. "You've got ten minutes, Declan."

"Ten minutes," he mumbled. "Got it."

Jasmine hit him one last time, then tossed the pillow onto his back. She crossed around the bed, leaning into me to whisper, "He's sad."

"I think he's sleepy."

Jasmine shook her head as if I were an idiot, then crossed through to the bathroom.

I glanced at Declan, who appeared to have gone back to sleep. But I knew it was exceedingly unfair to ogle him when I'd just been attempting to flirt with Kett in the next room. I turned away, stepping back out into the living room and partially closing the door behind me. It was odd that Jasmine thought Declan was sad just because he preferred to sleep past dawn. Though perhaps I had missed something in our interactions the previous night.

A dark-haired, slim woman abruptly appeared between me at the bedroom door and Kett at the far window.

I flinched, involuntarily glancing toward the main door to the suite, though it seemed highly unlikely that she could have opened and closed it without me noticing. I forced my gaze back onto the woman, which was where my attention should have been in the first place—on the threat that had just apparently teleported into the room.

Though how a vampire could have appeared that way without the use of magic—or at least not any magic I could feel—was a mystery to me.

Kett turned from the window, eyeing our uninvited guest with a sneer. "A text message would have been more appropriate."

She strolled across the space between them, laying her hand on his arm. She was about three inches shorter than me, with dark-brown hair pinned back except for too-short, curled-under bangs. Those were even more dated than her oversized cat's-eye sunglasses, high-waisted cigarette pants, and ballet flats.

"There was a time when we didn't need such mundane means to communicate, my boy."

"Thankfully, those days are long gone."

She lifted her face to his, whispering, "For now."

A shiver ran down my spine.

She laughed scornfully, as though responding to my unease. There was something so practiced, so completely arrogant, about her that I easily shook off my instinctual fear and stepped farther into the room. Despite the fact that I was still clothed only in a silk shift, hand-knit socks, and my pashmina, I squared my shoulders and lifted my chin, indicating without speaking that I expected to be formally presented.

Kett's gaze flicked to me. A slow, satisfied smile curled his lips.

The dark-haired vampire swiveled her head—the movement utterly inhuman—to gaze at me over her shoulder.

"Her?" she asked derisively.

"Do you bear a message?" Kett asked.

"Do you have manners?"

"None learned from you."

She laughed mirthlessly. "From your connection to the human world, then."

Kett sighed.

I wasn't certain I'd ever heard him express so much emotion in a single breath. And in that moment, I understood that the dark-haired vampire's use of the endearment 'my boy' had been intentional.

I was standing before Kett's maker.

I suddenly found myself hoping that I was wrong about her ability to teleport. Then I fervently wished that teleportation wasn't the 'gift' she'd inherited from her maker, Kett's grandsire. Because the idea of a vampire who could teleport and who was more powerful than the executioner himself was nightmare inducing. Even for me.

"Wisteria Fairchild," Kett said, blithely offering introductions as if I hadn't just been silently, and rather rudely, assessing every inch of his maker. "Scion of the Fairchild coven. Reconstructionist."

"And your chosen," the dark-haired vampire added mockingly. She removed her sunglasses, keeping her gaze riveted to me.

Kett inclined his head.

"You always had a thing for witches."

"This time, the choice was not my own."

"Yes. You've made your dissatisfaction well known," the woman said. "And now I see why." She eyed me.

Kett stiffened angrily.

I threw my head back, laughing. Two could play the haughty game, and I'd learned that game from teachers who could run circles around the dark-haired vampire. She was out of practice, and my mother personified arrogance and disdain.

I stopped laughing as abruptly as I'd begun. Then I eyed Kett's maker coolly.

She frowned.

Kett's lips twitched. "Estelle, maker of Kettil the executioner and elder of the Conclave, child of Ve."

I noted, as I was sure Kett intended, that Estelle held no titles of her own. So she wasn't an elder of the Conclave, even though she was older than Kett—by his own accounting—by at least a hundred years.

"Ve?" I asked.

"Still your tongue, witch," Estelle snapped. "His name may not bless your lips."

I raised an eyebrow in Kett's direction.

He inclined his head slightly. "You will call him grandsire."

"Not if I have any say in it," Estelle said, smoothing her hair back from her face.

"Audrey Hepburn," I blurted out, finally putting together what was so familiar about Estelle's contrived look. She would have been better off channeling some of the famous actress's charm, not just her iconic style.

Jasmine abruptly pushed through the bedroom door, shouldering past me. "What the hell is going on in here?"

Behind her, the faint sound of the shower emanated from the bedroom's en suite. I was relieved that Declan wouldn't be too quick about joining us and potentially complicating the situation even further. What with his penchant for blasting vampires.

Estelle's dark gaze fell on Jasmine. Her expression turned predatory, sweeping over my best friend's tousled blond curls and voluptuous curves, barely contained within a bright-blue tank top and cotton pajama pants printed with all different kinds of cheese.

"Oh, yes." Estelle sighed affectedly. "I like this one."

She stepped forward, already lifting her hand toward Jasmine as if to beguile her.

Kett placed his hand on Estelle's arm, halting her forward momentum.

She frowned, glancing down to where he held her in place. "You dare?"

"I do dare," he said. "Test me."

A fierce, almost gleeful anger spread across Estelle's face. And for a heart-stopping moment, I thought she was about to slaughter all of us. Then her features smoothed, and she smiled.

"Illuminating," Jasmine said. Then, completely ballsy, she reached forward, offering to shake Estelle's hand. "Hi, I'm Jasmine."

Kett loosened his hold on his maker. Estelle glided across the room, clasping Jasmine's hand in her own as if it were something precious. "Hello, darling one. I'm Kett's sire."

"Pleased to meet—"

Estelle shrieked. Sweeping Jasmine's curls back from her neck, she carefully lifted my cousin's chin. Red flooded the whites of her eyes, but whether from blood or magic, I wasn't sure. Still holding Jasmine's chin, she spun back to snarl at Kett.

"It wasn't me," he said mildly.

"A witch," she snapped. "In your territory!"

"He has been destroyed."

"What's up, almighty vampires?" Jasmine took a step back from Estelle. "Us mortals don't follow."

"Your bite marks," Kett said.

Jasmine lifted her hand to her neck. The bites had healed months before—and without scarring, thanks to Rose and some liberal doses of my mother's salves.

"Though..." Kett said, feigning thoughtfulness. "His maker still lives."

"Tell me," Estelle demanded, then she turned to Jasmine. "I shall make him pay for the transgressions of his progeny, my sweet witch. To ravage someone as lovely, as full of light as you, is dreadful. Such blood should be savored, cherished."

"Yale," Kett said bluntly.

Estelle stilled, withdrawing her hand. She'd been about to caress Jasmine's cheek. "Yale," she echoed darkly.

"Yes, Yale. Your maker's new favorite toy."

Estelle didn't take her gaze from Jasmine. Narrowing her eyes, she nodded thoughtfully. "These things can be managed."

She turned back to Kett. "I approve of this one," she said. "The same blood runs in her veins. You may make her my grandchild."

"She would not survive the transition," Kett said, though not unkindly.

Jasmine shrugged. "This isn't news to anyone."

Estelle frowned, then shook her head at Jasmine as if she'd spoken out of turn. "I say she would."

"Your ability to sense magic was always wanting." Kett somehow managed to even sneer with a sense of detachment.

A terrible energy shifted between them, causing me to grit my teeth and Jasmine to take another step back. It was obvious that Estelle wasn't accustomed to anyone questioning her, especially not her own progeny.

Behind me, Declan stuck his head into the room, echoing Jasmine's entrance. "What the hell is going on in here?" His hair was wet, his shoulders dappled by water as if he'd just stepped out of the shower. He was, in fact, completely naked except for the towel he held cinched around his waist.

Estelle sighed as if heaven had just opened its gates to her. Then she abruptly appeared beside me, facing Declan. I hadn't seen her move. And, again, I hadn't felt any magic. She was just suddenly standing shoulder to shoulder with me.

Declan flinched.

"You…" She reached for him dramatically. "You, I will take myself."

"The hell you will," Declan snarled.

Estelle's magic shifted, stilling in that way that Kett's energy did when he was planning to take some sort of most-likely bloody action. Terror raked my brain as I twisted, stepping back and thrusting myself between her and Declan.

Her lip curled in a snarl. She lifted forward on her toes, perhaps readying to grab me.

I slammed my hand against her chest and—impossibly—shoved her across the room. She slammed against the bar that ran the length of the far wall, the dark wood crumpling beneath her impact.

"Oh," Jasmine moaned. "That's going to be difficult to explain."

Estelle vanished and reappeared again, standing suddenly before me and shoving her nose against mine. "You dare, witch," she snarled.

Calmly, I pressed my fingertips against her chest, now intentionally channeling all the magic I could into the bracelet on my wrist. "Declan and Jasmine are under my protection. You will not touch either of them without explicit, uncoerced permission."

Declan snorted, indicating with that single sound that he'd die before he gave a vampire permission to touch him.

Estelle stepped back—not from any unease, but simply to get a better look at the magical artifact I wore on my right wrist. I allowed my arm to follow her, keeping contact. Her chest was as hard as Kett's, though she was slighter in build. Almost gaunt.

"The bracelet isn't as easy to dismiss," Kett said wryly. He hadn't moved from the window. The sun had fully risen behind him, casting a rosy glow across his shoulders.

"Neither is the dowser's power," Estelle said. Her tone was neutral, so I didn't get a sense of how well she knew Jade. Her gaze flicked back to me. "The boy is enchanting. I trust you can empathize with my reaction. Might I suggest you keep him near?" She glanced over at Jasmine. "In fact, keep both of them near. They will slake your newborn thirst well."

I opened my mouth, readying a vehement protest of her exceedingly disturbing suggestion.

Estelle disappeared.

Kett sighed again, harshly. "The message?" he asked, lifting his gaze to the sunrise-tinted ceiling.

A thick parchment envelope landed on the coffee table beside him.

Jasmine looked at me with wide eyes. "Teleportation?"

"Apparently."

Declan swore under his breath in Creole as he retreated into the bedroom, presumably to find some clothing. He dropped the towel on the floor, giving me a fantastic view of his hindquarters. I quickly reached for and shut the door, turning back to find Jasmine smirking at me.

Kett had opened the envelope and was reading its contents. "Yale will need some time before he is able to answer questions."

"Time?" I asked. "How much time?"

"However much time it takes him to reabsorb the blood that he's been drained of. Apparently, he attempted to escape a few days ago and paid heavily for the infraction. None of the elder vampires will feed him, and human blood will take longer to revive him."

"Okay," I said, my heart sinking deeply in my chest. "Okay, well…we take the timeline that Jasmine is piecing together of Yale's movements and we keep looking for other locations. And…other missing children."

Jasmine nodded, already settling down in front of her laptop. "I'm going to focus on the time between Chicago and Litchfield. We know New York is a possibility somewhere in there."

"I'll order breakfast. We're going to need more than the fruit and juice we picked up." I retrieved the room service menus from beside Jasmine's elbow.

"Declan is getting coffee and something…donuts or bagels," Jasmine said. "Maybe you could check in with Lavender, ask her about Coral? Maybe they've accessed more of her memories."

I nodded as I turned back to knock lightly on the bedroom door, wanting to retrieve my phone from charging on the bedside table. I was more than happy to be directed toward some useful effort. Hanging around waiting for opportunities to collect reconstructions was wearisome, which was why I was usually called in only at specific times during an investigation.

"Why is New York a possibility?" Kett asked Jasmine quietly.

"We figure that's where the vampires connected us," she said. "You and me."

I knocked on the door again.

"Yeah!" Declan called from inside the room. I took that as an invitation to enter.

"Kett?" Jasmine whispered behind me. "You can still see the bites?"

My heart squelched as I darted into the bedroom to grab my phone. And so I didn't have to hear Kett's answer.

"She's not all right." Declan spoke quietly from behind me.

I wheeled around to face him, pleased to discover he was fully clothed in his typical black T-shirt and jeans.

"She was okay," I said. "But ... maybe she was just hiding it."

He nodded. "I'm glad she moved in with you."

"It's the investigation, I think. Even before we tied Yale to Ruby's kidnapping. But I ... I guess we could hand it off."

"No. I get that it's personal now. But she'll be fine with us to balance her. Though honestly, I wish the vamp wasn't here. I ... " Declan clamped his mouth shut on whatever he was going to say, then shook his head.

"Yale's involvement makes this a Conclave matter," I said.

He nodded, not meeting my gaze. "Right. Okay. I'm going for coffee. You like a dark roast, no cream or sugar. Yes?"

I couldn't help but smile a little. He had just pretty much described himself. Physically, Declan was the complete opposite of Kett. Dark haired and dark skinned. Tall and bulky, rather than chiseled and lithe. And maybe, just maybe, that complete contrast was good for me, for my heart. Maybe that would give the vampire and me a chance to cement the bond that was being forced upon us.

Declan laughed lightly, responding to my grin. Smirking, he turned to grab his money clip and keychain from the bureau. He hesitated, brushing his fingers across the twelve tiny reconstruction cubes that decorated the keychain. The reconstructions I'd collected with him in mind, and which I'd sent to him for every birthday we'd spent apart, even though we hadn't been in contact.

I tore my gaze away from him, scrolling through the contacts on my phone for Lavender's information.

"Wisteria," Declan said, not looking up from the tiny, softly glowing cubes. "It's more than the assault, than the kidnapping, for Jasmine. She … we … we're both struggling with losing you."

Unbidden tears flooded my eyes. I struggled unsuccessfully to keep them in check. "I know," I said, finding my voice. "I know. It would be the same for me." Leaving the tears that had fallen to trail down my cheeks unhindered, I met his gaze. "But … it's selfish of me. But I won't lose you. You or Jasmine. If I accept Kett's offer, I get to keep you."

I pressed my hand across my chest, pausing to breathe against the block of pain lodged there.

"You don't know that Jasper would come after us," Declan said softly.

"You felt him take the estate magic back."

"It's his to wield."

"It isn't. Not how he chooses to wield it."

"So you're going to be the Fairchild moral compass now?" The edge was creeping back into his voice.

I wiped the tears from my face.

Declan grimaced, turning away to angrily stuff his keys and money clip into his pockets. "I … I find it difficult to talk to you. About this, about anything."

"But you have Jasmine," I said. "And she'll have you. And that has to be enough."

"You're just so goddamn rational about it," he said, snarling.

"I try to be."

He nodded stiffly, then left the room without another word.

And I cried. As silently as possible, I stood between the messy beds that had held the only two people I loved in this world just an hour before, and I cried. I cried for all the sleepy evenings I was going to miss. I cried for all the coffees and breakfasts we wouldn't share. I cried over losing Declan again, having already lost him once before. Having lost what might have been between us. I cried.

Then I gathered my sorrow tightly into my chest, just as I gathered magic into a reconstruction cube. I held it there, breathing through it, absorbing it. And I recalled Jasmine laughing, leaning into Declan in the restaurant in Litchfield. I remembered his smile and their ease together.

They were going to be okay without me.

I went into the bathroom and splashed water on my face. Then I dug around in Jasmine's makeup bag for her under-eye cream, hoping it had magical properties, because I certainly needed all the help I could get.

Finally, I called Lavender for an update on Coral. Putting aside my pain, putting aside the looming future, because Ruby might still be alive.

And if she wasn't?

Then Kett had made me a promise. For Ruby. For Jasmine. And I'd make certain that Yale paid.

Chapter Five

"I've got nothing," Jasmine said, throwing her hands up in the air as I entered the main area of the suite.

"You've been looking for five minutes," I said, glancing up from the notes I was still typing into my phone from my conversation with Lavender—a transcript detailing our two minutes of stilted communication, which had only served to inform me that she and Nevada hadn't uncovered any additional leads into Ruby's whereabouts.

"No, I mean I've got Yale's movements mapped out." Jasmine was perched over her laptop, which she'd set up on the desk in the parlor area again. "From New York to Chicago, then to Los Angeles. But I don't have anything else connecting him to LA."

"And any other missing witches?"

"None that I could find who fit the timeline. And nothing registered with the Convocation."

I sent my notes to Jasmine, who grunted in acknowledgment when they popped up on her screen. I tried to think about the many ways an Adept like Yale could hide from magical investigation—and all the ways he might kidnap a witch such as Ruby, who wouldn't necessarily be immediately reported to the Convocation. "What about local law enforcement?"

"For a missing witch? How would I even make the distinction from mundanes? I need to figure out where Yale lives, or lived. Like, whether he maintained a residence where he could have been keeping Ruby."

I nodded, content to follow Jasmine's lead. Not finding any substantive evidence to support Kett's theory of Yale's possible predilection for feeding on children, or at least on young Adepts, was a positive outcome. One missing child was enough.

"Where's Kett?" I asked.

"Who knows? Doing whatever he does when he needs to feed but can't ask to feed on us."

My jaw dropped.

Jasmine snorted. "He's too pale. Even for him. His magic is more present in his eyes. I get the impression he has a hard time being around the three of us. You know, without tearing our throats out. You heard his maker say that thing about him and witches? And here I thought I was unique." She laughed, softening the wry twist of her voice.

"Actually, I was putting the flight crew on notice." Kett's blisteringly cold voice emanated from behind me. "I thought it would distract Jasmine, so I stepped into the hall."

I glanced over my shoulder.

The door to the corridor was slowly closing behind Kett, his phone still in hand. He raised an eyebrow at me. "We're heading to LA?"

"Are we?" I asked.

"Yep," Jasmine said, completely nonplussed over being overheard. "I've verified another car rental on Yale's credit card. In Los Angeles for three days at the beginning of January. So after New York and Chicago, but before he drew my attention in Connecticut. He also withdrew more cash from an ATM there. So I'll keep digging, but we might as well be on the jet heading there while I do."

"All right. You're the lead investigator."

"And don't you forget it." Jasmine flashed me a grin. "We'll head out as soon as Declan gets back with breakfast. What's taking him so long?"

"Well, you did demand the best coffee," I said.

"For you, Betty-Sue." Jasmine jumped up from the desk, packing up her computer and other electronics. "For you."

Hustling by, she kissed my cheek, offered Kett a saucy grin, and exited into the bedroom.

I called after her. "I got nothing new from Lavender, by the way."

"I already read your notes." Her voice faded as she crossed past the partially open door, getting ready to pack and change.

"She implied that the sooner we found Ruby, the better." I pitched my voice a little louder so my best friend could hear me. "Which wasn't particularly helpful." I looked at Kett, including him in the conversation. "The witch, Lavender, intimated that having Ruby back could possibly help the reader deal with the block on Coral's mind."

"Lavender's a delightful witch." Even practically yelling from the other room, Jasmine's sarcasm was unmistakable. "So caring. And professional."

I looked at Kett questioningly. "Based on the weeping bite marks already on Coral's neck at the beginning of the reconstruction, Yale bit her, then exerted his...powers of persuasion. Is that...normal?"

"The gift is different for everyone," Kett said. "Beguiling victims is generally within every vampire's abilities. Clouding a mind, taking a snippet of time so you may feed, is a combination of the influence of venom and a vampire's skill at wielding forms of telepathic magic. What Yale has done is…rash, clumsy. There was absolutely no way he wasn't going to be caught."

"Can you undo it?"

"No. I am no healer."

"The reader, Nevada, has no experience with this. The Convocation is seeking out a telepath with some understanding of vampires. So far, they've been unsuccessful."

"Most vampires aren't so stupid."

"Can Yale fix it?"

That question gave Kett pause. He tilted his head thoughtfully. "And if he could? You know that he would demand a favor for doing so."

"He can bargain for his undead life."

A slow smile spread across Kett's face.

"What?" I asked. "I can be Machiavellian. I'm a Fairchild, after all."

"I don't think you are," he said softly. "You are much, much more."

Heat flushed my cheeks at the compliment. At the hint of tenderness backing his words.

Jasmine popped her head back into the room, wearing only a pretty pink lace bra, low-slung jeans, and a wide grin. "I can be cunning too, you know."

Kett inclined his head.

I laughed. "No one doubts it."

She shrugged. "I'm not a fan of games, but you don't have to shield me so much. Either of you."

She retreated back into the bedroom before I could respond.

I glanced at Kett, offering him a smile. "I should change too."

"We should discuss my maker … Estelle … " I could tell that he really didn't want to talk about any such thing, but it was lovely that he was willing to offer.

"Do you make me justify my crazy family?"

"The ones I've met, Jasper excepted, aren't in the same league as my maker."

I shrugged. "They're comparatively young yet."

"Estelle, to whom you understand you will likely be bound, plays games that take centuries to unfold."

I nodded, ignoring the way my stomach twisted at the idea of such a timeline. "You haven't met my mother yet. Or Dahlia. Trust me, Estelle is out of practice."

Kett laughed abruptly, then appeared surprised that he had done so. Grinning, I followed Jasmine into the bedroom to change and pack. I, however, closed the door behind me.

Kett had a white SUV in the hotel parking lot. We drove to a private airport just outside the city center, finding his Learjet waiting for us. So, despite the intermittent showers and thick fog that had encased the city that morning, forty-five minutes after Declan returned with coffee and donuts, we were on our way to the West Coast.

Upon climbing into the jet, Jasmine immediately commandeered one of the white leather center seats and began plugging in every device she owned.

"Remember to charge your phones," she said bossily as I settled into the seat across the aisle from her and Declan took the one seat in front of me, rotating it to face Jasmine and me.

Neither of us argued. Though I'd barely used my phone, I didn't want to do anything that could possibly dampen Jasmine's renewed energy. And Declan had just been silent since arriving back in the hotel room, emitting that brooding quiet that should have driven me crazy—but which instead made him crazy endearing.

And that said way more about me than it did him.

Kett disappeared for the takeoff, which seemed to be his regular routine, and I found myself wondering if he actually had anything to do with piloting the jet. Or maybe he was simply such a control freak that he couldn't leave such things to mere mortals. Perhaps life became even more precious when you could live forever. I cast my mind back, recalling Kett's behavior when we'd confronted the necromancer Teresa Garrick in a graveyard teeming with zombies. How he'd laughed. How he seemed to relish the challenge that a necromancer of power had presented.

We'd left a massive mess that evening, and—

I sat upright in my seat, unaware that I'd been lightly dozing while the plane leveled off. "Jasmine."

"Yeah, babe?" Jasmine muttered around the rainbow-sprinkled chocolate donut she'd brought with her onto the plane.

"What if you looked for unusual events?" I asked. "In LA, in early January."

"Like what? A mass slaughter that the Convocation didn't notice?"

"Like a mess that was small enough to not get the authorities' attention. A mess connected to a child. A witch not necessarily registered to the Convocation."

Jasmine was staring at me. "That's a little vague."

"Like...like..." I racked my brain, formulating the thought and trying to offer possibilities at the same time. "Magical events that could have been explained away, but which might indicate that Yale screwed with other people's thoughts."

"People reporting missing time? Again, too vague to track down with any efficiency."

Declan was watching me intently as he sipped a coffee. I noticed the three copper-and-raw-gem rings he wore on his right hand. I'd only gotten a glimpse of them before. Normally, he kept them shielded from view. I lifted my gaze to meet his, and he curled his lips, noticing my attention. Then he stretched his legs across the aisle, settling them only inches from my own.

Each of the three nested, hammered-copper bands he wore contained a single birthstone—a raw topaz, a sapphire, and a fire opal, representing each of our birthdates.

We all carried our past, our connection to each other, differently. Jasmine had her tattoo, I had my bracelet, and Declan apparently had his rings. Though it was likely that those rings served double duty. Raw gems and copper were perfect for storing the energy spells he wielded so skillfully. That, along with his blasting rod, was the type of magic Jasper would have taught Declan once his talent asserted itself.

Declan.

Jasper.

"Like Declan…" I said, continuing as if I hadn't become lost in my own thoughts. "Declan's birth wouldn't have been registered with the Convocation. Your mother wouldn't have bothered, would she? Not being a witch?"

Declan frowned, but then he twirled his fingers, inviting me to continue.

"And when Jasper came for you in New Orleans, who knew? Who would have noticed?"

Declan laughed edgily. "A vampire would have had a difficult time snatching me, even at nine."

I looked triumphantly at Jasmine.

She shook her head, though. Doubtful. "Jasper knew Declan existed. He must have used some sort of blood-based spell to track him. With Grey's blood… or mine… " She frowned thoughtfully.

"And if a vampire was hunting witches? What do you think they hunt by? Blood."

"And unaffiliated witches would be easier to snatch," Declan murmured.

"You knew what you were, Declan," I said. "Even at nine. But what if you hadn't grown up with a magical parent? What if you'd been born with a recessive gene?"

"The Academy tracks magical manifestations," Jasmine said.

"When they're strong enough to register," I said. "When an Adept reaches puberty, say. But Yale took Ruby knowing her mother was practically alone in the world. If Jon hadn't come back when he did… "

Jasmine's fingertips hovered over her keyboard. "I still have no idea where to start."

"Police reports," Kett said, strolling through from the front of the jet. "Strange animal attacks. Odd disappearances. Panicked calls to 911 by children that were later deemed pranks."

"Los Angeles is a large place," Jasmine groused. But her fingers were already flying across the keys of her laptop.

Kett's gaze settled on Declan as he slipped into the seat in front of Jasmine, then rotated it so all four of us were facing each other. "The heart attack or stroke of an elderly caretaker," he said thoughtfully, adding to his list of possibilities for Jasmine to research.

Declan eyed him, a deep frown etched across his face. "What are you implying, vampire?"

"Not everything happens naturally."

"What are you saying?" I asked, aghast. "Are you thinking… Declan's grandfather?"

"I don't know anything for sure," Kett said. "But the timing is suspect, isn't it?"

Declan clenched the arms of his seat, jutting his jaw out angrily. "Losing my grandfather put me on the streets. What the hell would that benefit ... " A terrible realization flooded through him.

"Oh, no," Jasmine gasped, pausing her search. "That's not ... that's ... crazy."

"You think Jasper murdered my grandfather." Declan's voice was flat, emotionless.

"I'm saying it was easier to extricate you from New Orleans abandoned, rather than tied to family." Kett's tone was stiffly dispassionate. "You indicated you would have fought if a vampire had tried to take you."

Declan didn't answer, his lips tightening until they were just a strip of white cutting across his tanned face.

"How easy was it for Jasper to pick you up?" Kett asked. "What did he do to convince you to come with him?"

Declan's eyes cut to Jasmine, then to me.

"Did he have pictures? Of Jasmine? Of Fairchild Manor?" Kett asked silkily.

"Enough," I whispered. Then I strengthened my voice. "That's enough. This isn't a game, Kett."

A tense silence settled around us. I glanced out the window. Miles and miles of gray cloud shielded the earth from my view.

"My apologies, Declan," Kett said coolly.

Declan lifted his hand, waving off the vampire's sentiment.

Jasmine applied her fingers to her keyboard again. The renewal of her incessant tapping instantly soothed me.

"I know what to look for now," she said.

Declan shifted his seat back, closing his eyes. He brushed his ankle against mine. In response, I curled my foot around his leg, offering a touch of comfort. Then I remembered that wasn't my role anymore ... or that it soon wasn't going to be. I pulled my leg away, meeting Kett's silvered gaze instead.

After another fifteen minutes of listening to Declan's quiet snoring and Jasmine's typing, I slipped back through the sleek jet to the bathroom. I wanted to freshen up, though I knew I was doing so more as an excuse to keep busy rather than from any actual need. It would likely be warmer in Los Angeles, though, so a change of clothing might be in order. Any outfit that required nylons would definitely be out and inappropriately dressy for a visit to a group home.

Still thinking over what items of clothing I'd packed, I opened the door to the bathroom to return to my seat. Kett was leaning back against the far wall. His posture was slumped. Casual. As if he waited for women outside of bathrooms all the time.

His woman.

Me.

My breath caught in my throat.

He lifted his silvered gaze to me, curling his lips in an expectant smirk. As if he was gleefully anticipating the tongue-lashing he deserved for needling Declan with suppositions and innuendo about his grandfather's death.

Except I wasn't going to give him the satisfaction of fulfilling his expectations that I'd be typical and trite. Instead, I lifted my chin archly. "If you were any other male, I would think you were looking to join me."

"I'm patiently awaiting an invitation."

My jaw dropped. I scanned his face for sincerity. Kett's smile twisted, turning almost self-deprecating. I glanced up the aisle toward the passenger cabin, where I could see

Declan's long legs and a section of Jasmine's riot of curls as she bowed over her computer.

"Asleep," Kett whispered. "And otherwise occupied."

I looked back at him, knowing that in a moment he'd hold his hand out to me—always inviting me to touch him, always careful to not overwhelm me.

"I'm not a victim," I said matter-of-factly. "Yes, Jasper abused me. He abused us all, but I don't…I have a more difficult time with my mother, actually. Of her not protecting me when I came to her. Jasper is just…ill. Damaged. Likely abused himself."

"So the literature would suggest."

I laughed quietly. "You've been reading books about abuse victims?"

"No," he said. "I've been reading books about abuse survivors…since January."

Since Kett had offered me a sexual relationship. Since he'd offered to be my lover. To compete for my affections, if that was what it took for me to accept his offer of an immortal existence with him.

I took a step, closing the space between us just enough so that I could gather his thin cashmere sweater in my hand and pull him toward me. He came without resistance. Or at least he made a show of ceding control. I couldn't have moved him otherwise.

I tugged him against me. Our thighs and hipbones brushed. Then I stepped back into the bathroom, acting on a sudden desire to be without thought. To be without obligation.

In two-inch heels, I was only a couple of inches shorter than him. He flicked the door closed behind us, turning away only to flip the lock.

I pressed against the hard length of him, molding myself against his body. I lifted my gaze to his, seeing nothing in his gaze but the silvered blue of his eyes. Hovering my parted lips over his, I breathed him in. He smelled like breath mints. Peppermint, maybe.

I laughed quietly at the idea that an ancient vampire had freshened his breath for me.

Kett ran his fingers up my bare arms. His touch was featherlight.

I darted the tip of my tongue into his mouth, but withdrew it before he could close the kiss. He laughed huskily, the sound running through me. I shuddered, turning my head slightly away. His breath whispered across my neck.

He brushed his thumb across my nipple, coaxing it to harden in an instant even through my dress and bra. Shivers of desire fluttered in my stomach.

I moaned softly.

Then, even before I'd registered the movement, he had me propped up on the counter beside the sink with his hand up my dress. I wrapped my right leg around him, spreading my left leg so he could slip his fingers between my thighs. I gasped as he made contact with me through my underwear, then pushed the lace fabric aside, pleasure flooding away the embarrassment of opening myself to him so eagerly, without words, without even a kiss.

I arched back into the hand he held steadily at the small of my back, pressing my center into his fingers. Abandoning myself to the orgasm that was already curling my toes and burning through my nether regions.

I moaned, swallowing the need to vocalize as I convulsed underneath his steady touch, swiftly climaxing.

He eased his pressure, whispering into the skin of my neck, "Another?"

I opened my eyes, finding him only inches away. I lifted my hand to caress his face, running my fingers over his firm lips. "Who says no to seconds?"

He chuckled, rubbing a finger against me in a slow but steady circular pattern without further prompting.

I gasped as I wrapped my hand around his wrist, delaying the pleasure, but not denying it. I leaned forward and pressed my lips to his ear. "Bite me."

"Not today," he said. "I want you clearheaded and focused on me, Wisteria Fairchild. Not befuddled by my venom, which won't have the same effect on you when you've been remade."

He lifted an eyebrow, as if asking me to argue.

Not dropping my gaze from his, I loosened my hold on his wrist. He slipped his fingers through my wetness, slowly increasing the rhythm of his touch. I kept my gaze locked to his until my breathing was once again ragged.

"So...take you as you are, as you will be to me?" I asked. My voice quivered with pleasure. "You...we...won't drink from each other when I'm remade?"

A deep-red haze rolled across his eyes. "Oh, we will drink from each other. Deeply."

He kissed me then, darting his cool tongue into my mouth. I met him with my own, matching the steady rhythm of his fingers.

I orgasmed a second time without warning, nearly falling off the counter as pleasure liquefied my limbs.

He grunted with such satisfaction, with such a human sound, that I had to laugh breathlessly.

"Thank you," I said.

"You are welcome to anything I have to give, Wisteria. God knows, you'll have to take my shortcomings as well."

I snorted quietly. "God knows?"

"I'm open to the idea of an ultimate creator. I just know that divinity had no hand in my second incarnation."

I traced my fingers across his cheekbone, then down along his jaw. "Well...I have to believe that our choices...our deeds define us. Even if we are only...good enough."

"Good to a few good people," he whispered against my neck. "I can do that."

"A conversation for another time." I licked his neck lightly, running my tongue up his carotid artery. And for the first time since we'd entered the bathroom, he was the one who shuddered involuntarily.

I smiled against his smooth, hard skin, feeling exceedingly wicked. Then I spent some intense time figuring out where else he liked to be touched...or licked, as the case might be.

"I've got a half-dozen possible incidents that I could dig deeper into," Jasmine said before I'd even made it back to my seat. "Including a fire with no probable cause that will likely be ruled arson any day now, a couple of siblings remanded to state care after their grandmother had a stroke, an unusual animal attack, multiple reports of flashing lights in an abandoned warehouse...and Jack Harris."

Jasmine spun her laptop so I could see the screen as I settled back into my seat. "Twelve years old. Reported as running away from his group home on January 4."

"And?" Declan spoke up though he remained inclined back in his seat. I'd thought he was asleep.

"Every window on the first floor of the facility was broken," Jasmine said. "Completely shattered that same morning. No one knows what happened."

I leaned across the aisle, peering at the picture of a mixed-race boy with dark-blue eyes on Jasmine's screen. He looked closer to ten than twelve. "They could have at least updated the picture," I said. "Are they saying Jack broke the windows?"

Jasmine shook her head. "Someone made a call to 911 from the group home number. I'm trying to get access to the recording. The police investigated, but it's still listed as an open case. I connected the missing person report, which was filed two weeks after, to the broken window incident myself. I'm not sure the police have done so yet."

"Does Jack have a history of running away?" Declan straightened up in his seat.

"Yeah."

"That's why they haven't connected it yet."

"What are you saying?" I asked. "That the police would write off a twelve-year-old's disappearance?"

"I'm saying that a boy who's run away repeatedly and is currently living in a group home has fewer advocates. That's all."

I leaned farther out of my chair, attempting to read the file Jasmine had found on Jack. "You think it was wild magic?"

"I think there's a chance," she said. "Declan broke windows multiple times when we were younger."

"Training incidents," her brother groused. "It's doubtful that an unregistered fledgling witch would have the amount of magic it would take to inadvertently break every window on the ground floor."

I glanced to Declan. Caught in a death echo I'd inadvertently reconstructed outside of a circle in October, I'd unknowingly lashed out and broken every window in a funeral home in an attempt to free myself. Still, he was right. Though that was ample evidence that such an incident could result from a burst of emotionally fueled wild magic, I was no fledgling.

I reached across the aisle to turn Jasmine's laptop, but she batted my hand away. "Don't you come any closer. I can't replace my computer while we're in the air."

Nodding to acknowledge her concerns, I scanned the screen from a distance. "Mom dead, father unknown. He's been in the system for six years? Why hasn't he been adopted?"

"Keep reading." Jasmine ran her finger up the laptop's trackpad, scrolling down so I could read more of the file.

My gaze snagged on his date of birth as she scrolled past. "Wait," I murmured. "Wait. Go back."

Jasmine obligingly scrolled back up the page.

I stared at the date on the screen. September 9. "That has to just be … a typo."

Jasmine pivoted the laptop back so it faced her. "What?"

"His birthday."

Jasmine's jaw dropped. "I … I didn't bother looking closely. The missing person's report simply lists him as twelve years old."

"What?" Declan asked. "He isn't?"

"Can you confirm it?" I asked. "Find his birth certificate?"

Jasmine nodded, her fingers already flying over the keys.

"I just love playing the game where you don't answer any questions," Declan said, exceedingly heavy on the sarcasm.

I settled back in my seat, glancing at Declan, then looking out the window. "He was born on the same day as me."

"Okay, so? It's a weird coincidence." He glanced between Jasmine and me.

"Ruby Cameron was born on the same day as you," I said.

Declan frowned. "Yeah? That's … odd."

"Yeah, odd."

"And if Jack was a witch…is a witch, how did Yale track him down?" I asked. "Are there any other reports of odd incidents?"

"If. If Yale tracked him down," Jasmine said, correcting and cautioning me at the same time. "We're jumping to conclusions without much to base them on…other than Kett's belief that there would be more than one kidnapping, Yale's car rental, and some broken windows."

"Why hasn't he been adopted?" I asked quietly. "Because he's…different? Because weird things happen around him when he gets upset, so he's been deemed violent?"

"Harris isn't a typical witch surname," Declan said, offering counterpoints rather than outright disagreeing with me.

"Could be his father's name," I said. "Could be a name his mother took during a previous marriage. Could be that the witch magic skipped a generation or two."

"Could be that the kid's a psychopath," Jasmine said. But her fingers stilled on her keyboard before I could counter her argument with the fact that the police report would probably have indicated Jack had broken the windows if that was the case. "It's not a typo." She looked up from her screen, locking her gaze to mine. "Okay. So that's officially weird."

I nodded. "I'll need to get into the group home."

"Too bad they'll have replaced the windows by now," Declan said. "We could get in under the guise of being a work crew."

Jasmine snorted. "Please? Wisteria as a glazier?"

I laughed. "You think you could pass any better?"

"I'll be the one in the car, glued to my computer."

I leaned my head back. "If we were Kett, we'd just buy the building."

I was totally joking as I said it, but Declan and Jasmine glanced at each other thoughtfully.

"Don't be crazy," I said. "We can't buy the building."

Jasmine's fingers hit the keyboard again as she muttered to herself. "The group home must be funded with some combination of private and government money. It's doubtful they're funded well enough to own the building outright. So who does?"

"We can't buy the building just because I need to reconstruct residual magic we don't even know exists."

Grumbling, Declan pulled out his phone, then levered himself out of his seat. "I'll call Grey."

"Good, good," Jasmine said absentmindedly.

They were both completely ignoring me. "Absolutely not!" I cried. "The proper channels of … we'd have to submit a requisition to the Convocation."

"Which would take weeks," Jasmine said. "Plus, we'd have to prove that something actually occurred on the property to justify the financial outlay. And to do that, we'd need to have already obtained the reconstruction you want to cast."

Declan wandered forward toward the galley, then poked around in the cupboards with his phone pressed to his ear.

"There has to be another, easier way," I said.

"Like one that doesn't involve our parents?"

"Like one where we pose as social workers or police investigators," I said, helplessly casting around for ideas.

"Yeah? Which one of us is going to pull that off? Kett?" Jasmine giggled.

Declan stepped up beside Jasmine, phone still pressed to his ear. "Grey wants you to email him the details. He figures it's a good tax write-off for a Fairchild trust."

"Of course he does," I muttered.

Jasmine hit a key on her computer. "Done!"

Declan continued looming over me with the phone pressed to his ear. Grinning, he abruptly waved a bag of chips that he'd been hiding behind his back in my face. "Corn chips!" he crowed.

I grabbed for the bag. He jerked it just out of reach.

"Really? I can get my own chips."

"Last ones," he said, wagging his eyebrows and the bag at me again. A muffled voice came over the speaker of his phone, pulling his attention away. He addressed Grey, stupidly taking his gaze off me. "Yep, still here."

I lunged out of my seat for the bag. Corn chips had always been my favorite when we were kids.

Declan shouted as we stumbled sideways, grappling for the bag. He managed to tear it from my grasp, but not before we'd ripped it in half.

Corn chips rained down all over Jasmine's head and shoulders.

"Geez, guys!" my best friend shouted.

Declan's booming laugh reverberated around the cabin. I collapsed against him, giggling madly.

"Ah. I thought someone was being murdered," Kett said coolly from behind us.

Jasmine gathered a handful of chips from her laptop. "With corn chips?" she asked teasingly. "Or was it the laughing that confused you, vampire?" She shoved the chips in her mouth, happily chewing while she returned to work.

"What?" Declan spoke into his phone. "No, no one is being murdered, Grey." He sauntered away, chatting quietly with his father as if he did so every day. I still wasn't certain whether he and Grey had ever forged a real relationship despite Dahlia's vindictiveness—and despite the abuse Declan had suffered under Jasper's so-called tutelage. But if he and his father had managed to bond, then Declan forgave much easier than I did.

Kett tilted his head as if waiting for something. Something from me.

I simply smiled at him, then plucked a chip from Jasmine's abundant curls and ate it. "Salty," I said appreciatively.

Jasmine collapsed over her laptop in a fit of giggles.

Kett raised an eyebrow, closing the space between us. "Might I suggest some real food?"

"Not sure why," I whispered, grinning saucily. "I certainly haven't done anything to build up an appetite."

A frown flashed across Kett's face, then his lips twisted questioningly as he contemplated my innuendo. He brushed his fingers against mine. The gesture, the need for contact, felt almost involuntary. As if his previous touches had all been well considered and carefully implemented.

"Still," he said, stepping away abruptly, "I'll have the steward put something together quickly. Before we land." He crossed through the jet, passing Declan leaning back against the wall of the galley.

"It's going to be okay," Jasmine said quietly. "We can get used to the vampire. If it has to be him."

I combed my fingers through her curls, loosening a few more of the corn chips trapped in her hair. "What do you mean?"

"When he turns you," she said, looking at her screen rather than up at me. "It doesn't mean you have to go away."

I stilled. All the joy that had warmed me just moments before was draining away. "I...I think it does. I don't think they...the Conclave...and I'm not sure..."

Jasmine reached up, grasping my hand harshly but still not looking at me. "Just ask him. Like with Ben staying with Teresa—"

"She's a necromancer, Jasmine. And I think it only works because Ben is...weaker. Because Kett thinks he isn't strong enough to be around other vampires yet."

"Just ask him." She loosened her grip on my hand, returning to typing.

I watched her hands flying across the keyboard, suddenly desperately wishing I could drop my shields and get a glimpse of her magic dancing around the laptop. But I didn't want to inadvertently burn out her computer.

I glanced over at Declan—but stopped short when I saw Kett standing a few feet down the aisle, watching me. I was suddenly conscious of a tear trailing down my cheek, wiping it away as I turned from his dispassionate gaze.

Vampires didn't stay with their human families. They gained immortality and invulnerability, but they didn't get to keep their old lives. Mostly because their loved ones wouldn't be safe. Unless your mother was a necromancer, such as in Ben's case. Or if your maker was able to impose his own control over you, as with Yale's brood. If I was going to be remade, it was to save Declan and Jasmine not to inadvertently tear their throats out myself.

"Does your iPad have enough protection on it that I can use it?" I asked Jasmine, keeping my tone as professional as I could.

"Yep. For a bit at least." She handed the tablet to me.

"Could you send me everything you've compiled on Jack Harris so far?"

Jasmine acknowledged my request with a grunt.

I sat down diagonally across from her, lifting my gaze to Kett. He was still watching me from the aisle. I gestured toward the seat beside me, offering him what I was sure must have been a sad smile.

"Have you had any luck with a place of residence?" Kett asked, crossing up the aisle toward us and settling into the seat I'd indicated. "LA seems an unlikely place for vampires who cannot bear the sun."

"Still stymied," Jasmine said. "I'm running checks on Valko, Amaya, and Mania. But you know those are totally fake names."

"Try Garrick," Kett said.

I glanced at him. "You think they might have taken over a property owned by former vampire hunters?"

"I think it's an unexplored connection."

Declan threw himself into the seat opposite me, then leaned over, trying to read off Jasmine's screen.

"Don't you dare read over my shoulder," she groused.

A message flashed across the screen of the iPad I was holding. I tapped it, accepting the airdropped file Jasmine had sent me.

"I can't just sit here," Declan said.

"Kett says the steward is bringing food," I said absently. I began reading the files and the brief history that Jasmine had compiled for Jack Harris.

"I'm not a teenager, Wisteria," Declan said. "Easily assuaged by the promise of food."

Silence fell as three of the four of us read from various electronic devices.

"What kind of food?" Declan finally asked.

Chapter Six

In the end, Grey didn't have to buy the building that housed the group home from which Jack Harris had gone missing to get us access. He simply had to indicate that the Fairchild Foundation was considering a major donation and that we wanted to assess the home in person.

We landed at yet another private airfield in LA at a little after one o'clock in the afternoon. Traveling west and two hours back in time had its benefits. And, as was becoming commonplace, Kett had a large white SUV waiting for us. Since we were about to clandestinely investigate a group home in a suburb of Los Angeles, though, he'd swapped out the Cadillac or BMW models he preferred for a Jeep Grand Cherokee. And as soon as we hit the bumper-to-bumper traffic on the first highway, I was lost. Without GPS, I'd have been stranded in the City of Angels forever.

I'd been to LA and Santa Monica a few times, on contract for the Convocation. But all I could remember of the trip from the airport to the group home was the hour and a half I spent trapped in traffic amid massive urban sprawl. And palm trees in every yard.

The weather was warm enough that I hadn't packed any appropriate clothing, so I had to pair a black silk blouse with a cutout lace trim along the V-neck with my two-tone-weave navy-and-black slacks. In the heat of the day, I would swelter whenever I stepped outside of an air-conditioned vehicle or room. Not knowing how long we'd be in the city, we'd left our luggage with the plane.

Kett parked a block away from the nondescript three-storey building that housed the group home. A light sweat had already pooled in the small of my back by the time we stepped into the lightly air-conditioned entranceway.

In an office to the right of a small waiting area, two women were chatting quietly, one younger and taller than the other. Grey had arranged for us to meet with the director of the facility, but I hadn't caught her name.

The dark-haired older woman stepped forward to shake Kett's hand, opening her mouth to speak as she touched him. Then she just paused.

The second woman stood utterly still, holding what looked like pamphlets as she gazed at the vampire blankly.

Kett tilted his head slightly, not taking his gaze from the first woman, who I assumed was the director. "Most of the residents are away on a field trip," he said.

Apparently, he was reading the director's mind. I'd known Kett was skilled at ensnaring multiple mundanes at the same time, but not that he could pluck information out of people's heads while he did so. Perhaps it was the physical contact that gave him such access.

"I'd like to view the upper floors first," Kett said. The compulsive power underlying his words brushed against me.

Declan swore under his breath. His expression was stony, his attention riveted to Kett.

"Of course," the director gasped. "Please. This way." She stepped around us, toward a wide set of stairs leading up.

Kett glanced at the second woman, possibly an assistant or an administrator of some sort. She smiled dreamily. Then, not taking her gaze from the vampire, she followed the director.

As the administrator passed her, Jasmine plucked one of the pamphlets out of her hand.

Declan shook his head grimly at his sister.

She shrugged nonchalantly, deliberately ignoring how obvious it was that Declan was disturbed by the vampire's magical prowess, rather than by her actions. "What? It might have different information."

"I'll case the exterior," he growled, pivoting so quickly that his leather jacket slapped against my leg.

"Please look for residual pockets," I said.

"I'm not an idiot." He slammed his hand against the entrance door to open it, not bothering to pause or look back as he exited the building.

Jasmine opened the pamphlet. Kett and the two women disappeared up the stairs.

I glanced around. Because the police report Jasmine uncovered had indicated that all the windows had been broken on the main floor of the group home, I immediately opted to check a large common area off the entrance for residual magic. Trying to appear like a casual observer looking to make a hefty donation, I wandered through what appeared to be a recreation room, replete with old couches, board games spread across randomly spaced tables, and shelves overflowing with well-worn books.

As expected, the windows had all been replaced.

But a large pocket of residual magic hovered around the couch nearest the windows at the back of the room, radiating out as if something magical had exploded. I didn't even need to lower my personal shields to sense it.

"Score one for the tech witch," I muttered to myself, though I didn't really feel like celebrating the discovery.

I glanced through the windows behind the couch, seeing only an empty basketball court and some picnic tables. Back the way I'd entered the recreation room, Jasmine was glued to her phone, hovering in the entranceway.

Catching my cousin's eye, I nodded. She immediately fished some premade spells from her bag—most likely distraction spells—as she crossed through the recreation room. She placed the first one at a door that stood open to a dining area and a large kitchen.

As I paced a circle around the pocket of magic I'd found, Jasmine triggered the spell and closed the kitchen door behind her. Then she crossed through the room to a second doorway leading to a hall that likely bisected the remainder of the main floor. She closed that door as well.

Unfortunately, the arched opening leading to the entranceway was just that—an opening. I wasn't sure Jasmine had anything as advanced as a mirroring spell—magic that would reflect whatever the person entering the room expected to see—among her collection of premade spells. I might have attempted to surround the entire room with a second circle, as I'd done with the swing set in the park, but the area was large and we didn't have much time.

So I swiftly placed my candles instead, keeping my circle tight and assuming that I'd be able to shift it if I needed to. I would let Jasmine worry about any possible foot traffic.

My hasty circle snapped into place with a mere thought. The residual contained within immediately resolved into a massive cloud of light-blue magic. The reconstruction itself needed no coaxing, as if the residual were eager to reveal what had happened four months before.

Underneath my raised palms, the magic churned, becoming streaked with red. Then the light in the pocket of the room I'd manifested shifted into what looked like early evening.

Yale appeared, having apparently just set a dark-brown-haired, dark-skinned, lanky boy on the couch.

As the scene I was reconstructing continued to run backward, energy ricocheted against the edges of the circle. I gasped involuntarily. Shattered glass—having exploded outward—resolved into windows behind the couch.

I glanced away from the magic playing underneath my palms, looking over toward Jasmine hovering near the entranceway.

"It's him," I said. "Yale."

She looked grim as she nodded, as if my findings were expected. "Find me something to track."

"I'll try." I returned my attention to the circle. The magic was fading, eroding the image. Then it dissipated.

Instead of immediately replaying the scene I'd collected, I pressed my palms to the edges of the circle and carefully moved it around the entire room. I checked for any other residual, but found nothing substantial other than a streak of red-blurred movement toward the entranceway. Along with what I now assumed was Jack Harris's wild magic along the windows.

I was just settling the circle back at its original location when Jasmine called out.

"Bus pulling up."

I hastily grabbed an oyster-shell cube out of my bag, setting it down in the center of my dormant circle. Then I swiftly replayed and captured the reconstruction in the cube at the same time. I usually preferred to replay a scene before collecting it, concerned that I might miss an important element. Because once I collected it, I couldn't zoom or shift the reconstruction's perspective. But at least I'd confirmed Yale's involvement. And that the boy, Jack, was a witch. Hopefully, we'd find other clues, and possibly some dialogue, on playback.

The main door slammed open. Over a dozen chattering teenagers poured into the building as I tucked the cube into my purse. I grabbed my candles, snuffing them as I went.

Jasmine practically stumbled away from the onslaught of teens, most of which headed toward the stairs off the entrance, presumably up to their rooms. After glancing over at me, my best friend snatched what looked like a small stone away from the archway connecting the entranceway to the recreation room. A second wave of kids piled in after her, barely bothering to look in my direction while I attempted to remove the spell on the door to the kitchen, my hands still full of candles that hadn't hardened yet.

Jasmine darted across the room to grab a spell from the third door—though not before a teen had tried to use it, then wandered away looking completely confused.

I made a beeline for the entrance, drawing some assessing looks my way. But the teenagers didn't question my presence in their space, which made me sad. A stranger in their midst was obviously not unusual. It didn't seem as though they felt any sense of ownership over their surroundings, or even found any comfort in them. Not enough to defend their territory at least.

Jasmine caught up with me. "Anyone else in the reconstruction? Anyone we need to question?"

"Not that I saw. But I didn't get time to replay it."

My cousin glanced behind us. The teenagers were settling onto couches or continuing to wander deeper into the facility. "Someone else had to have seen Yale."

"Someone most likely noticed when Jack abruptly disappeared from the room," I said grimly. "But what are the chances we can figure out who they are? And if we do identify them, what are the chances they answer our questions?"

Jasmine nodded. "Let's look at the reconstruction in the car. And see if Declan found anything outside." She opened the door as she fished her phone out of her back pocket. "And I should probably text Kett to let him know he can let the vulnerable humans go about the rest of their afternoon normally."

The neighborhood surrounding the group home had an eighties feel to it. Stuccoed ranchers were everywhere, all of them with sun-faded exterior paint, empty driveways, and gravel or other drought-friendly lawns. Plus more palm trees.

The hazy day continued to be too warm for me. Once more, I had managed to break out in a light sweat by the time we made it back to the white SUV, which Kett had thankfully parked in a bit of shade.

Declan was waiting for us. "Nothing of significance around the exterior." He held open the back driver's-side door for me, then crossed around to climb into the seat behind Jasmine, who had taken the front passenger seat. "Too much time has passed. If there was anything to find."

Leaving my bag and candles on the floor by my feet, I placed the reconstruction on the armrest between the front seats.

Declan eyed it grimly. "Yale?"

"Yes," I said.

"I've reported Jack Harris's disappearance to the Convocation," Jasmine said, still bowed over her phone. "And that he's an untrained, unaffiliated witch. They can get the local coven to start looking for him or other family members."

"Is there an organized LA coven?" Declan asked. Then he answered his own question. "Santa Monica, maybe."

"The Convocation is fine with us continuing to investigate?" I asked. With two missing witch children now identified, it was likely that a team with more seniority and experience than Jasmine or me would be brought in. Not necessarily instead of us, but to take over and lead the investigation.

"Kett won't work with anyone else," Jasmine said. "Or that's what I told them, anyway. We have access to any resources we need. And a no-limit expense account."

"Less red tape. Wow," Declan said. "Generous."

"You know it is, Declan," Jasmine said sharply. "Kett's involvement is the only thing keeping a lid on all this. And keeping us involved. Yale is unknown to the Convocation, especially since no one knows he also kidnapped me."

Since I had pretty much murdered two vampires last January, with Jasmine instigating the murder of a third by Kett's hand, we had decided to not report my best friend's kidnapping to the Convocation authorities. But now that we knew Yale had been kidnapping young witches, I was already beating myself up over the idea that keeping that secret might have been a mistake.

"Are we waiting on the executioner to view the reconstruction?" Declan asked.

Jasmine eyed me through the seats. "Is it as bad as the last one?"

"I don't know," I said, though I couldn't imagine too many things being worse than what Yale had put Coral and Ruby through. "I had to grab it without playback. But ... the boy fights. The broken windows make that obvious. So if Yale tried to ensnare him, he was unsuccessful."

The driver's-side door opened and Kett slid into the SUV, passing a battered Nike shoebox to Jasmine in the same motion.

"Ah, crap," she said. "What fresh hell is this?"

"Jack's room has already been stripped down and re-assigned," Kett said smoothly. "They kept this. Only this."

Jasmine pressed her hand to the lid of the box. "This is the sum total of a twelve-year-old's life?"

Kett didn't answer her.

Jasmine shook her head forcefully, wordlessly passing the shoebox back to me. I opened the lid, quickly glancing through the contents—a random assortment of keepsakes, including a basketball game ticket stub, worn photos, and a tiger's eye. My stomach squelched wretchedly.

"Magic?" Jasmine muttered.

"Nothing of immediate significance." I managed to keep my tone even.

"I'll go through it," Jasmine said stiffly. "After we view the reconstruction."

I nodded, gratefully replacing the lid on the box and setting it on the middle seat between Declan and me.

I reached for the reconstruction, which was still sitting on the armrest console between the front seats.

Declan brushed his fingers across my knee comfortingly before placing them next to mine. Kett and Jasmine twisted in their seats, touching the other two edges of the cube.

I triggered the playback.

Within the reconstruction, Yale suddenly popped into existence. He hovered over a dark-haired, dark-skinned boy seated on the threadbare couch by the back windows of the recreation room. It was early evening, definitely after the sun had set but before full dark.

"Jack Harris," Jasmine said, confirming that she also recognized him from the picture she'd found attached to his file.

"Like I said, dude," Jack said, sneering up at Yale, "we don't know you."

"We?" Kett asked.

I paused the playback, studying the still image of the ruddy-haired vampire looming over the lanky boy. Yale was clad in a thin fisherman sweater and jeans artfully torn across the knees. Ironically, Jack was similarly attired, though his jeans weren't intentionally ratty. "See the way Jack's sitting on the couch?" I said. "I'm fairly certain there's someone seated to his left. Someone without magic for the reconstruction to manifest, just as we couldn't see Luci in the reconstruction of Colby's rising."

"With the pink pencil," Kett said, sounding almost impressed.

"Someone he's protective of," Declan said. "By the angle of his shoulders."

"Jack's shielding someone from Yale, even though it's obvious he's frightened," Jasmine said. "See the whites of his eyes? The way he's gripping the edge of the couch with his left hand?"

"Continue, reconstructionist," Kett said.

I allowed the magic to flow underneath my fingertips and the scene started to play again in real time.

"You don't want to be here," Yale said, glancing around the room disdainfully. "Here is ridiculous. You're better than this. You know you are. I can take you somewhere where your talents will be unleashed."

Jack glanced to his left as if listening to someone else speak. His expression was tense, wary.

"Can we see Yale's face?" Kett asked.

"No, sorry. I had to grab it quickly. No other angles or zooming."

Within the reconstruction, Yale shifted, reaching forward and moving so quickly that his arm blurred. He snapped his fingers in front of whoever was sitting to Jack's left. "That's enough from you."

Jack flinched, pushing away from the vampire. Then, realizing he wasn't about to be hit, he glanced over at the invisible person beside him. His tense expression drained into disbelief.

"What did Yale do?" Jasmine whispered. "He can't kill someone by snapping his fingers, can he?"

"Ensnared," Kett said. "Calling his or her attention to him with the finger snap. Then once he had eye contact, he took control."

I swallowed away the discomfort that rose with Kett's explanation. I had just watched the executioner beguile two humans so that I could collect the reconstruction we were currently viewing. As such, being morally outraged at Yale's ability to do the same was hypocritical.

Within the reconstruction, Jack reached for the unseen person seated next to him, shaking them. "What have you done?"

"It's no matter to you, fledgling," Yale said. "You will come with me. Willingly."

I could hear the magic in Yale's words, even if I couldn't see it.

But Jack simply leaned across whoever was on the couch beside him, shielding them with his body. "Like hell I will."

"Interesting," Yale murmured. "Not many witches, and certainly none untrained, can shake off the compulsion of a vampire."

Jack's face crumpled into heart-wrenching fear in response to Yale identifying himself as a bloodsucking immortal creature. Even with his mundane upbringing, Jack would know to be wary of such things—and might have been even more so because he wielded magic himself, un-controlled and unintentional or not. The boy's eyes darted around the room, looking for help but afraid to call out.

"Brave," Declan said. "He doesn't want to get anyone else involved."

"Shortsighted," Kett said. "I doubt Yale has the ability to hold more than one or two enthralled at a time. Even a vampire wouldn't want to involve too many mundanes, for the risk of attracting the attention of the Conclave."

"Before or after he slaughtered all of Jack's friends?" Jasmine sneered.

"I have already apologized for not being omnipotent, witch," Kett said coolly. "I am also not the only one in this vehicle who has allowed so-called evil to go unchecked."

"Hey," Declan said, though his protest felt halfhearted. Because Kett was right. No Fairchilds—not even the three of us—had much of a moral leg to stand on when it came to comparing reputations.

"Pay attention," I said. I had paused the reconstruc-tion for their round of bickering, then restarted it just in time to see Yale reach for Jack.

As the vampire's fingers brushed against his arm, the twelve-year-old flung himself back on the couch. Then, without him speaking a single word, wild magic exploded from him—a completely instinctual casting.

The wave of energy buffeted the vampire, shattering every window in the room.

Yale stumbled back from Jack, momentarily pressing against the outer edge of the tight circle I'd cast. Then the vampire lunged forward in a blur of red-streaked magic, snatching Jack off the couch and disappearing from the reconstruction.

"He'll be powerful," Declan said. Then he added heav-ily, "If he's still alive."

"He's alive," Kett said.

I lifted my gaze from the cube, already nodding in agreement as I met the vampire's dispassionately certain gaze.

"What?" Jasmine asked, glancing between the two of us.

I tapped the cube. "Unlike with Ruby, Yale made Jack an offer."

"I can take you somewhere where your talents will be unleashed," Declan quoted. "Ah, shit."

Kett nodded.

"He's collecting young witches," I said. "But to what end? And why break the streak by kidnapping Jasmine?"

"Maybe kidnapping Ruby and Jack was what Yale thought I was going to uncover," Jasmine said thoughtfully. "When he realized I was investigating for Kett."

"But then why try to set up the meet-and-greet with the Conclave?" Declan asked, shaking his head. "It doesn't add up."

"Or Yale was playing two games at once … " I kept my gaze on Kett. "And the connection between kidnapping the children and Jasmine was nothing but coincidence."

"You still think he's kidnapping the kids for someone else? Maybe for a fee?" Jasmine asked. "I haven't found any obvious financial connection. And the second so-called game? Something to do with Jasper? Something to do with the Conclave?"

I shook my head, addressing Kett. "I need to speak to Yale."

He nodded, but he didn't look pleased. "I'll make another call."

"Good," Jasmine said. "There's a diner across from the group home. We're going to get some hopefully perfectly greasy fries while we figure out our next step. And, side note, if I was a creepy vampire, the diner is exactly where I would have sat to stalk my prey."

"Not in a shadowed doorway?" Kett asked blithely.

"Nope, that would draw too much attention. But buying a few coffees a couple of evenings in a row ... that's the place."

Kett nodded thoughtfully, then exited the SUV.

I tucked the reconstruction into my bag.

Jasmine opened her door, glancing back at me grimly. "Bring the shoebox."

Declan grabbed the box before I had a chance to, though, then climbed out of the vehicle. I followed at a slower pace, my mind whirling with questions. I had a terrible feeling that there was more to the investigation than a vampire snatching witch children. But what that might be, I didn't know.

As we walked the block and a half to the diner on the opposite corner from the group home, Declan fielded a phone call, frowning at his screen. Jasmine and I continued on as he fell back to take it.

Kett had disappeared before I'd exited the SUV, and I didn't bother asking Jasmine or Declan as to his whereabouts. It was unlikely the vampire had shared his itinerary with either of them. I had asked him to facilitate a conversation with Yale, and I knew he would try to make that happen.

The diner didn't appear to have a name, or any signage. Its exterior brick had been painted over in brighter patches of green, presumably covering graffiti, and the 'Help Wanted' sign taped on the front door was sun bleached. Thankfully, though, the air-conditioning was on full blast and the vinyl booths along the length of the front windows were clean.

A clock on the wall told me it was approaching four in the afternoon as Jasmine and I commandeered the center booth that a pink-haired server waved us toward. A group of teenagers sat in the far corner, away from the windows. I wondered whether they were from the group home, or were maybe visiting friends who resided there. I wondered also if the invisible person who Jack had tried to protect in the reconstruction was among their number, though I had no urge to interrupt their intermittent conversation.

Drawing unnecessary attention to Jack's kidnapping was a bad idea. The kind of idea that got mundane minds wiped. And magic was tricky even when it wasn't being used on the nonmagical, making it unlikely that whoever had been next to Jack could have shed any light on the situation anyway. That was what was so inherently satisfying about reconstructions. Not even the most skilled Adepts could hide their wrongdoings when revealed in one of my collections. I just had to find the right moments. Then eventually, slowly but surely, we'd figure out what had happened to Ruby and Jack.

Upon sitting, Jasmine immediately opened her laptop and began systematically digging through and logging the contents of Jack Harris's keepsake box.

I was seriously pleased to find that the diner offered old-fashioned milkshakes, ordering three—chocolate, strawberry, and vanilla—when the server approached the table with glasses of water in hand.

She was young enough that I briefly wondered if she lived at the group home, or at least knew some of the residents. But again, it would have felt intrusive to ask, and I wasn't sure how it would benefit our investigation. So I kept quiet, letting Jasmine discreetly wield her tech magic across the table from me.

Jasmine would uncover our next lead. I had contributed as much as I realistically could with the reconstruction, but I still felt oddly restless. Plagued by the nagging feeling that there was some connection I was missing at the root of our investigation. Perhaps it was simply that I was at loose ends personally—with whatever was going on with Lark that needed my attention, and the formal inquiry I'd vowed to open into Jasper's nefarious deeds.

All of it needed to be dealt with before the time limit on the contract with Kett ran out. And I hated it when my personal life intruded on my professional life. I also had no idea how to initiate contact with Lark unless I was standing within the brownie's personal territory, whether my apartment or Fairchild Manor.

And even though I was concerned enough that I might have asked my Aunt Rose for a favor, sending her to the manor in search of the brownie and incurring a debt by doing so, it was highly unlikely that Lark would appear for the healer of the Fairchild coven. Brownies were notoriously selective about who they chose to communicate with and serve, following a code that had more to do with personal preferences than any sort of easily defined morals.

Through the front windows, I saw that Declan had followed us to the diner but not entered. So apparently, I wasn't the only one who was restless. He was slowly pacing back and forth in the tiny parking lot that occupied the front half of the diner's property, his phone glued to his ear. His responses to whomever he was speaking to appeared to be short and brusque. Perhaps Grey had called to follow up on the group home visit. Or perhaps Copper was checking up on him. Declan looked up and met my gaze through the window, and I smiled rather than dropping my eyes. I was tired of feeling guilty about staring at him. He was my concern, always.

Declan ended the call, shoving his phone back in his pocket and striding into the diner. He nodded to the server, who nearly walked into the stools lining the front counter upon seeing him. She recovered her step without Declan noticing her interest in him, and he slid into the booth next to Jasmine.

"All right?" she asked, not looking away from her laptop.

He grunted, grabbing a menu.

"Wisteria ordered milkshakes."

"Good," he said. "And?"

I shook my head.

Instead of waiting for the server to return, Declan exited the booth abruptly and approached the cash register. I heard him order onion rings and fries, along with a bacon-cheeseburger. The pink-haired server stared resolutely down at her notepad as he spoke. Her cheeks were pink as well.

"They've broken up," Jasmine said quietly.

"Who?"

"Declan and Copper. She's been texting. He moved out while she was away. Which, if he wasn't my brother, I would have said was a pretty vile play."

"Might have been a long time coming, but badly timed," I said, instinctively defending Declan though I knew nothing about his relationship. I'd never met or even spoken with Copper. "Wait. You've been reading his text messages?"

She shrugged.

"Do you read my text messages?"

"Yeah, because you put all your secrets in writing."

Declan slipped back into the booth. "What secrets?"

My heart hollowed suddenly, and I looked out the window. "I don't have any secrets from you. I never did. All I have is what is, what will be. The unalterable future."

Jasmine glanced up from her screen. "Wisteria—"

"No," Declan said sharply. "We aren't doing this here. Not now."

Jasmine shut her mouth, accepting her brother's rebuke without protest. Though she pressed her ankle against mine underneath the table as she slid one of the photos from Jack's keepsake box across to me. "Jack's mom."

I glanced at the smiling woman in the picture. She was holding a tiny baby. Then I flipped it over. Two names and a date had been carefully printed on the back. *Jack and Melody Harris. April 2005.* The handwriting looked childish, as if it might have been Jack's, not his mother's. My heart pinched.

I flipped the picture back over and focused on the joy etched across the woman's face.

"He would have known how much she loved him," I whispered. "How much she wanted him, just by having this picture." The photo was worn at the edges from being handled. I slid it back to Jasmine but she didn't pick it up.

"More than we had," Declan said. "And we survived."

"So far…"

Movement out the window drew my attention. A dark-green rental car pulled into the lot, taking one of the three empty parking spots.

"I have a picture of Dahlia holding me as a newborn," Jasmine said. "She sure as hell ain't smiling in it."

Declan snorted, laughing.

A tall, thin woman stepped out of the rental car, her shock of coppery red hair shimmering in the sunlight. She glanced up at the diner—where the sign should have been—then down at her phone, as if she wasn't sure she was in the right place.

"You ever notice how all the witches we know who are named Red, or Carmine, or Scarlett all have red hair?"

I said, trying to change the subject. "Though I think Ember Pine dyes hers."

"I don't know any witches named any of those things," Declan said.

The server appeared at the edge of the table with our milkshakes, hesitating with the distribution of the different flavors.

"In the middle works," I said. "Thank you."

"Okay." She placed down the chocolate shake, which Jasmine immediately snagged.

Declan grinned, shaking his head for my benefit while the server placed down the strawberry and the vanilla shakes. Then I smiled back, eyeing him.

He snorted. "You're the one with the sudden red obsession."

I laughed, snagging the strawberry for myself. With Jasmine's and Declan's heads both bowed over their shakes, I caught sight of the red-haired woman as she entered the diner. "It's not all that sudden," I said, taking a wholly satisfying slurp of my strawberry shake. "The woman who just came in has red hair."

Declan grunted, drinking down his vanilla shake at a remarkable rate.

"Although," I said, watching the woman as she scanned the interior of the diner, "in this light, her hair is more copper than truly red."

Declan went very still. Then he slowly twisted in his seat, following my gaze.

"And … "—I focused on the woman—"I think she might actually be a witch. That's odd, isn't it? Did the Convocation say they were sending someone?"

Declan swore viciously under his breath in Creole. Or at least his version of it.

The woman locked her blue-eyed gaze on our table, heading our way with a look of utter determination. Declan darted out of the booth, crossing back through the aisle to physically block her progress.

"What the hell?" Jasmine muttered, craning around to watch Declan hustle the witch back out of the diner.

As they moved, the copper-haired woman kept glancing over her shoulder, as if she were trying to get a better look at Jasmine and me.

"Enter complication number five," Jasmine muttered.

"Number five?"

"That's Copper."

I immediately transferred my attention out the front window, my heart squelching in my chest in an entirely new, terrible way. Declan was leaning over the witch, even as tall as she was, talking to her a mile a minute.

Copper.

"Not so broken up," I said, rubbing my chest as if that might ease the pain lodged there. Then I dropped my hand when I realized that Jasmine was watching me.

"Just because she's making a last-ditch play for him doesn't mean anything."

I dragged my gaze away from the drama in the parking lot. "And what did you mean, complication number five? Are you counting? What are the first four?"

She grinned at me saucily. "You figure it out."

I laughed, somewhat incredulously. Then, against my will, my attention was drawn outside again. Copper met my gaze through the window, then gestured toward me.

Declan spun around. His jaw was clenched, his shoulders tight.

I tried to offer him a smile. But, more than a little chagrined at being caught staring, I ended up grimacing instead.

He threw his hands up, frustrated. Then, having come to some decision, he charged back toward the door.

A satisfied smile flitted across Copper's face. She lifted her chin, strolling after Declan as if she had all the time in the world.

"She's playing him," I murmured, not at all happy with the observation.

"She's a woman, isn't she?" Jasmine said.

"Hey!"

"I mean, dealing with a guy like Declan. You're either straight up and take what happens in stride, or..." She shrugged without finishing her thought.

Declan barreled toward the booth, nearly colliding with the server carrying plates heaped with fries, onion rings, and his burger. She cried out, but managed to avoid dumping the food.

"Excuse me," he said gruffly, stepping back and allowing her the space to set the food down on the table. While waiting, he locked his intense gaze on me, but I couldn't read his expression.

The server stepped away from the table. "I'll get you more napkins."

"Thank you," I said, keeping my gaze on Declan.

A flood of emotion washed across his face—a mixture of frustration, regret, and anger. Then he angled his shoulders to the right, allowing Copper, who'd been standing behind him the entire time, access to the table.

I slid out of my seat, standing up to greet her.

"Copper Sherwood, witch." Declan's tone was stilted as he forced himself to make proper introductions. "Wisteria Fairchild, reconstructionist, and my... my..."

I actually wasn't technically his anything. We weren't really related. And it was unlikely he wanted to introduce me as his former sweetheart. If that was what we'd even been.

"... my sister's cousin."

I reached my hand out to Copper. "How do you do?"

She looked surprised by my offer to shake, flexing her hand but then not reaching out herself.

Jasmine laughed huskily. "Good call, Copper. Dissing Wisteria is the perfect way to endear yourself."

Anger flushed Copper's face.

"Would you join us?" I asked, sliding back into the booth.

Declan crowded in next to me, forcing me against the window and away from Copper.

"Jasmine," Copper said, perching on the very edge of the seat and eyeing the food spread across the table distastefully. "Attached to your laptop like always."

"Yeah," Jasmine said snarkily. "Because missing kids are just so boring."

Copper looked aghast. "I didn't know what you were working on."

"Oh? Just thought we were on a vacation?"

"Of course not. I knew you were here on a case, but … " She trailed off, locking her distressed gaze on Declan as if silently seeking support.

Declan reached across the table and retrieved his milkshake, allowing his ex-girlfriend the freedom to handle the situation on her own. It seemed pretty clear that she had completely set up this meeting. Though to what end, I wasn't sure.

"You were in town?" I asked politely. "Or you live in town?"

"No," Declan said unhelpfully, digging into the fries.

"I was in Santa Monica, delivering some items that couldn't be shipped to a client," Copper said, not quite meeting my gaze. "When I checked in with him, Declan mentioned he was coming to LA as well. I was … I was hoping to meet you."

I wasn't entirely certain how to respond. "Well, I'm glad. Though I'm not sure how long we'll be in town."

Jasmine frowned at her brother, possibly at the confirmation that Declan had broken up with the witch while she was away from home. If they were actually broken up. Copper's desire to meet me, and the fact that she'd known we were at the diner, seemed to contradict that.

Kett appeared at the door to the diner, scanning the windows before he entered. I lifted my hand, drawing his attention. He nodded but then frowned, noting that our booth was full.

"Who is that?" Copper asked, craning her neck to follow my gaze.

Neither Declan nor Jasmine answered her.

Kett drew what looked like a hotel keycard out of his pocket, nodding in the direction of the SUV.

"Do you still have the car keys?" I asked Jasmine.

"Second set," she said.

I nodded to the vampire. He disappeared.

"Kett booked a hotel. He's leaving the keycard in the car."

A text message pinged through on Jasmine's phone. She scanned it. "He sent me a map link."

"Kett?" Copper asked, overly brightly.

I answered as pleasantly as I could. "A work colleague. As Jasmine said, we're unfortunately tracking two missing children."

"Missing?" Copper asked in that same bright tone.

I eyed her coolly and quietly, becoming more and more bothered by the coincidence of the witch just happening to show up. Troubled by her interest in Kett and our investigation.

She began to fidget.

Declan straightened in his seat, his gaze on me.

Jasmine closed her laptop, then drew it to her chest protectively.

"Why are you here?" I whispered.

The copper-haired witch's gaze flicked to Declan, then back to me.

"Wisteria." Voicing my name as a warning, Jasmine snatched her cellphone off the table.

"Do you have something to do with the children?"

"No!" Copper cried, aghast.

"Do you know why they've been kidnapped?"

"Kidnapped? No! Of course not. I—"

"Where has Yale taken them? To what ends?"

Her eyes flicked to my hands on the table—and to the bracelet on my wrist, which was glowing so brightly I could see it on the edge of my peripheral vision.

"I don't know what you're—"

"The timing is odd, isn't it?" I asked. "Showing up now? Talking about just wanting to meet me, and asking about Kett in that bright, fake tone. Like you don't already know who he is and how he's connected to all of us."

Declan wrapped his hand around my wrist, covering my bracelet. I could feel the sparks of his magic on my exposed skin. "Wisteria," he murmured softly.

Copper's face crumpled. Suddenly and desperately sad, she dropped her gaze from me.

I looked over at Declan.

"I don't think Copper is involved," he said soothingly.

"No," I said, suddenly aware that I'd almost just attacked the witch across the table from me. Almost accused her of kidnapping children. "I...I'm sorry." I glanced over at Copper. "The case...the children..."

She nodded.

"I understand you're here for Declan," I said. "I...I just need some air. Would you let me pass?" I directed my question to Declan.

He nodded, slipping out of the booth. "I'll pay," he murmured as I slid out past him.

I nodded.

"Maybe I could help," Copper said. "I'm proficient in tracking spells, and—"

"Thank you," I said, rudely cutting her off but really needing to move beyond the current awkwardness. "I'm sure that would be appreciated. Jasmine?"

Then I escaped the confines of the diner, abandoning my best friend to deal with Declan's helpful girlfriend. A girlfriend who I'd almost blasted across the room.

I stepped outside, practically gulping down fresh air despite the heat. The case had me terribly on edge. There was something I was missing, something that we were all missing.

Maybe it was another coincidence, like Copper just showing up unannounced...or maybe it was a specific co-incidence that we'd shunted to the side, unexplored.

The shared birthdays.

A coincidence that I was afraid to explore further.

Because if Ruby sharing a date of birth with Declan and Jack sharing mine was deliberate, then Yale kidnapping witches for his own means made even less sense. Because if the shared birthdays actually meant something, then this was about us. About Jasmine, Declan, and me.

Something connected to the three of us was getting children kidnapped.

I pressed my hands to my face, surprised to find my skin cool even as I felt overheated.

Jasmine slipped out of the diner behind me.

"I need you to do something for me," I said, rushing the request before she could speak, before she could ask me if I was okay.

"Anything. Always."

"I need you to find the third missing child."

"Third? Wisteria, we have no evidence—"

"Find me the missing witch with your birthday." I turned around to meet her gaze. "I know it's a nearly impossible request, especially if Yale targeted another unregistered fledgling... or has kidnapped multiple children, all with different birthdays. But please... just prove me wrong on this one point... please. Then I'll be able to move on."

She nodded.

"I know you're busy tracking Jack and Ruby," I said.

"No," she said. "I'm just compiling evidence, looking for clues. I've got nothing. I'm hoping Kett talked to Yale." She glanced back to the diner.

Inside, Copper was gazing up at Declan as he paid the bill at the cashier.

"We didn't even touch the food," I said mournfully.

Jasmine linked her arm through mine. "It gets worse. Copper just volunteered her services, and she's a damn good witch."

"Maybe it's good she's here, then. Good for Declan... and you."

"Yeah, because both of us are so eager to replace you."

"That's not what I... never mind."

"Fine."

"Fine."

"I still get shotgun."

I laughed. "It's yours. Always."

Jasmine sniffed, satisfied with my capitulation. I turned away from watching Declan and Copper. Maybe they could repair whatever had broken between them. And either way, I had no business being heartbroken about any of it.

Because I was tied to Kett, whether or not we were lovers. Whether or not I had any choice in the matter.

Chapter Seven

I curled up on the couch of the luxury hotel suite that Kett had booked for us—and that I'd already forgotten the name of—while Jasmine's fingers danced over the keyboard of her laptop at a light-oak desk near the window. Despite the fact that darkness had fallen across the city while Jasmine worked, Kett hadn't reappeared yet. And Declan and Copper had 'gone for a walk' hours before and never returned. So they were either fighting or having sex in some other room.

I had fallen asleep with the contents of Jack's keepsake box carefully laid out across the coffee table before me. We had hit a dead end. Well, I at least had no idea what the next step in our investigation was. Jasmine still had a few threads she was pulling on, though, including the coincidences of the shared birthdays.

"Dawn Fairchild," Jasmine murmured, rousing me from my light doze.

"Dawn?" I asked, racking my brain for a possible familial connection. "A cousin?"

"If she is, she's way down the line. I'd have to piece together a family tree." Jasmine paused, reading whatever she had just pulled up on her screen. "She's seven. The only registered witch to share my birthday."

"October 7," I murmured. "Parents?"

"Um…Dean and Amy."

"They didn't opt in for weird witch names."

"But they named their daughter Dawn." Jasmine's fingers flew across the keyboard. "Okay, the mother, Amy, is registered with the Convocation. But maybe she's nonpracticing. And Dean doesn't use the Fairchild surname. I've got a fairly recent picture."

She turned her laptop slightly, angling the screen so I could see the photo of a brown-haired, green-eyed girl with tanned skin and a missing front tooth.

I laughed. "Lucky her. She gets the magic but not the Fairchild bland-blond thing."

"Hopefully her teeth grow in straight."

"They have braces for that, you know."

"They have magic for that, you know."

"Right. Well, braces are cheaper unless you carry enough Fairchild blood that the family potion master is required to gift you with a teeth-straightening elixir. And Dawn isn't Fairchild enough for that. Lucky her times two."

"Jasper got one from Violet for Declan," Jasmine said.

"Did he? I don't remember that…"

Jasmine glanced over at me with a smirk. "You liked his crooked teeth."

I smiled but didn't respond.

She returned to her keyboard. "Let's see…no missing person report, and…I…oh…" She exhaled sharply, as though all the air had been forced out of her lungs. "They…they're dead."

I straightened up on the couch. "What? All of them? When?"

Jasmine's fingers danced. The light of her computer screen flickered across her face as she opened and closed multiple windows. "A car accident … "

"When?" I got to my feet. "When?"

Jasmine stilled, then looked over at me. "January 25, 2017."

"More than a week after Kett took Yale to London." I slumped back down on the couch, feeling oddly defeated. Though I should have been pleased that I'd been wrong about the possible pattern, at least for witches affiliated with the Convocation. We had no way of tracking unregistered witches. "Okay, then. That's … good. We can focus on Ruby and Jack. I'm going to text Kett."

I shifted off the couch, straightening my silk blouse and crossing toward my bag, which I'd left on the entertainment sideboard next to the TV. "And I should check in about Coral," I said, pulling my phone out of my bag.

"Hmm," Jasmine said, only half listening to me and still glued to her screen. "I checked in with Lavender about an hour ago. They're bringing in a healer to work with the reader."

I glanced up from my phone. Jasmine was flicking through pictures of a crumpled, charred car wreck.

"Are those … " I stepped as close to her laptop as I dared. "Are those crime scene photos? How do you get hold of these things?"

"You don't want to know."

I shook my head, texting Kett as I crossed back to the couch.

Any updates?

"This is weird," Jasmine said thoughtfully. "They had a memorial service."

"Most people do."

"No, I mean as opposed to a funeral. There weren't any bodies to bury."

My stomach soured. "Yeah. The accident looks bad."

Jasmine started flipping through pages and pages of information again, the images reflecting across her face. She looked tired. And sad. And though both states were entirely logical given the situation, I found myself wishing she were smiling and happy.

"It takes a really hot fire to completely consume a body," she said. "That requires fuel."

"Cars carry a lot of fuel."

"Right … except the investigation is still open. Into the accident. The authorities haven't figured out the cause."

"Most accidents usually involve another vehicle."

"Exactly. Or, say, brake failure."

"And neither is possible?"

"Well, look at the damage to the front end of the vehicle … "

"I really don't want to."

Jasmine snorted. "I mean, it looks like it hit something. But no other car was found at the scene. And any vehicle that caused that much damage probably wouldn't have been able to drive away … or at least there would be evidence that a second vehicle was at the scene."

"And … brake failure?"

"Flat road. No damage to the nearby trees … or the gravel at the edge of the road."

"Did a magical investigation team sweep the area?"

Jasmine eyed me grimly. "Not yet."

"Could a car hitting a vampire create that sort of damage?" I asked.

"I don't know any Adept who could get hit by a car and not be at least severely injured."

"And Yale was in London," I murmured.

"Supposedly."

"It could all still be a coincidence."

"Yeah. It could be."

My phone pinged. I glanced down at the screen to see a text from Kett.

>*I'm in San Francisco. Don't leave LA without me.*

San Francisco? Since when? "Are there any vampires in San Francisco?" I asked. Jasmine had lived in the city off and on for many years.

She shrugged. "Rumors, maybe. Why?"

"Apparently, Kett has jetted off there."

"Classic. Vampires, always team players."

Ignoring the enigma that was Kett for a moment, I called us back to the subject at hand. "Was the car accident in Connecticut?"

"New York State."

"What's the protocol? Do we ask the Convocation to send a team to look into the accident?"

"Not without more than my hastily put-together guesses."

"Or my hunch."

Jasmine shrugged. "I could look into the family more. Find out if there was anything nefarious going on, any reason they'd be targeted. If their deaths aren't just a weird, unexplainable accident."

"But logically, we should be focusing on Ruby and Jack."

Jasmine sighed. "I'm not sure I'm getting anywhere tracking them either."

"Have you uncovered any other bank accounts somehow connected to Yale? Any large deposits around the time of Ruby or Jack being kidnapped that you could trace back?"

"Nope. Though I've really got nothing substantial on Amaya, Mania, or Valko. Money could have been routed through them, using their real names. I could make the assumption that an immortal being with three dependents would have needed more money than I've uncovered, so there could be other accounts, other caches."

"Three former dependents."

"Yeah. Yale's bank account will be pleased there aren't so many mouths to feed."

"Sick, Jasmine."

"You started it."

"So as far as we reasonably know, Yale kidnapped, and likely killed, two witch children. Because he has a thing for young, magical blood."

"Yep. As long as we ignore the fact that we have no idea why Yale would target these specific victims. Especially because it's likely that Jack himself didn't even know he was magical. And we ignore that Ruby and Jack have the same birthdays as Declan and you."

"Ignoring the birthdays as coincidence, Yale's witch, Mania, could have crafted a spell to identify and track Adepts."

Jasmine shook her head. "Her specialty was poisons, combined with some low level of warding magic. Or she purchased spells that she combined with her potions. Crafting a spell sensitive enough to track underage witches, that's detailed work." Jasmine paused, thinking. "Most witches specialize in flashier magic. I know of one witch I went to the Academy with who could do it."

"And Dahlia," I said.

"Well, if you want to bring Fairchild witches into it, anyone in the main coven could probably do it. Maybe even Rose. Or you, now. If you felt like it."

I gave her a look, keeping us on task rather than discussing what magic I was willing to wield. "Which likely puts all the Convocation members on our list. And … Copper?"

Jasmine eyed me for a moment, then nodded.

"Okay. So then, if that is the case, why would a witch employ a vampire to kidnap children? And why would Yale bother, if not for money?"

"We already know one vampire who'd never turn down a willing witch," Jasmine said. She was quoting Kett from when he'd caught us talking about him in the dark hallway of a funeral home.

I sighed, pressing my thumb and forefinger to the bridge of my nose. "I prefer it when the clues just naturally link up and lead to each other."

Jasmine laughed. "That's because you're only brought in when the clues are there to collect, or there's a scene to reconstruct. Investigations take months. You … you and Declan should probably go home. I can call when I need you."

"I'm not leaving you," I said gruffly.

"You're restless, Wisteria. And feeling useless. I'm accustomed to this part."

I slipped off the couch, wandering to the windows. The buildings stretched out on either side of the hotel were a blur of lights, blocking any chance of stargazing. I couldn't see the moon. I let my gaze drop to the street, which was bustling with traffic and pedestrians despite the late hour. Between the sealed windows and the air-conditioning continually running, I couldn't hear anything from outside.

"We still have a few months," my best friend said. "Before … before you leave us. You probably have things to do. Things—"

"I don't," I said sharply. "I'm fine here. With you. Don't get rid of me before I'm ready to go."

The silence that fell between us felt strained, contrary to our normally comforting moments of quiet companionship.

I kept my gaze out the window, though I saw nothing. Just waiting for Jasmine to start typing again. She didn't.

"Do you think you will be ready?" she whispered. "To go?"

I shook my head, not answering because I didn't have an answer. Maybe it had been stupid to delay at all, once I'd known I had no choice but to accept the terms of the contract. I wasn't sure what I was accomplishing with the delay. Maybe a clean break would have been better for all of us.

Except... I'd already walked away from Jasmine and Declan once. And I wasn't sure I was strong enough to do so again. Not yet.

"Let's go to New York," Jasmine said, struggling to keep her tone light. "I can work remotely, and you can follow up on your hunch. If something is up with the car accident that has nothing to do with our case, we'll have the Convocation open a file and send another investigative team."

I waved my hand helplessly. "There must be other things you need to do in LA."

"Like what? Question Jack's friends? Asking what? It was obvious he didn't know Yale. Though, by his exact wording, he'd rebuffed the vampire at least once previously. We saw as much as anyone else saw in that room, of the kidnapping at least. Probably more, with Yale ensnaring Jack's companion. Jack doesn't have any credit cards, and the thirty-five dollars in his bank account hasn't been touched."

Jasmine closed her laptop, standing to stretch. "There's a safe-deposit box in his mother's name, which he likely gets access to at eighteen. So it maybe holds bonds of some sort, or family heirlooms, or even information about the Adept, if his mother had magical roots and didn't tell Jack. But if it was something the state could have seized to fund his upkeep, they would have."

"If I wasn't here, hovering and bothering you with hunches, what would you do next?" I asked.

"Keep tracking Yale. There must be another credit card or bank account. I don't even know how he got from Chicago to LA, then back to New York. He has to be flying. Otherwise, the cars he's rented don't make any sense. Unless he just randomly exchanges rentals... but even then, how is he paying for the gas? Or do vampires somehow get by on way less cash than the rest of us need just to exist?"

"Maybe he simply takes what he wants, then wipes people's memories of the transaction. He might resort to using his credit card, or cash, only if he can't manipulate the situation. Say, if too many people are around."

Jasmine stared at me aghast for a moment. Then she snapped her mouth shut and shook her head. "Text Kett. Tell him we need the jet to go to New York. He won't let you go without him, so when he shows up, we'll grill him."

"It's difficult to grill someone who just doesn't answer questions."

Jasmine tilted her head. "He's warming up."

I offered her a smile. My heart was still heavy, though, so it wasn't a particularly sunny smile.

"Do you think the stores are still open in the lobby?" she asked thoughtfully.

"I can call down and ask."

"Let's go buy bathing suits and sit in the hot tub," she said. "I can afford a break, especially since I'm pretty much just spinning my wheels without a new direction."

Jasmine lifted her hand to me, and I took it. She tugged me forward into a hug. "Though you'd probably prefer an expensive meal first. Check and see if the restaurant is still open. We'll charge it to the Conclave. Serves them right for letting vampires run wild."

She let me go. I reached for the phone on the corner of the desk.

"And then," she said, drawing out whatever she was about to proclaim, "I'll research Copper a bit. Just in case your 'coincidences' are actually something, and not just rampant jealousy over how much time she's spent in Declan's bed."

I picked up the phone, tilting my head thoughtfully as I dialed down to the front desk. "Declan isn't really the bed sort."

"Eww! Wisteria!"

"You started it."

The desk clerk answered. "How may I help you?"

"Hello," I said. "Are any of the restaurants still serving dinner? And can any of them accommodate a table of two in the next ten minutes or so?" I glanced up at Jasmine with a grimace, then added, "Actually, that might need to be a table for four."

Jasmine lifted her lip in a fake snarl, then pulled out her phone. She took my hint to text Declan, inviting him and Copper for a late dinner.

"Our main restaurant would be happy to accommodate your party in fifteen minutes," the desk clerk said. "We're featuring a sushi bar tonight, and I can request that they hold it open for you. Would that work?"

I woke to a faint wash of moonlight streaming across the bed. And for a breath, I waited, listening for whatever had roused me. Listening for Kett visiting in the dark again. But when nothing more happened, I rolled toward the windows.

Jasmine was perched on the opposite edge of the king-sized bed, looking out at the sprawl of bright city lights beyond the windows. Her knees were tucked to her chest.

"Jasmine?" I whispered.

"I'm okay." Her voice was hushed but bright. "Just awake."

I tugged the covers up to my neck, curling my arm underneath my pillow. I had almost dozed off when she spoke again.

"I told Dahlia," she said. Her tone was still steady and clear. "Before I left Connecticut this last time. I told her what he'd done."

"Valko?" I asked sleepily.

"Jasper."

My uncle's name and Jasmine's admission felt as though they had suddenly sucked all the air out of the room, leaving my chest heavy and constricted. I waited, suspended in that airless space, for my best friend to elaborate. She often spun tales about our life together—half of which I swear hadn't actually happened in the way she rendered them. But we never talked about Jasper or her parents.

"She didn't want to believe me," Jasmine finally said. "She said you'd polluted my mind." She laughed harshly.

The sharp sound pooled in my stomach, giving rise to a flush of anger. "As if you can't think for yourself," I said, sitting up. My hair spilled down around my neck and shoulders.

"He told me I was beautiful..." Jasmine's voice cracked.

I was scrambling across the bed and wrapping my arms around her before I'd even thought to move.

She grasped my forearms as if steadying herself. Then she forced herself to continue. "He told me...that he couldn't hold back with me, like he could with you and Declan...because I was just so beautiful."

I squeezed her tightly, fighting my own tears. Wanting to keep that moment focused on Jasmine, and not on our shared pain.

"I was older then, of course," she said. "Fourteen ... fifteen ... sixteen. On the edge of being a woman, he said. So I suppose it was ... different than when we were younger."

She fell silent.

I remained still, my arms cinched around her shoulders. Barely daring to breathe for fear of upsetting the delicate balance of her confession. Of causing her more pain with the wrong reaction or with ill-chosen words. I didn't know what else to do. I didn't know how to make any of it better, other than being there and holding her.

"Dahlia ... " she said. "I think she believed me in the end. I mentioned his birthmark. The one just above his genitals. And her face sort of ... crumpled. Then I got up and left." Her voice became strident. "I left her there with it. She followed me to the door and she just kept repeating that she hadn't known. That I hadn't ever said anything. I kept walking." Fiercely, she wiped the tears from her face. "I'm so tired of crying about it."

"Valko biting you ... assaulting you has brought it to the surface," I said. "It will fade again."

"I'm not sure I want it to fade. Some part of me wants ... blood ... vengeance. On them all."

"I know. I understand."

"He's not going to let you stay," she whispered. "He's too careful. Of you. And me."

She meant Kett. She meant after I was remade, transformed.

"You'll never be without me," I said. "Not if I can help it. Even if we can't be in the same ... space. Isn't that what Skype is for?"

She laughed. The sound was harsh, soul bruising. But it was a laugh.

"Come back into the bed," I said. "Under the covers."

"I'm not cold."

"I am." I slid back on the bed, making sure to keep my hand pressed to her back as I moved. Tucking my legs underneath the covers, I lifted the duvet, coaxing Jasmine away from the edge near the window.

She settled in beside me without further protest. We lay there for a few moments, side by side with only our hands linked.

"What was I supposed to say to them all those years ago?" she said. "I woke up in the hospital and you were gone. They came to me, already questioning what you'd told them. They thought you were lying to protect Declan. They thought the deal you'd made was the truth. That in leaving, in running away, you'd admitted as much."

"They wanted to believe the lie."

"I don't think they really cared one way or the other. Like on some level, what Jasper did to us was expected. Maybe even mimicked from their own upbringing."

"For the accumulation of power," I said. "For the fortification of the coven."

"Yes."

"Are you glad you told Dahlia?"

"I am...though it felt cruel while I was doing so. She hasn't tried to contact me since. And that tells me everything I needed to know."

"Maybe she doesn't know how to fix it."

"Maybe she really doesn't give a shit."

The sky outside had begun to lighten. As if on cue, I noticed that the traffic noise had increased. Without the air-conditioning running, even the triple-paned windows couldn't completely muffle it.

"When Kett remakes you," Jasmine said, sounding suddenly sleepy. "Even if you can't stay here with me, you'll be able to email more. And FaceTime. I don't think vampires have the same issues with technology."

"I'm sure I'll be able to get my crypt wired with Wi-Fi."

Jasmine laughed, proving she was more awake than she sounded. "I can totally imagine Kett rocking a mausoleum. He likes being a monster."

I chuckled.

"Will you like it?" she asked. "Being a monster?"

I opened my mouth to say that I wouldn't like any aspect of being a vampire. Then I thought about all the implications of her question. "If I survive."

"You'll survive," Jasmine said. "That's why Kett chose you. Or at least one of the reasons. Like Jasper always said, you're the power, Declan is the force, and I'm... " Her voice trailed off.

"The heart?"

"Yes. That's better than simply 'pretty.' "

"It's the truth. Can you imagine Declan or me without you? Who would we love?"

"Each other."

"You know what I mean."

"I do, but I think you're wrong. I think you suppressed your ability to love the way you suppressed your magic. Because without power or emotions, you couldn't be manipulated."

"See how well that worked out for me?"

"There's always a choice," she murmured. "Even in the deepest darkness."

I fell into a light slumber as the sun rose, sleepily regretting that we hadn't pulled the curtains, but unwilling to break contact with Jasmine in order to get up and close them.

"Will you be my guardian demon, Betty-Sue?" Jasmine whispered the words, hushed as if she was wary of waking me. "Will you watch over me when you're the monster in the dark? Will you bring me the blood and vengeance I crave?"

My heart constricted with a terrible pain, a terrible need to declare my intention of watching over her for every day of her life. But I didn't know. I didn't know who I'd be when Kett remade me.

Jasmine might believe that there was always a choice, even in the deepest, darkest moments. But I knew without question that there was always a payment to be exacted as well. Immortality and invulnerability would come with a heavy price. One that I would be forced to pay, first with my humanity and possibly my soul.

And second... well, that remained to be seen.

Chapter Eight

I bumped into Copper—literally—in the hotel corridor while on the way to breakfast. I had the uncomfortable feeling that the witch might have been lying in wait for me, but immediately quashed the uncharitable thought with a forced smile.

"Good morning," I said.

"Wisteria," Copper said, speaking as though she'd prepared what she was about to say, "I feel like I've intruded…but it's just that you, and Jasmine, are so important to Declan, and when the opportunity presented itself…" She trailed off, offering me a curl of a smile instead of finishing her sentence.

I got the distinct feeling that I was supposed to complete or reciprocate the sentiment. Unfortunately for her, I was terrible at making friends or saying things I didn't actually mean. So I simply nodded. "Let me make sure Jasmine is actually joining us."

Copper's face blanked, then she nodded stiffly.

I turned back to run my keycard through the door lock, feeling bad for excluding the witch even though this wasn't the time or place for bonding. Then a thought came to me.

"Copper?" I called back over my shoulder.

She paused a few steps up the hall, turning back expectantly.

"Do you know of any way to contact a brownie?" I asked. "When not on their territory, I mean."

"You...a brownie bonded to a certain family? Or an estate, you mean? Bonded to you?"

I nodded. "Yes. There must be a...well, not a summoning spell, because—"

"That would just be wrong!" Copper exclaimed. "They are sentient beings. A blessing. Not some magical creature to be presumptuously summoned."

I eyed her. "Yes. As I was saying."

Copper twisted her lips. "My immediate family isn't so blessed. But I understand that the main New York office of Sherwood and Pine have such a connection. I could make a call."

"That would be appreciated. I'm concerned for the brownie's welfare. Lark, bonded to Fairchild Manor."

Copper nodded curtly, obviously trying to keep her opinions to herself as she retrieved a phone from the tan-colored purse looped over her forearm. Then, as if forcing herself to speak her mind, she said, "A brownie is more than capable of taking care of herself. Perhaps more so without witch interference. If she hasn't contacted you, I would suggest it is her choice."

"I understand your opinion and your reservations, Copper. Thank you for your assistance in this matter."

"Of course," she said. "I'm always pleased to aid a Convocation specialist, and..."—she hesitated as if reminding herself—"... a friend of Declan's."

She stressed the word 'friend' a little too sharply, then appeared momentarily mortified with herself.

"We do what we can," I said, attempting to be kind. "For the people we care for."

She nodded awkwardly, returning her attention to her phone.

I unlocked the hotel room door. Jasmine had promised that she'd be right behind me when I stepped out.

Just inside the door, I found my best friend leaning back against the wall next to the closet, texting or playing a game on her phone.

She grinned at me saucily. "Is the coast clear?"

I shook my head at her. She must have heard me speaking to Copper before the door swung closed behind me. "Breakfast," I said.

"Right behind you," she said. "As always."

"Yeah, you've really got my back."

She laughed, and I couldn't help but grin at her. Copper was going to have a dreadful time making a place in Jasmine's life, but some part of me was glad to know that the witch would at least try.

I stepped back out into the hall, quashing the mournful thought. I wasn't gone yet. I had at least one more breakfast to enjoy with the two people who meant more to me than anything else in the world. Whether I had to begrudgingly put up with Copper's presence or not.

When breakfast was done, Jasmine, Declan, Copper, and I piled into Copper's rental car, which she had arranged to have picked up at the airport. Then we headed out to meet up with Kett and the jet. Everyone seemed consumed by their own thoughts—excepting Jasmine, who kept up a steady stream of chatter detailing her progress with the various threads of her online investigation.

I wasn't certain that Declan had said a word since we'd murmured our good mornings at the table in the restaurant. Whatever was going on between him and Copper obviously hadn't healed overnight, and I was starting to feel sorry for the witch. But given that she was here, we needed to drag her with us across the country. I was about to reconstruct a large event—if there was magic involved in the car accident that had claimed Dawn Fairchild's family. And Jasmine's distraction and cloaking spells weren't anywhere near as effective as having a talented witch on site would be, especially one who could adapt her magic quickly if we needed her to.

Moments after we arrived at the private hangar and boarded the jet, Kett disappeared to wherever he went when we took off, and we all settled in for the six-hour flight. The vampire had been completely close-mouthed about what he'd been doing in San Francisco, and I hadn't bothered needling him. If he'd obtained pertinent information, he'd share it.

After the jet took off, Declan leaned back in his seat, swiveling it to face me. He hadn't removed his sunglasses, so I wasn't certain if he was settling in to sleep or preparing for a conversation.

I glanced over at Copper, who'd sat directly across the aisle from Declan. The copper-haired witch had been looking at me, but she quickly returned her attention to the collection of spent spells she had arrayed on her table. She had chalked, then closed, a tiny circle around her workspace and was renewing Jasmine's collection. I kept my personal shielding up, layered even more tightly than I usually held it, not wanting to affect her casting. And I was surprised that she was willing to pull from her personal reserves in such a fashion, with no connection to the earth. She was either quite powerful, capable of storing magic on her person—likely in an object similar to my bracelet—or she was overly confident in her abilities.

I knew that not many items similar to my bracelet existed. At least not among the general population of the Adept, who didn't have some sort of a relationship with an alchemist. As far as I knew, Jade Godfrey was the only such alchemist of our era, and she didn't sell objects of power.

Kett slipped back through the passenger cabin, pausing to tower over me. He was carrying three objects—a brown, leather-bound book; what appeared to be an ornate chess set; and a box of Ghirardelli chocolates.

He handed me the book and the chocolates. "Go join your cousin on the couch," he said almost gruffly.

I started to laugh—but then I felt the magic radiating from the book. I slipped out of my seat, taking Kett's offerings and looking at him questioningly.

He flicked his gaze to the book I held in my hands. "That doesn't leave the jet. The bastard wanted my blood for it. Thankfully, I had an excuse he couldn't counter. Your imminent remaking. So I had to trade an open-ended favor to get it. It will return to its owner in three days, or if it falls into the wrong hands."

"Well, I'm intrigued." I smiled softly. Then, impulsively, I kissed his cheek lightly before I stepped around him and shoved the box of chocolates in Jasmine's face.

My best friend looked up from her laptop, squealed, and tried to snatch the box from me.

Laughing, I pulled it from her grasp, then wandered back to the white leather couch at the back of the passenger cabin, pretty much dragging her and her laptop along with the lure of chocolate. The couch was a feature of the slightly different model of Learjet that Kett had brought back from

San Francisco. I briefly wondered if he'd made the change solely so that Jasmine and I could sit together.

Glancing back at Kett, I was surprised to find him watching me. He smiled, then took the seat I'd vacated, facing Declan. He then swiftly pulled out a table and set up the chess game he'd been carrying, his hands moving in a blur.

"Declan," the vampire said, blunt yet inviting.

Declan dropped the pretense of sleeping, straightening his chair. He removed his sunglasses and eyed the executioner for a moment. Then he barked, "White."

Kett spun the chess set.

"The vampire is making friends," Jasmine murmured. Her mouth sounded full, because it was. She'd already opened the box of chocolates. I hadn't even noticed her grabbing it from me a second time.

Of course, the magic emanating from the book I held was fairly distracting. I frowned at my best friend as she popped the second half of the first chocolate she'd purloined into her mouth.

"What? It's a soft center...strawberry...mmm. You only like the caramels and clusters."

I snorted, settling beside her on the couch with the box of chocolates between us.

Jasmine chortled to herself, shifting her laptop farther away from me.

I placed the book in my lap, running my fingers along its supple leather binding. It was an easy guess that the magic it radiated was the timed spell that would return it to its owner in three days—along with whatever spell could possibly determine what the 'wrong hands' were.

"What is that?" Jasmine asked, leaning her shoulder against mine.

I opened the book. Scrawled across the first page was the handwritten title:

The Chronicles of Ve
Collected by a child of his blood
Without permission.

Jasmine sighed with so much pleasure that I almost laughed. Except I was fairly certain I was holding a book filled with information that could get me killed. If I hadn't already been slated to die.

"Without permission," Jasmine whispered. "Child of his blood. Kett?"

"No," I said. "Ve is his grandsire. Estelle's maker."

"Right. So...this was the mysterious trip to San Francisco?"

"Apparently."

Jasmine looked up at me. "He's preparing you."

I nodded.

"Well, then. Turn the freaking page."

"Don't take notes," I whispered. "At least not where Kett can see."

"He can see I'm reading it with you. He practically told you to invite me."

"No," I said. "He gave me the book and told me to come back here on the pretense that he wanted my seat. And now he sits with his back to us."

"Plausible deniability."

I laughed. Then I sobered as I ran my fingers across the black-inked lettering of the title. I couldn't be completely certain without retrieving the contract from my bag, but I thought the handwriting might be the same. Which meant that whoever had written the chronicle also drafted contracts for the Conclave, or at least had drafted the contract that tied me to Kett. Ember and her associates had assumed it was constructed by a sorcerer, so maybe the vampire in question had once been such an Adept. Before he became a child of Ve and a sibling of Kett's maker, Estelle.

I kept my thoughts to myself—not wanting to bring the contract up with Jasmine if I didn't need to—as I flipped the first page.

Then I spent the next five hours eating chocolate and learning about ancient vampires, blood wars, and the origins of the Conclave.

By the time I was done, I was exceedingly glad that Kett had indicated we'd be avoiding London for as long as possible. Because I was about to inherit a great-grandsire who had fashioned himself as a god on more than one occasion. And who could likely destroy me after my remaking merely by focusing his capricious will in my direction.

Of course, the text I'd been reading might just have been an elaborate mythology. But something about the 'without permission' tag underneath the title told me that the chronicler, at the very least, held what was contained within the book as the utter truth.

Dawn's family lived in Rye, a relatively small city in Westchester County, New York, close to the Connecticut border but not right on top of the main branch of the Fairchild coven. As Jasmine had originally guessed, we were distant cousins, but it was likely that Amy, Dawn's mother, didn't actively pursue magic. This made me wonder if Dean, Amy's husband, had any inkling of the Adept world. That had to be a fine line to walk for a husband and wife, especially if Dawn showed any magical proclivity.

It was evening by the time we landed at yet another private airfield and climbed into yet another SUV—with Copper tucked into the back seat between Declan and me.

This time, the behemoth vehicle was dark green and a rental, meaning Kett hadn't been able to source his preferred make and model. I didn't catch the name of the airport. But then, they were all starting to blur together. And it was the destination, not the trip, that held the most importance for me. I always felt useless through the distance in between.

As we neared the site of the accident, Jasmine pieced together a working narrative for the incident we were about to investigate. "Based on the last charges on Dean's credit card, it looks like the family were on their way home from dinner and a movie. The accident took place about five minutes from home, which is near enough to a wildlife sanctuary to be relatively remote. At least they died together."

"No," I whispered, staring out at the dark, tree-lined street blurring past my window. "Each of them would have wanted the others to survive."

Jasmine didn't respond.

Kett pulled over onto a wide gravel shoulder a few moments later, stopping at the exact point Jasmine had punched into the GPS.

We climbed out of the vehicle into tree-shrouded darkness. The headlights illuminated the immediate area, but there weren't any streetlights. The houses were spaced far apart and back from the street, not offering any light of their own.

"The accident took place there," Jasmine said, pointing ahead of us.

"How do you know?" Copper asked.

"Burn marks," Declan said grimly, walking in the direction Jasmine had indicated. A few steps away, he activated a small flashlight and began scanning the narrow two-lane street.

Kett slipped off into a dense row of trees beside us, some of which were still leafing out. At a guess, he'd be making a quick check of the perimeter. I buttoned my trench coat, tucking my silk scarf into the lapel. New York was chilly compared to LA, but not uncomfortable.

Jasmine set up her laptop on the hood of the SUV as I wandered after Declan, opening my witch senses and seeking any residual magic.

The headlights on the SUV winked out. Copper, as per protocol, had been silently trailing along behind me so she didn't interfere with my sensing. But now she murmured something quietly and light bloomed behind me. With another whispered command, she fixed the light-blue orb she'd called forth over our heads. It was high enough that it would look like a streetlight to a casual observer, and wouldn't interfere with any reconstruction.

A car passed as I traversed the remainder of the half-dozen yards between the SUV and the site of the accident. I paused at the edge of the gravel, shoulder to shoulder with Declan, practically able to taste the residual magic coating the immediate area. Copper coaxed her orb slightly closer, until it illuminated the dark marks along the asphalt.

"Wait until this next car passes." Declan was looking farther up the road. "Then we can get closer."

"No need," I said, raising my voice so Jasmine could hear me. "There's more than enough magic here to attempt a reconstruction."

Beside me, Copper nodded in agreement, sweeping her arm forward. "Concentrated magic here. Likely at other points just off the road, setting up some sort of masking."

Jasmine jogged over to join us.

"Witch magic?" I asked Copper, wanting to confirm what I could sense.

"Feels like it. Could be purchased spells, of course."

Headlights swept across us from a car slowly approaching in the opposite direction.

"Then there are probably at least two other points farther up the road in both directions," Jasmine said grimly.

"For redirecting traffic that night. They would have been timed spells, since no one found the vehicle until the fire had burned itself out." She turned to me. "I seriously hope this is some weird, isolated incident. But you should reconstruct it before I report any of our findings to the Convocation."

I nodded.

The car slipped past us, then slowed further to turn into a nearby driveway. I caught sight of a young girl with light blond hair watching us from the back seat. She might have been around the same age as Dawn. Maybe even a schoolmate, given that we were only a few minutes from Amy and Dean's home.

Declan crossed into the road as the car passed, crouching down to get a closer look at the burns.

"It will take me a few minutes to redirect the traffic," Jasmine said.

"I'll cast a large circle, rather than a mobile one," I said. "Grab it all at once."

"One circle?" Copper echoed. "The integrity—"

Jasmine curtly cut the witch off. "If Wisteria says she can do it, she can."

Copper nodded stiffly, apparently still questioning my abilities as a reconstructionist. But I came by my skills honestly. I deserved my reputation, so it wasn't ego or posturing to suggest I could collect such a large area in one pass.

"I'll set the distraction spells," Copper said. "They'll be stronger if anchored here, rather than using the premade I gave you. Moving vehicles are more difficult to reroute."

"I'll come with you," Jasmine said. "So I can document any residual you might pick up from previously laid spells."

"Of course. Then I'll place a shielding around the reconstruction circle itself. About five feet out? Will that disrupt your casting, Wisteria?"

"Not if you cast first."

"I'll need to physically hold a circle that large in place," Copper said. "To ensure its stability. But doing so will also allow me to adapt quickly if a car or a person manages to bypass the distraction spells."

Momentarily dropping her professional guise, she glanced over at Declan. Crouched over the burn marks on the pavement, he continued to ignore us as he brushed his fingers along a number of gouges I could see near the marks, but which would have been hidden to plain sight from farther away.

Copper headed back to the SUV without another word.

"Be ready," Jasmine said. Then she followed the other witch.

Declan looked up, catching my eye. "Looks like my magic," he said, sweeping his flashlight across the marks. His tone was hollow and heavy.

"It doesn't feel like your magic." I pulled the first of my candles from my bag, not willing to participate in any conjecture. Not yet. I needed to focus in order to cast a precise circle as large as I anticipated needing it.

I crossed to the very edge of the shoulder, carefully placing my white pillar, then shoring it up with loose gravel. I straightened, eyeing the trajectory toward the next point. My red candle—representing fire—would need to be situated in the middle of the road. So I'd have to wait for Jasmine's signal that the traffic had been successfully diverted before I placed it. Once I began, I preferred to set the candles in place in succession, pacing the edge of the circle and laying magic in my wake in a single direction, usually clockwise. Even though that precision wasn't always necessary, I'd stick to it with this casting. I had only a limited time to capture what I assumed was a large-scale magical event, so I needed to be meticulous.

Kett appeared on the edge of my peripheral vision, obviously attempting to slow down so he didn't startle me.

I offered him a tight smile.

"The witch is almost done on the northern edge," he said. "She is skilled."

"High praise."

"But annoyingly disruptive."

I involuntarily snorted out a laugh. "Don't tell Declan," I said. "He'll ask her to stay just to continue to annoy you."

"It's Declan who she is disrupting."

I let my gaze wander across the road. Declan was walking along the opposite edge, as if looking for any evidence that the mundane crime scene investigators might have missed.

"I have inserted myself into your life similarly," Kett said almost musingly. "You all seem to have accepted my presence. Begrudgingly, perhaps. But you don't extend the same courtesy to the witch."

"We got off on the wrong foot. And Jasmine doesn't like her."

"And what Jasmine likes, you and Declan go along with."

I glanced at him. "I think we try. Why?"

Kett didn't answer me, staring off into the distance.

I brushed my fingers across the top of his hand. "Kett?"

He turned to me with a slight smile, almost as if he hadn't realized there had been a gap in our conversation.

"Thank you for the book," I said.

He nodded. "You left it on the jet."

"As instructed."

He stepped closer, bowing his head slightly as he whispered. "You will be easier to protect...after. Less vulnerable."

My stomach fluttered with a sudden burst of nerves. "Are you ... is there something you aren't telling me?"

He laughed quietly. "Many somethings. Which would you like to know first?"

"I wasn't being literal."

"You don't need to be so careful with me, Wisteria. I'm not changing my mind. I'm not requesting your immediate fulfillment of the terms of the contract. You may still change your mind."

"I won't."

I spoke more forcefully than I'd intended, drawing Declan's attention. He frowned at me from across the street, then glanced both ways for traffic.

"Our conversations are never straightforward," I grumbled under my breath as Declan jogged across the road.

"Agreed." Kett's whisper brushed against my ear. "We do better with fewer words." Then he was standing a step away from me.

I quashed a smile at his attempt to flirt.

Declan joined us, fishing his phone out of his pocket and glancing at the screen. "They're done with the outer spells."

"Good." I stepped back to the white candle I'd already placed, waiting for Declan and Kett to clear away from where I needed to establish the circle.

Then I deliberately and steadily paced toward the next point, focusing only on the feeling of the gravel, then the pavement underneath my feet, and of the magic I was laying in my wake.

One by one, I carefully situated my four candles in one of the largest circles I'd ever attempted to cast. Then I retraced my steps, lighting each candle as I passed.

I could sense Copper pacing alongside me, about five feet away as she constructed a second circle around mine.

A secondary layer of protection. She appeared to be using salt rather than candles. Given the amount of salt needed to trace a circle of such a wide diameter, I guessed that she either carried a spelled bag, or she'd asked Kett to have supplies waiting for her in the SUV.

When I reached the green candle—for earth—at the northern point in the middle of the road, I paused before lighting it.

Copper closed the salt line behind me. She glanced around, making sure Jasmine, Declan, and Kett were standing inside her circle but outside of mine.

She met my gaze.

I nodded.

She reached for the magic she'd seeded into the salt, calling up her circle swiftly and efficiently. Her subtle energy brushed my senses, but I didn't pause to admire her proficient casting. We couldn't hold off traffic for long without drawing attention, though thankfully, the road didn't appear to be particularly busy.

I crouched, lighting my green candle with a sustained exhale rather than a snap of my fingers, thus allowing a final breath of my magic to seep into my circle. Then I straightened as I raised my hands, palms facing forward. Reaching out for the magic I'd carefully laid in my wake, I called my circle into being.

The residual magic captured within the circle exploded, a wash of power battering the edges of the reconstruction.

I gasped at its intensity, but the energy didn't fight me. Rather, the magic pooled underneath my palms as if eager to be revealed.

"Everything okay?" Jasmine asked.

"Yes," I said. "But give me a moment before you tap in, please."

Jasmine and Declan could watch the reconstruction just by touching the edge of my circle, but I was concerned that they would off balance the energy if they did so before the residual revealed its source.

"Show me," I murmured to the torrent of power now captured in my circle. "Show me how you came to be."

The light within the circle brightened slightly, still evening but without the intermittent cloud cover. A sprinkle of starlight appeared overhead. The energy shifted, coalescing into a massive form in the middle of the street. Then it burst into flame, which I should have been expecting.

Momentarily blinded, I squeezed my eyes shut. The magic pulsed underneath my palms.

"It's a lot of power," I said shakily, blinking to clear my sight. Then I breathed deeply to settle further into the casting.

"As expected," Kett said from somewhere behind me.

"Initial impressions?" Jasmine said, keeping me on task.

"It's evening. Fire." I focused on the reconstruction playing backward within the circle.

The shape that had appeared in the center of the street was a car completely engulfed in flames. I could see its edges but no details within. And though it might have been unprofessional, I was glad I couldn't see the occupants of the vehicle being burned alive.

The fire shifted as if snuffing out, but I knew that was just a product of viewing everything backwards. The reconstruction was still forming, meaning I was seeing the moment the fire started, but without me perceiving its cause.

The scene blurred, moving too quickly for me to distinguish specifics. Except I thought I might have seen a door opening, just before the crumpled front of the car smoothed itself out. After a moment, the car shot backwards, out of my reconstruction.

Then nothing, though the magic was still held inside the circle with formidable intensity.

There was just the empty road.

"There's no...there's nothing," I murmured. "The car didn't hit anything."

Standing on either side of me, Declan and Jasmine glanced at each other over my head. I allowed the circle to go dormant, pressing the heels of my hands to my eyes.

"Nothing?" Jasmine asked quietly.

"I'm going to need to play it again," I said. "Slowly. Before I collect it." I glanced over my shoulder at Copper. "Do I have a little longer?"

She nodded, but shallowly. Holding an active circle was draining.

I turned back to the reconstruction. "You'll need to touch me," I murmured to Kett.

He slipped his hand through my jacket and underneath my silk blouse. Jasmine and Declan raised their hands to my circle. I activated the reconstruction again, playing it as slowly as possible.

Within the circle, the light shifted into late evening. Stars once again appeared, but I couldn't see the moon.

The headlights of a vehicle appeared at the far edge of the circle, quickly resolving into a gray sedan. I immediately slowed the playback, taking the time to observe every last detail. I had to meticulously capture it all in this pass, so that we could review it in the cube.

A brown-haired male was driving the sedan, turning to laugh at something the dark-blond woman in the passenger seat had said. A girl was sitting in the back seat, leaning sideways so she could look through the front seats. There wasn't enough light to determine skin or eye color from this distance, but I was certain we were watching Dawn and her parents seconds before their fiery deaths.

The car crept toward us, almost painfully slowly, but no one asked that I quicken the playback. I had to have missed something in the initialization of the reconstruction. Or someone. Cars didn't just crash into nothing.

A wash of dark blue appeared between us and the car. Witch magic by its color, though I couldn't pick up the tenor.

I paused the playback, zooming in on what appeared to be a fissure of energy streaking across the pavement.

"Some sort of barrier spell?" I asked. "With a delayed trigger?"

"Strong enough to stop a car?" Jasmine asked doubtfully.

I reoriented the playback, allowing the scene to continue playing out in slow motion.

The front of the car hit whatever spell had been laid across the road.

The bumper crumpled.

Within the car, Dean's laughter dissolved into a look of sheer panic. He clenched the wheel.

The hood of the car buckled.

Amy screamed, slowly flung forward against her seatbelt. Her terror exploded out of her in a wash of bright, vibrant-blue magic. Then, a breath before the windshield shattered, she somehow gathered all the power she'd generated and wrapped it around Dawn, whose eyes were wide and terrified.

The magic Amy had called forth drove the back passenger door open and ejected Dawn from the car.

The girl hit the pavement and rolled across the street. When she came to a stop, she was lying insensible on the gravel shoulder.

More magic exploded from within or below the vehicle, and it was immediately engulfed in flames.

I paused the playback, needing a moment to calm myself.

"She…" Jasmine said. "What was that? Did Amy just…"

"Used her own life force to save her child," I whispered. Because other than perhaps Kett, I was the only one there who knew what that sort of magic felt like. Many years ago, I'd used the dying life force of our brownie, Bluebell, to cripple Jasper. To save Declan and Jasmine. I had used the darkest of magic without a thought, and I could still feel the stain it left on my soul. But Amy had used that magic out of love, devotion…

I took a shaky breath, fruitlessly wiping away the tears streaming down my face. Kett shifted his hand on my back, but I couldn't feel any comfort in his cold touch.

Declan cleared his throat. "Yeah. You hear of things like that. Mostly with healers, but…"

We all stood silently for a moment, staring into the frozen reconstruction. The car in flames, and the little girl lying on the side of the road.

When I thought I could express myself without breaking down, I spoke. "The explosive spells in the car were timed, yes? Previously set?"

Declan nodded. "Looked like it. I don't think the car had sustained enough damage to explode like that. The gas tank is in the back."

"It wouldn't make any sense to kill anyone," I said grimly. "Not until he had Dawn. So he would have waited to trigger the spells. Luckily for him, Amy took care of getting Dawn out of the vehicle."

"Him?" Jasmine asked. "Yale was already in London…"

I didn't respond, knowing that what I was about to suggest would come across as farfetched. Born of my own psychosis rather than actual facts. I triggered the reconstruction again, allowing it to play through to the end.

Magically fueled flames ravaged the car. On the edge of the road, Dawn raised her head, seemingly groggy, though she didn't appear to have a scratch on her. Which explained why the police hadn't found any blood at the scene. Amy's magic had cushioned her child's fall.

A terrible realization flooded across Dawn's face. She thrust her arms forward, opening her mouth to scream.

Then she disappeared.

I paused the playback, rewinding it to play the moment of Dawn's disappearance over again. Then again. Back and forth. I'd missed this in the initial collection as well, though I wasn't surprised at that. It had all taken only a moment in real time.

A thin cloud of magic shifted over top of the girl right before she disappeared.

A blue haze.

"Kett," I said, "I apologize, but I need you to step back for a moment."

The vampire dropped his hand from my back without questioning me.

I kicked off my shoes, taking deep breaths. I reached for the magic within me, for the magic underneath the pavement and in the very earth. I gathered the energy I found there, then filtered it into the reconstruction circle. Directing this extra pulse of power toward Dawn specifically, I allowed the reconstruction to play through again.

Someone or something stepped up beside the girl, reaching down and scooping her up in his arms right before she disappeared. Right before she was swallowed by whatever intricate and powerful spell her kidnapper was using to mask his presence.

I rewound the playback one more time, pausing with the cloaked image of the kidnapper highlighted by the extra power I'd pumped into the reconstruction.

"Him," I said grimly.

Jasmine and Declan stood silently by my side, staring at the form of the person standing over Dawn. There was nothing particularly distinctive to go on. The powerful Adept I'd revealed was either a tall woman or a somewhat slight man.

But I knew instinctively who it was that I'd almost managed to unmask.

I knew that only one person would be capable of hiding his magic from me, from my reconstruction. Only one person would seek out and kidnap witches with the same birthdays as Declan, Jasmine, and me.

A cool relief flooded through me, loosening my limbs and steadying my resolve. Without another word, I allowed the reconstruction to fall dormant, fishing an oyster-shell cube out of my bag and crossing through my circle. I set the cube down and channeled the magic I'd collected into it.

When I was done, I lifted the brightly glowing cube, holding it by my fingertips. Gazing at it with great satisfaction, I whispered, "Got you, asshole."

Then I turned back to the group waiting for me at the edge of my circle, taking immediate control of the situation. "Copper, please remove your barrier and your distraction spells before we attract any more attention."

"Of course." She quickly dropped the spell she was straining to maintain.

"Thank you. Jasmine, I'll need the flight logs for the Fairchild jet."

My cousin's face creased with confusion.

Kett laughed huskily, getting to where I was leading more quickly than the others. Then, with his phone to his ear, he crossed back to the SUV.

I crouched down and snuffed out my green pillar candle, dissipating the magic of my circle.

"We need somewhere to regroup," I said, crossing to collect the rest of my candles. Jasmine and Declan trailed after me as if they were in shock. "Rose's?"

"No," Declan said bluntly.

"Wait, wait," Jasmine said, grabbing for my arm. "What are you saying? Why would the flight records of the jet help with this? If...if a Fairchild was involved here, they'd just drive. We're only hours away from Litchfield."

"We're not worried about connecting him to this accident. I've already done that. We're looking to connect him to Chicago and LA."

Jasmine's jaw dropped. Her mouth hung open incredulously.

I leaned down, snuffing out my red candle.

Declan swore viciously under his breath.

"You...you're saying..." Jasmine shuddered, unable to complete the thought.

"I'm saying Yale handed Ruby and Jack off to Jasper. Who likely flew them somewhere in the jet, which is why we kept losing Yale's trail. He wasn't keeping, or feeding, or housing them."

"The power of three," Declan muttered. "The birth dates."

"Yes," I said. "He's creating another trio."

"That's...you're leaping to conclusions," Jasmine said. "We all know the tenor of Jasper's magic. That wasn't it. And...and...what he did to us had nothing to do with any birthdays."

"It does now. Whatever spells Jasper spent years crafting to bind us, he wants to utilize them again. They must have used magic or runes that tie to those particular dates." I shrugged. "Or perhaps he's just insane, and the matching birthdays simply bring him some sense of order. Or maybe he just wanted to get our attention. But if Jasper can conceal himself that effectively from reconstruction, he's figured out how to mask his magic." I glanced over at Declan. "Which is why you thought it was similar to yours."

He grimaced in unwilling agreement. "There might be only one reconstructionist in the world who could have exposed him. You."

I nodded, though a streak of terror slipping along my spine momentarily threatened my poise. "We should assume that he expected that. Me. Us. Without Yale to hide behind, he had to kidnap Dawn himself. He's not stupid. He expects us to figure it out."

"All right. We regroup at Amy and Dean's." Declan nodded his head toward the road. "They lived near here, right? The house should be empty. If it isn't, we'll go to a hotel."

"This is insane," Jasmine muttered. "We need more evidence. So much more."

"Prove me wrong, then," I said quietly. Then I realized that someone was watching us, listening to our every word.

Copper was standing just at the edge of my peripheral vision.

I frowned at the witch. "We need those distraction spells down."

"I'll help you," Declan said, turning away.

Copper smiled at him as if he'd just told her she was the most beautiful thing he'd ever seen. He walked away without noticing.

I crossed to pick up the rest of my candles. Then, mired deeply within my own thoughts, I slowly walked back to the SUV.

Jasmine trailed silently behind me.

Kett was waiting for us, leaning back on the hood of the vehicle.

Jasmine crossed toward the passenger side without a word, but I called out to her before she climbed into the SUV.

"I'll need to know where he is, Jasmine," I said. "Here or on the island."

She lifted her bright-blue eyes to meet my gaze. "I'll ask Rose, if we tie him to Chicago and LA. But as soon as I do...he'll know. He'll know we know. So you need to be sure this is what you want to do, Betty-Sue."

"I am."

Jasmine nodded. Still moving as if she might be in shock, she climbed into the SUV but didn't close the door.

I pinned my gaze on Kett, knowing he'd overheard everything I'd already said to Jasmine and Declan.

His slightly amused smile faded at whatever he saw in my expression. His chiseled features settled into his typical detached demeanor as he stood upright, watching me carefully.

When I was certain I had every bit of his attention, I spoke. "I need to talk to Yale."

"I'm working on it."

"Listen to me closely," I said, stepping into his space. My tone felt dark even to my own ears. "I'm calling in a favor, or cashing in a chit, or whatever it takes."

"You don't have any favors banked."

I raised my chin haughtily. "No? I rescued the executioner of the Conclave from a horde of zombies. And I didn't implicate the Conclave in Jasmine's kidnapping." I ground out the next three words. "Get me Yale."

Kett's marble-carved face went utterly still. The red of his magic glinted in his silvered eyes. Then he arched an eyebrow. "As you wish."

I nodded stiffly. Then I retreated into the back seat of the SUV, ready to replay the reconstruction over and over until I had every pulse of its magic memorized.

Chapter Nine

We regrouped in Amy and Dean Fairchild's tidy, three-bedroom home. A real estate *For Sale* sign sat at the turn into a long driveway that ran through a treed front yard. And though it was still furnished, the house itself was dark and unoccupied. It should have felt disrespectful—using the home of people I was fairly certain my uncle had slaughtered. But remembering Amy's wild casting, her completely unselfish attempt to save her daughter's life, I decided that if we were convening a war council, then the living room of the woman whose child I hoped to rescue was the perfect place to do so.

Upon entering, Jasmine had immediately commandeered the six-seat glass-topped table in the dining room, plugging in her various devices. Declan disappeared deeper within the house. Kett opted to stay in the SUV and make more phone calls. Or perhaps he was keeping an eye on Copper as the witch set distraction and minor cloaking spells around the immediate perimeter of the house.

Though the house was situated back from the road and shielded from any neighbors' view by trees on either side, Copper's due diligence was appropriate and completely by the book. Given our collective headspace—muddled verging on overwhelmed—I wasn't sure that Declan, Jasmine, or I would have remembered to take such precautions.

After making a quick circuit of the main floor, I paused at the front windows of the living room, which was situated just off the entranceway and adjacent to the dining room. Other than furniture, no personal objects remained.

Overhead, the quarter moon made an appearance in the dark, cloudy sky, momentarily washing across the SUV in the driveway, the well-trimmed lawn, and the dark border of trees surrounding the modest property. Not seeing Kett, I assumed he'd wandered off somewhere. Then the moon disappeared behind another cloud.

"I've got it," Jasmine said hollowly from behind me. "Flights into Chicago and LA on the days Yale kidnapped Ruby and Jack."

I nodded, glancing back through the living room over my shoulder. My cousin hadn't turned on the dining room light, and in the glow of her laptop screen, she looked drawn, tired, and terribly sad. I wasn't surprised or particularly vindicated by Jasmine's confirmation of Jasper's involvement, but it was clear how it was affecting her. And I had no idea how to help her, other than to rescue the children and make it through the coming confrontation—in whatever form it was going to take.

"We're going to need more before we can take this to the Convocation," Jasmine said. "Some evidence of an agreement between Jasper and Yale. Payments. Meetings. Some sort of traceable communication at a minimum."

"You would have found that already," I said. "We need to hear it from Yale directly."

"He'll never go on record. Why would he even talk to us?"

"Call Rose, would you?" I ignored Jasmine's question, having no doubt that Kett would make Yale talk to us, willingly or not. And how that came about didn't matter anymore.

"And tell her what? That Jasper is kidnapping kids?"

I shook my head. "Wait until we have all the last pieces in place. Just find out where he is. We're going to have to figure out what to do about the kids."

"Do?" Jasmine echoed. "We're going to rescue them."

I turned away from the window, moving past the comfy-looking couch and the matching recliner armchairs into the dining room. Jasmine held my gaze steadily. I'd misread her. She wasn't shocked or distraught. She was quietly—even desperately—angry.

Reaching across the glass table, I brushed my fingers across the back of her hand. She shivered at the touch of my magic. "You know that if any of us confront him face to face, it won't go well."

"For him," Jasmine said darkly.

Declan appeared in the kitchen doorway behind his sister. "Pizza has been ordered."

"You found someone to deliver?" I asked.

He shook his head. "I have to go pick it up."

"My hero," Jasmine said, twisting around in her chair to bat her eyelashes at him. "Where's Copper?"

"Resting." His gaze settled on me. "Only Wisteria can cast and hold a circle for that long without needing to at least nap afterward."

"Or Jasper," Jasmine said, resting her chin on the back of the tall chair. "That masking spell was...masterful."

Declan grunted, reluctantly agreeing.

"I suspect I can break it." Keeping my voice hushed, I skirted the table to stand closer to both of them.

Jasmine looked up at me.

"If the tribunal requires it. I'll recast the circle and try. Closing down the road will be simpler with the Convocation's backing."

Declan shook his head. "They won't let you present. Jasper will counterfile, barring us from the trial. If they need it, they'll have to find another witch to try to remove the masking spell."

Jasmine nodded. "He'd be stupid to not get us removed from the investigation team. Which is why we have to find the kids first, before we present our evidence."

"What?" Declan asked. "You want to confront Jasper directly? You want to get the kids killed?"

Jasmine waved her hand offishly. "I'm compiling our evidence and application, aren't I?"

"Do the flight records have him going anywhere else since Amy and Dean were killed and Dawn was snatched?" I asked.

Jasmine shook her head. "Nowhere else unusual. Chicago. LA. Then Litchfield to Barbados and back, three times."

"Indicating that he's in Connecticut now?"

She nodded.

"Makes sense," I mused. "Since he just regained control of the manor..." A flush of realization flooded through my chest so harshly that I actually gasped. "Oh, God. Lark."

"Lark?" Declan asked.

"The brownie," Jasmine said.

"He...he must have used the kids to break our hold on the estate magic," I said. "That's why Lark asked me to come. You don't think...he wouldn't have. I assumed that he'd train them...not...not..."

"You're leaping to conclusions again, Betty-Sue," Jasmine said. "Jasper isn't rash. Slightly stupid to use the jet, but not rash."

"Who would know?" Declan said. "Other than us, who else would bother looking to connect Jasper to the kidnappings? Like I said, I doubt another reconstructionist would have even noticed the damn masking spell. Jasper isn't even slightly stupid." He scrubbed his hand across his face wearily. "I'm getting the pizza."

He crossed past me, then stepped back to hold his hand out to me. When I brushed my fingers across his, he closed his hand around mine firmly. His touch was warm and steady.

"He hasn't killed the kids."

"Yet."

"Yeah, yet." Declan sighed harshly. Then he squeezed my hand and released it.

I curled my fingers into a fist, holding onto his warmth as best I could.

Declan strode off through the living room and into the front entrance. "Where's that damn vampire? I need the keys."

"It doesn't need a key to start," Jasmine called after him. "Kett leaves them in the car, just press the ignition."

"Fancy," Declan said sarcastically. Then the door opened and shut.

I smiled to myself, glancing back at Jasmine. She was watching me, her expression hard and hooded.

The smile drained from my face.

"We aren't going to leave Jasper with the kids a minute longer than they have to be," she said. "Protocol or not."

"I know," I said. "Let's just try to get the coven on our side first."

She nodded stiffly, then returned to building her report.

Copper wandered into the living room, blinking sleepily. "Declan?"

I smiled at her as kindly as I could. "He's gone for pizza. But perhaps there's some tea in the cupboards?"

Jasmine shifted out of her seat with a put-upon sigh. "I'll make it. The estate is trying to sell the house. They don't need the stove broken." She crossed back through into the kitchen with Copper trailing after her. "When we get Dawn back, she'll need the money."

Unbidden, the thought came to me of what would happen if we didn't get Dawn back...and how the Fairchilds were going to be on the hook for way more than a broken stove.

Forcing myself to focus on more immediate concerns, I called after Copper. "Have you heard back from Sherwood and Pine? About Lark?"

The witch shook her head. "Not yet. I just checked my messages."

Suddenly weary with all that was to come and all that I had yet to figure out, I slowly followed the other two witches into the kitchen.

A ruddy-haired vampire was sitting on the far kitchen counter, next to the open door to the back patio. He was clad in a misshapen blue sweater, torn jeans, and dirty sneakers, his green-eyed gaze riveted to me.

Yale.

I paused in the doorway of the dining room, the first one to notice him.

To my far right, Jasmine flinched a moment later, pinning Copper behind her against the stove. Copper's jaw dropped and stayed down. Jasmine was gripping a stainless steel kettle so harshly that I thought she might hurt herself before she got a chance to brain the vampire with it.

"That trick is a little overused," I said snidely. "Isn't it, vampire?"

Yale grinned at me spitefully. "Wisteria Fairchild. My lovely soon-to-be shiver mate. You called. And now I'm here. The fact that there was no threshold to impede my entry confirmed my welcome."

"The owners of this property are recently deceased," I said. "But you know that already."

His smile faded from his face. "I haven't killed anyone in a long time, Wisteria. Such things are liable to draw the attention of the executioner."

"And that's exactly what you wanted."

"Was it?"

"Tsk-tsk, Yale." Estelle clucked her tongue as she strolled in through the back door, sweeping her gaze disdainfully across the kitchen—more functional than stylish—and the two witches still pressed against the stove. "I told you to wait."

Kett was right behind his maker. My stomach churned at the idea of Estelle simply appearing in the backyard with Yale in tow, indicating that not only could she teleport across vast distances—perhaps even all the way from London, England, to Rye, New York—she could do so with another person.

"No," Yale said, correcting Estelle snottily. "You asked."

"I'll pay closer attention to my wording next time." The dark-haired vampire turned to me, sweeping her hand toward Yale. "Wisteria Fairchild. A gift. To cement the bonds soon to be formed between us."

"Yes," Yale said, overly brightly. "A temporary reprieve from the dungeons. Though my shackles are simply less visible." The vampire kept his mossy-green gaze glued to me.

"Without my blood, you'd still be insensible," Estelle said.

"Without your blood, I'd still be free."

"If it was my choice," Jasmine said, slamming the kettle down on the stove, "you'd have been destroyed along with your rapist progeny."

Estelle narrowed her eyes at Yale. "So you did condone the ravaging of this beautiful witch."

"You can discuss the details another time, perhaps." Kett swiftly closed the distance between us, situating himself just behind my left shoulder.

A look of utter annoyance flitted across Estelle's face. "You called in a favor, Kettil. We're here."

I didn't like the idea of Kett owing anything to his maker. Though perhaps he'd simply collected on an old debt rather than incurring a new one on my behalf.

Along with Yale, who still hadn't taken his gaze off me, everyone else in the kitchen turned to look at me expectantly.

"You're working with Jasper," I said.

"Working with? No." Yale smiled, tight-lipped.

I could practically feel the loathing rolling off him. And for some reason, instead of feeling intimidating, it emboldened me. I deliberately stepped forward until only a couple of feet separated me from Yale still seated on the counter.

Slightly off to my left, Estelle could have reached out and touched me. Kett kept pace behind me, showing rather than saying that he'd support whatever I chose to do.

I tugged the sleeve of my black silk top back from my wrist, freeing my bracelet to dangle over the back of my hand. I tilted my head in Estelle's direction, indicating I was addressing her even though I kept my gaze on Yale. "We were just going to make some tea," I said.

"Ah," she said, angling her gaze toward Jasmine. "Something warm would be lovely. Earl Grey?"

Jasmine nodded, crossing to the sink to pour water into the kettle. After setting it on the stove, she bustled around the kitchen, gathering a teapot and mugs.

Yale flicked his gaze to Kett behind me. "I'm here, as requested. I could have refused."

"I don't speak for Wisteria," Kett said.

Yale returned his gaze to me, then glanced down to the bracelet teeming with magic on my wrist.

"You had a deal with my uncle, Jasper Fairchild," I said. "I'd like to know the particulars."

"Ask your questions then, witch."

"You kidnapped Ruby and Jack for him."

A smile stretched across Yale's face. I didn't know him well enough to judge, but he looked paler and slimmer than the last time we'd met. "I didn't catch everyone's names."

"You snatched a young girl from a park in Chicago," I said. "And a boy from a group home in LA. I have the reconstructions."

Yale's gaze flicked to Kett again.

"I haven't handed the evidence over to the Convocation yet," I continued. "But I doubt the Conclave would hesitate to do whatever it took to maintain a smooth relationship with the witches. Whether your blood has any potential value or not."

"There is no need to threaten me further." Yale leaned back nonchalantly.

"Then speak plainly." I was keeping as cool and collected as I could—when what I really wanted to do was torture the answers out of him with my bracelet. "Detail your actions from the moment you made contact with Jasper Fairchild."

Yale took a breath as if relishing the opportunity to tell the tale. But I could see by the way he clenched his hands that he wasn't pleased to be confessing anything.

"Jasper contacted me in October of last year," he said, leaning forward so our eyes were level. His magic brushed against me, against my mind.

I curled my lip scornfully at his feeble attempt to ensnare me, or at least to beguile me.

He laughed without mirth, then waved his hand offishly. "I was to be something of a backup plan, you see."

"He wanted you to turn him. To remake him," I said. "If Kett didn't."

"Exactly. But the wheelchair was a problem." He flicked his gaze to Kett, then back to me.

"You didn't think your blood could heal him," I said. "So he had a secondary plan. The children."

"I actually don't know what he wanted with the kids," Yale said dismissively. "Witches kidnapping witches isn't any of my business. I was just the intermediary."

"And what were you to get out of it?" I asked. "Money?"

"Of course."

"But that's not all."

Yale shrugged.

"A position of power," Kett said. "Within the Fairchild coven."

"Being nomadic does wear after a century or so," Yale said. "I'm sure you understand, Executioner."

Kett stared Yale down until the younger vampire turned his gaze back to me.

"So if Kett didn't remake Jasper, you were supposed to?" I asked, just to clarify.

"If he got himself out of the wheelchair, even if only temporarily."

A flush of self-loathing ran through me at his confirmation. I'd allowed my ingrained hatred for Jasper to cloud my judgement, never following up on how he'd managed to be walking around with only a cane for support when I last saw him. I pushed away the self-recrimination, forcing my focus onto the task at hand.

I glanced over at Jasmine by the stove. My best friend stood with her arms crossed, silently sneering at Yale.

"And kidnapping Jasmine? Was that your idea or Jasper's?"

Yale didn't answer.

I narrowed my eyes at him, then allowed a smile of anticipation to spread across my face.

A muscle in his jaw tightened.

I lifted my right hand, placing my fingers on his knee and just barely keeping my bracelet from touching him.

"Don't make promises you can't keep, witch," he said.

"I never do."

Estelle chuckled.

The kettle started to whistle. Jasmine removed it from the stove and began making tea.

"Shall we retire to the parlor?" Estelle asked, already stepping farther into the house.

I didn't move.

Yale flicked his gaze to Kett, then looked back at me.

Kett stepped away, herding Copper through into the living room. Jasmine followed them with a teapot and mugs on a wooden tray.

I didn't move. Neither could Yale, not with my hand on his knee.

"It's just me and you now." I spoke softly, completely nonthreatening.

"They can still hear us," he said crossly.

"But they're not close enough to stop me from hurting you." I smiled.

Yale laughed.

"Do you blame me?" I asked coldly. "For Mania and Amaya?"

Any and all expression faded from his face. "Why would I blame you?" he whispered.

"Who do you think destroyed them?"

The red of Yale's magic flashed through his green eyes as the muscle in his jaw clenched again. I knew I was pushing him too far, that he might well be able to kill me before Kett could get back to the kitchen. But if I was going to get through the next couple of days, I was going to have to face off with a monster far more powerful than the vampire perched on the kitchen counter.

"Did you think it was Kett?" I asked, leaning toward him seductively. "It wasn't."

"You?" he spat derisively.

I let the bracelet touch his knee, allowing its magic to lightly lick against him. To give him just a tiny taste of its destructive power.

He flinched as he hissed through his teeth, holding himself stiffly in place.

"Yes. Me." I lifted my hand from his knee.

"Why make an enemy of me, Wisteria?" he asked. "When it would only benefit you, during your transition, to be—"

"Friends?"

"Cordial."

"You touched Jasmine," I said, finally allowing some heat to seep into my tone. "No one touches her without her permission. How do you think Jasper got in that wheelchair?"

Yale nodded as if he'd already known what I was capable of doing. "I can see why the executioner picked you over him."

"Thank you."

"It wasn't a compliment."

"I know."

He laughed, but the sound was forced. "Going after Jasmine and Kett was a joint decision. The idea was to take the blood of the executioner. With it, I might be able to get Jasper out of the wheelchair."

"And if the executioner killed you and all your brood?"

Yale cast his gaze to the tile floor. "I never thought it possible. I gathered that Jasper didn't either, that he didn't know the extent of the executioner's...strength. Apparently, I was played."

"Or...maybe with Jasmine, Declan, and me out of the way, courtesy of you, Kett would have been forced to remake Jasper."

Yale lifted his gaze to meet mine. "Your uncle never asked me to kill you. Any of you. You're important to him. Somehow." He grinned nastily. "Maybe he just wants the pleasure of killing you himself."

"That must be it," I said.

Yale slid down off the counter. In my heels, we were almost the same height. I didn't step back.

He leaned into me, whispering, "London will be a revelation for you, Wisteria Fairchild. I look forward to seeing you there."

"You owe me a favor, Yale," I said, ignoring his attempt to intimidate me.

He stepped to the side so he could eye me incredulously. "I've paid my debt by answering your questions. And trust me, I've paid my debt to the Conclave twice over."

"Perhaps. Though they don't know what you did to Ruby and Jack, do they? They don't know how you've destroyed Coral's mind. All of them witches. The Convocation is going to take exception. And the Conclave won't risk their wrath, not over a masterless rogue."

"What do you want?" he snapped.

"You'll go to the Academy Hospital and help the reader heal Ruby's mother. And I won't turn the evidence of your involvement over to the Convocation."

He laughed sneeringly. "You can't turn that over. It ultimately implicates your uncle."

"Don't worry about that, vampire. I'm burning that all down in the morning."

"Plan to die with him, do you? Because that's the only way you're taking Jasper Fairchild down. I might be a vampire, but I know power when I feel it."

"I'm already slated for death."

Some emotion I couldn't identify twisted across Yale's face. "You Fairchilds are all the same."

"I'm not sure you know enough of us to make that judgement call. Though I can't really disagree. For our conflicting purposes, at least."

We stared at each other for a long moment, neither of us willing to back down or to continue the conversation.

"Estelle won't agree," he finally said. "And my movements are restricted at present. Thanks to this little conversation, I'll be under her thumb for a decade, at least."

"And if Estelle does agree?"

He shrugged, taking the moment to step back from me. "I've never tried to reverse the process..."

"The reader and the healer likely only need to...see you in action."

He grinned. "Any time or place. For you, Wisteria."

I shook my head. "I won't be there."

I turned toward the living room.

Yale snagged my arm before I could step away, drawing my hand gently toward him—though his grip felt as though it might turn intense in an instant.

"I look forward to renewing our acquaintance when you are…more. You will be an intriguing vampire." He brushed a cold, dry kiss over the back of my hand, obviously getting a better look at my bracelet in the process. "Might I suggest you leave the magical artifact behind when you come to London? Assuming you'll be able to wear it at all."

"I won't be there, either."

He raised his eyebrows in mock surprise. "No?" Then he leaned into me, whispering, "I hear differently. I hear the executioner is being called to heel, and that you are his punishment."

He paused, waiting for a reaction.

I gave him none.

"Oh, I like you, Wisteria Fairchild. I do hope the transformation and whatever Kettil has been drinking doesn't drive you mad."

Then he dropped my hand and sauntered into the living room ahead of me.

"No," Estelle said before I'd even made it to the edge of the couch. "Absolutely not. The Conclave would never allow a vampire to walk through the halls of the Academy."

I hadn't even made the request yet.

The dark-haired vampire was perched on the edge of an overstuffed recliner cupping a mug of tea in her hands, enjoying the warmth and aroma. But she didn't appear to be drinking it. Though she'd spoken to me, she was watching

Kett, who stood at the front windows overlooking the dark yard, his back to the room.

Copper was sitting as close to Jasmine on the couch as she could be without actually touching her.

Yale smirked at me over his shoulder, then crossed to stand by Estelle.

Jasmine rolled her eyes at me, but she didn't interject.

"Estelle…" I said.

"You may call me grandmama."

That stopped me cold. Kett actually turned to look at his maker. She smiled tightly at him, then lowered her face to her mug, smelling the tea. "I thought you'd appreciate the courtesy," she said to him.

"It's the implied strings that bother me," he replied coolly.

"Well, those are more than simply implied."

Kett turned his piercing gaze on me. "Please make your request, Wisteria. So we may move on."

I opened my mouth, but Estelle raised her hand to stop me from speaking.

"You will be Kettil's first child. Few vampires make it to elder status without expanding their bloodline, but still, I have only three other grandchildren. I suspect you will be my least favorite, but one never knows what the transformation… reveals. So perhaps I will be proven wrong. You will indulge me in this request."

I toyed with my bracelet. It was Kett's reaction that was causing me to hesitate. I knew through hard-earned experience that familial relationships—or, more specifically, the claim of a relationship—meant little when it came to love and trust. I rarely even thought of my mother or father by those titles anymore, preferring the distance that calling them by their first names enforced.

The Fairchilds—other than Jasper—might never go so far as to drain a family member of blood. But that simply meant their betrayals were subtler than I was suddenly imagining Estelle's would be.

That she would betray me the first chance she got, I knew for certain.

She was watching me play with my bracelet. A tiny smile graced her face. She looked more human, lounging on the recliner. Then I realized she'd changed her hair, smoothing it back from her face with a thin, jeweled band, and allowing the remainder to curl down around her shoulders. Kett's maker had updated her look, including a thin cashmere sweater over sleek, slim-legged black leather pants.

The transformation was subtle, but it spoke volumes. Estelle was preparing to live in the twenty-first century. I was immediately uneasy about what exactly the ramifications of that change of mindset might be.

I flicked my gaze around the room. Kett stood impassively by the windows. Yale looked bored out of his mind. Copper was snuggled so deeply into the couch that it was clear she was trying to hide from the three alpha predators currently holding court in the living room.

I looked at Jasmine.

"Better you than me," she said. Then she grinned, trying for saucy, though I could see her concern.

I dropped my hands to my sides, looking at Estelle steadily. "We request retribution…Grandmama," I said. "Yale has kidnapped three witches that we know of. And allowed his progeny to abuse at least one of them."

"The children were never near Valko," Yale snapped.

Estelle raised a hand to silence him, narrowing her eyes in Jasmine's direction.

My cousin lifted her chin pertly, tilting her head to the side. To me, her neck looked perfectly unblemished. But, as Estelle had already indicated, the vampires could still see Valko's bite marks marring her skin.

Yale clenched his hands, then immediately loosened them.

"Did you not teach your children to mind their manners?" Estelle didn't look at the ruddy-haired vampire beside her.

"Maybe Yale didn't have the control he thought he did," Jasmine said tauntingly.

"I did not know that the witch was under the executioner's protection," Yale said acidly.

Jasmine snorted. "Everyone in the room knows that's a lie," she said. "Even Copper."

Copper flinched at the mention of her name, sloshing her tea all over her lap. "Oh," she cried. Then she stood and took three quick steps away from the couch, likely intending to flee to the bathroom before she realized what she was doing—running from a room full of predators. She froze in place, visibly forcing herself to relax, then slowly continued out of the room.

"I was wondering if that one spoke," Estelle said, more annoyed than amused.

"When Yale kidnapped Ruby, he did so by convincing her mother that she didn't have a daughter," I said, trying to keep the conversation on track.

"Clumsily," Kett said.

"The mother, Coral, is slowly going mad as her mind... fights itself. I have a reconstruction. I can show you, the Conclave, and the Convocation how Yale bit, then forcibly coerced a witch."

Estelle waved her hand. "No need." Then she inhaled deeply, shifting back in the recliner as if carefully considering her options.

Kett shook his head. "State your terms, Estelle. We must move on."

"I shall need introductions," she said. "And Yale must be presented as a helpful contact, not the perpetrator."

"The team, including the reader, has seen the reconstruction," I said.

"Ah, well. Then what guarantee do I have that the Convocation won't pursue the matter? I have taken Yale as one of my own, for the near future. He must heed me, but I also must provide him with a certain amount of … protection."

"My guarantee," I said. "Jasper Fairchild will stand before a tribunal for these crimes. Yale's involvement would be mitigated by his willingness to help rectify the situation."

"And if he cannot perform as expected?"

"Has he done everything he can?"

"Let's suppose he has."

"Can you guarantee it?"

"If I wish."

"Then the same holds."

Two almost-solid beams of light cut through the windows, shifting along the walls as they crossed the room. I glanced outside, spotting the SUV coming up the drive. Declan was returning with the pizza. I wasn't certain that he'd be a great addition to the tea party.

I returned my attention to Estelle.

The dark-haired vampire set her tea down on a side table. Then she disappeared, reappearing directly in front of me before I could blink.

Jasmine swore under her breath.

I met Estelle's dark gaze without flinching. I was already in the deep end, past the point of no return—with the Convocation and my family alike. More involved in the formal business of the Adept world than I had ever wanted to be. But cementing deals with the vampires lingering in the living room was actually the least of my concerns at that moment. So with that thought, I extended my hand toward the dark-haired vampire standing before me. My white-picket-fence bracelet glowed light blue on my wrist.

Estelle smiled at me, revealing the tips of her teeth but no fangs. "I'll require a blood oath."

"No," Kett said.

"I don't dabble in black magic," I said. But I softened my refusal with a smile. "Grandmama."

"A token, then." She turned to look at Kett rather than me.

"No," he said again. "She is not to be bitten. Not now, and not when she has been remade."

"It won't be your choice then," Estelle said.

"Take her hand and her oath, or take nothing."

Smiling as if she'd gotten exactly what she wanted, Estelle clasped my hand. Though she held me delicately, I could feel the strength in her grasp. She could crush me without even trying. Had we both been witches, magic might have passed between us, indicating a light but binding oath. But vampires had other ways of enforcing their deals. Yale's unwilling presence in the house told me that much.

Estelle leaned forward, still grasping my hand between us. Her magic brushed my mind.

I didn't react. She was simply testing me.

Lifting up on her toes, she pressed a possessive, almost bruising kiss on my left cheek.

To my far right, the front door banged open in the entranceway. "Pizza!" Declan bellowed.

Estelle dropped my hand. Then she was gone. I glanced around me. Yale and Kett had vanished from the living room as well.

Jasmine groaned, flopping sideways on the couch. "It's worse when there's three of them."

Declan kicked the door shut behind him. I flinched at the sound, suddenly exceedingly aware that we were intruders in the house.

"Some help?" he asked, crossing into the living room balancing five boxes of pizza in one hand. He held a half-eaten slice in the other.

I turned to him, taking the top three boxes, then crossing through into the kitchen.

Jasmine slipped off the couch, following the food before she was even fully upright.

As I placed the pizza boxes on the counter, a pale flash from the other side of the window—the moonlight catching in Kett's hair—drew my attention to the backyard.

"Five pizzas?" Jasmine said from behind me.

"I didn't know what everyone wanted." As Declan set his boxes next to mine, he followed my gaze out the window.

Outside, Estelle was standing on the edge of the back patio with Kett. Yale was just a pale smudge at the edge of the yard.

I moved to the patio door, which was still open.

"Yale?" Declan asked Jasmine behind me.

She grunted in the affirmative, but her mouth was already full of pizza.

I took a step out into the cool night air. Kett glanced over his shoulder at me.

"Your grandsire isn't going to like her," Estelle said, not bothering to look back at the house.

"I know," Kett said.

"Tell me that isn't why you selected her. When the other two are completely adequate."

Kett returned his gaze to the yard—keeping his eye on Yale, who was leaning up against the high fence that bordered the property.

"I don't want adequate," Kett murmured.

"And neither does Ve." Estelle glanced back at me. "If you were hoping to avoid his attention, then Wisteria

Fairchild is the wrong choice. Keeping him slumbering is best for all of us."

And with that statement, she disappeared, reappearing beside Yale across the dark yard.

The ruddy-haired vampire flinched, then snarled at his own reaction.

Estelle grabbed his arm and they both disappeared.

All of which she had executed without a hint of magic. Or at least none that I could feel.

I took another step out onto the deck, pausing a few feet from Kett. "That's disturbing," I said. Then I added, "The teleporting." Clarifying that I wasn't referring to his conversation with Estelle.

"And yet you are not afraid." He continued to stare out at the dark.

Not fully knowing why, I closed the space between us, wrapping my hand through the crook of his elbow. "Well," I said softly. "You're here."

He turned to look at me. Surprise, followed by what I thought might actually be gratification, flitted across his face.

"Yes," he whispered, brushing a kiss across my forehead almost reverently. "I'm here. By choice."

"We'll be okay, then," I said, willing myself to believe the words as I voiced them.

"I never doubted it."

"Never?"

He smirked but remained silent on the subject. Smart vampire.

I dropped my hand, turning back toward the warmth of the house. Declan was watching us from the kitchen window. Beyond him, Jasmine was pulling plates from a cupboard.

"They'll be okay too," I whispered.

Again, Kett didn't answer me.

I crossed back into the kitchen, leaving the vampire to work through whatever was bothering him. But before I could close the door, he slipped through it behind me.

I joined Declan and Jasmine, taking a plate from the stack at the corner of the counter. They had spread the pizza boxes across the back counter, hastily setting the small table in the eating area with utensils and glasses of water.

"Where's Copper?" I asked. "Did you tell her there was pizza?"

"I heard," Copper said from the door to the dining room. Her gaze was on Declan. "I avoid white flour."

"The crust is whole wheat," Declan said, placing what looked like some sort of meat-lover's pizza on his plate. He tapped the box beside me, drawing my attention. "Smoked salmon for you."

I glanced at him, smiling my thanks.

He didn't look at me, placing a triangle of melted cheese and various sliced vegetables on his plate.

Copper unfolded her arms and begrudgingly took the last plate.

After making our selections, we settled around the four-seater table in the eating area, quietly replenishing calories. Kett remained standing by the back door, mostly looking out into the night but occasionally glancing over at us. I could feel his regard whenever it passed over me. But he seemed content to let us eat.

Declan pushed his empty plate back, then downed the rest of his water. He set the tumbler down with a thump.

Beside him, Copper flinched.

"Tell me." He glanced at Jasmine, then me.

"Still eating," Jasmine said. She was still working on the last half of her slice of Hawaiian.

I pressed my napkin to my mouth. "Yale kidnapped the kids for Jasper."

Anger flushed across Declan's face, but he didn't look at all surprised. "But he had to get Dawn for himself."

"Apparently."

"And how did he get out of the goddamn wheelchair?"

I sighed, standing to collect the dirty dishes but leaving Jasmine with her plate. "He'd progressed to a cane when I saw him in the bank."

"But he was in the chair in the reconstruction we saw in the house." Declan shifted back, stretching out his long legs.

I nodded, carrying the dishes to the sink.

"During the conversation with Yale?" Jasmine asked. "That was obviously staged."

"Obviously," Declan said. Then he muttered something else in his native Creole under his breath.

I plugged the sink, turning on the hot water and finding lemon-scented liquid soap, a tea towel, and a drying rack in the cupboard underneath. The kitchen was bare except for essential items, and had the feel of having been professionally cleaned recently. It made sense that the real estate agent thought it would be easier to sell the house if it appeared somewhat lived in.

Declan stood, shoving his chair back so quickly that it toppled over. He picked it up, then started to stomp out into the dining room.

Copper stood as if to follow him. But then she hesitated as he spun around and all but charged toward me.

I thrust my hands into the soapy water, calmly washing the dishes I'd collected. Declan filled the space behind me, agitated enough that I could feel his magic radiating off him.

"You're going after him," he said to my back. "And you're going to drag all of us with you."

"That's not a requirement," I said quietly. "I'd never want to get you or Jasmine hurt. But I think we have to act quickly. He's had the children for months." I looked over at Jasmine, still nibbling her piece of pizza at the table. "Did you find out where he is?" I asked. "Or where he might be keeping the children?"

"Not yet." She didn't meet my gaze.

"There's no question now," I said. "He's involved."

Jasmine nodded silently. Declan continued to pace the kitchen behind me. Copper seemed struck dumb, hovering by the kitchen table. I wasn't sure Kett was even listening. I rinsed the plate I'd been scrubbing and placed it in the drying rack.

"We take all the evidence and we hand it over to the Convocation," Declan said.

"Of course," I said. "After we get the children to safety."

"He isn't just going to let you have them, Wisteria," Declan said. "You think you can just show up on his doorstep, confront him with your evidence, and he'll crumple?"

I rinsed a second plate, not responding. Because even I wasn't that naive. But knowing what was likely to happen didn't change the events that were about to unfold.

"You aren't his goddamn keeper," Declan snarled.

"I think I might be," I whispered. "If not me ... us ... then who?"

Declan closed the space behind me, wrapping his hands over the edge of the sink on either side of me. "Just leave it, Wisteria," he whispered. His breath warmed the back of my neck. "Just hand it over. Just let the authorities do what they're supposed to do."

I rinsed the third plate, placing it carefully on the drying rack.

Declan pressed his forehead to the back of my head. "Just this once, Wisteria." His tone was laced with hope-filled pain. "Put us first. Choose us."

I spun toward him, suddenly flushed with anger.

He stepped back from me, already raising his hands as if he knew he'd overstepped.

"Choose you?" I cried. "When have I done anything else?"

"Right now," he said. "Right now, with Jasper and… " He nodded toward Kett.

I opened my mouth to launch into the tirade I'd been holding back for months, but Declan got started before I could collect my thoughts.

"We walk away," he said. "We three. We turn the evidence over to the Convocation and we build a life… together. We three."

A terrible sadness flooded through me, blunting my anger, and I struggled to hold it at bay. The last time things had come to this point with Jasper, I had walked away. Alone. But that wasn't an option anymore.

"The contract… " I murmured, twisting my soapy hands together in an attempt to steady myself.

"Screw the contract," Declan said. "The vampire can take Jasper."

"And when it goes wrong? When Jasper slaughters us all? Kett will have to kill his own child if he can't control him. You'd wish that on—"

"Yes," Declan snarled. "Let the Convocation take care of the coven and let the vampire deal with Jasper. That's the sane path. That's the right path."

He grabbed the tea towel I'd set out on the counter, swaddling my hands and drying them gently. "Fuck Jasper," he whispered. "Fuck the vampire. You love us enough to walk away, Betty-Sue." He tossed the towel onto the counter, pressing his warm hands to my face. "Please, please."

I reached up, wrapping my hands around his wrists.

He smoothed his thumbs across my eyebrows, kissing my lips lightly. "Please, please, my love. Come away with me."

My heart cracked. I lifted my tear-filled gaze to meet his golden-hazel eyes.

He saw my answer even before I vocalized it. A terrible sadness deadened his eyes, even as tears fell from my own. My heart felt like molten lead in my chest.

"And leave the children to a fate worse than our own?" I whispered.

He closed his eyes, pained.

"You could go," I whispered. "You and Jasmine…"

He dropped his hands, taking a step back. "That's never going to happen, is it? Even if Jasmine would leave—"

"I won't." My cousin spoke up quietly but forcefully from her seat at the kitchen table.

Declan grimaced. "Well, then." He started to turn away, then stopped. "You'd prefer to die, Wisteria. You'd prefer to die over being with me, truly loving me and Jasmine?"

"Yes!" I cried, suddenly unable to modulate my tone through the soul-wrenching pain his question provoked. "If that's what you want to hear! I'd prefer to die rather than have Jasper control me for one second longer. I'd prefer to die than live in a world corrupted by him. I'd prefer to die if it means you and Jasmine survive. That's how it's always been. So why would you think it would be any different in this moment?"

"And what do you expect us to do? Survive without you?"

I laughed harshly. "Yes. I expect you to survive. That's what you do, Declan."

He grabbed me then, crushing me against him and slamming his lips over mine in desperation. I accepted the kiss as best I could without submitting, without giving in to him.

He pressed his forehead against mine, our skulls practically grinding against each other. "And if I'm tired of surviving without you?" he whispered. "What about then?"

I didn't answer. I didn't know how to answer.

He dropped his hands, stepping away and exiting the kitchen before I could figure out what to say.

So I let him go. I had no more words. I had only the path forward, leading to the doom that had been waiting for me since I was sixteen. Since even before that.

I turned back, thrusting my hand into the sink full of soapy water, only to find it empty. I had washed all the dishes.

Something exploded outside. Something large. I flinched, then glanced over at Jasmine hopelessly. She and Kett were just staring at me. Copper appeared numb, even dumfounded, staring into the space in the middle of kitchen.

My best friend hissed with annoyance. "I'll calm him," she said.

"I'll go," Copper said, shaking off whatever had been anchoring her by the table. "Since Wisteria has made it very clear that she doesn't care what he wants or needs, I'll go and continue picking up the pieces that the two of you keep breaking."

Jasmine laughed nastily. "You do that, you deluded witch. See if it goes any better for you than it has already."

"Wallowing in darkness isn't heroic, Jasmine," Copper snarled. "Trapping Declan in your enmeshed garbage is self-indulgent and soul destroying. You might be blood, but you don't own him. And Wisteria has no ties to him at all, other than whatever your uncle did to the three of you. And magic, like hearts, can be broken."

"And you're the witch to do it, are you?" Jasmine's tone was dreadful, low and deadly.

But apparently, once Copper opened her mouth, she just couldn't stop voicing her opinion. She stuck her chin out. "And what if I am?"

"Don't let the door hit you on the way out," Jasmine said with a sneer.

Then she deliberately twisted out of her seat, turning her back on the witch and wandering across the room to hand me her dirty plate.

Copper looked as though she'd been slapped as she glanced in my direction.

I nodded to her. "Thank you for all your help, but I'd hate to drag you into anything beyond your role with the Convocation."

Copper's jaw dropped. "How dare you—"

"That's Wisteria's nice version of goodbye, Copper," Declan said from the doorway to the dining room. His voice was a laconic drawl, completely at odds with the wild energy swirling around him. "You don't want to be around the second time she asks you to leave."

Copper thrust her finger in my direction. "They're toxic, Declan. They're sucking the life out of you."

"No," he said, though not unkindly. "They are life. The only reason I exist at all."

"Can you hear yourself?" she cried. "That's ... that's—"

"The truth," Declan said. "A truth I never intentionally kept from you ... once it became relevant."

"But, Declan," Jasmine said, laying on the sarcasm and not bothering to look in Copper's direction. "She thought she could fix you."

Declan smiled, reaching a hand toward Copper. "There never was anything to fix. I am who I am. I am as I've been shaped. But also as I choose to be."

"And you'll stand with her? Despite everything, despite her preferring a vampire over you?"

Jasmine laughed harshly.

Declan scowled in his sister's direction. "I believe you've misinterpreted the situation, Copper. Which is fine, as you don't really know what's going on. And perhaps I should have asked you to leave more firmly when you showed up at the diner in LA."

Copper tried to interrupt him, but he raised his hand in her direction, meeting my gaze. "Either Jasmine or I, faced with the same options, would make the same choice Wisteria is making. Even if those choices tear us apart, two will hopefully be left standing."

"That was how it was always going to be," Jasmine whispered.

Declan nodded. "Perhaps."

Copper glanced between the three of us, then shook her head in frustration. "I won't always be waiting for you, Declan."

"Don't wait at all this time," he said.

Her jaw dropped. Then, grabbing her jacket and purse from the back of her chair, she stormed out of the room.

"Finally," Kett said, not having moved an inch from the back window throughout the entire exchange. "I'm at a loss as to what it is about you, Declan Benoit, that endears you to women."

Declan snorted. "Are you, vampire?"

"Don't pretend cat fights don't intrigue you, Kett," Jasmine said.

Kett lifted the corners of his mouth, smiling begrudgingly.

Jasmine snorted.

Declan sighed, ran his hand through his hair, and then followed Copper out of the room.

Jasmine eyed me. "You're quiet."

I glanced at her, meeting her questioning gaze with another request, rather than the answers she was seeking. "Find Jasper for me."

She swallowed, nodding. "Okay." She crossed into the dining room, reaching for her laptop.

I turned back to the sink to wash Jasmine's plate. And to prepare to face my uncle for what I was certain would be the final time for one of us.

"Will you go with me?" I whispered. I was staring at my reflection in the dark window over the sink, but speaking to Kett.

"Always."

"Does the contract restrict you in any way?"

"I cannot kill him." He chuckled darkly. "Not without permission."

I nodded, not surprised. "That's fine. The children are the priority. We'll worry about the consequences after we get them to safety."

"And should the ramifications become apparent before the children are rescued? Or if the children have already been killed? What then?"

I pulled the plug in the sink, allowing the soapy water to drain. Then I picked up the tea towel, finally looking at Kett as I dried my hands.

He regarded me impassively.

I carefully folded the towel, replacing it on the hanger on the back of the cupboard door. "Then I will wreak havoc on the Fairchild coven," I whispered.

"You'd seek justice in the blood of all your elders?"

"Which one of them is innocent? And who better to judge them than their own children?"

Kett smiled at me, the expression tight across his face.

"Will you go with me?" I asked, repeating the question now that he knew the full extent of my intentions.

"Always," he said again. Then he closed the space between us, brushing his cool fingers along my neck. "And then you will come to me, Wisteria Fairchild."

"I will fulfill the terms of the contract."

He tilted my chin back, ensnaring me—but with his eyes, not his magic. "Willingly. Not just because words inked on a piece of parchment compel you. Otherwise, I will take Jasper, whether or not I destroy him after he is remade."

I tried to nod, but he was holding me in place. I swallowed, frowning at his heavy-handedness, at his sudden demand for my ... commitment ... affection ... love?

Then he was gone, leaving me to my whirling thoughts. Apparently, I'd been wrong, or something had shifted between us.

The vampire wanted my heart as well as my soul.

Chapter Ten

"Wisteria," Jasmine whispered, brushing her fingers lightly across my arm.

I mumbled, refusing to open my eyes. I needed a few more moments of sleep. Even before fully waking, I knew that the day about to unfold was going to test my reserves more than any day had in over a dozen years.

I would face it, but I wanted to do so on my own terms. And well rested.

"I'm sorry," my best friend said. "But you need to wake up now, Betty-Sue."

It was the edge of panic in her voice that forced my eyes open. She was crouched before me at the edge of the couch, pressing the screen of her phone to her chest. Light glowed all around it. Dawn was threatening along the edges of the curtains, but it hadn't penetrated the living room yet.

We were still in Rye, New York. I didn't remember being woken from a dream, but... for a blissful moment, we hadn't been in Dawn's house. The house of her murdered parents. We had been in a place and a moment that was before whatever Jasmine was about to tell me. Before whatever had stressed her enough to wake me. But, by her expression alone, I knew we were in the midst of the after now. There would be no going back from whatever she was about to say.

"I found Jasper," she said without further preamble.

"Okay."

"I called Rose, like you asked. Like you wanted. But she...she wouldn't listen," Jasmine said. "I had to tell her everything before she'd confirm he was at Fairchild Manor. That he's been holed up there, except for his monthly treatments on the island, obsessing about reclaiming the estate magic."

"Okay."

"Wisteria! Are you awake?"

"Jasper's in Connecticut," I said, patiently proving I'd absorbed the information that had stressed her so badly. "We can fly or we can drive."

"No...listen to me. I told Rose everything. That you had reconstructions, plus Yale's confession, and that we had the flight logs. She still didn't believe me." She swallowed harshly. "Then I told her about the contract with the Conclave. She...didn't know."

I snorted with disbelief.

"And...she didn't take it well."

I shifted up on my elbow, my hair falling around my face. "What do you mean?"

Jasmine twisted her lips, worried but hesitant to tell me what was concerning her. "She said she was going to confront him."

"And?"

"And I can't reach her now."

"She's dodging your calls."

Jasmine looked up into the darkness above the top of the couch. Declan stepped forward, looming over me. Even in the dim light, I could tell just by the set of his shoulders that something was terribly wrong.

I glanced between them. Jasmine shifted her gaze. Declan rubbed his hand across his face.

"What did you do?" I asked, dreading the answer. Knowing that any sense of control I'd had over the unfolding situation—misplaced or not—was about to spin away.

They looked at each other, then back at me, remaining silent. As if neither of them wanted to be the one to tell me what they'd done while I'd been resting, while I'd been readying myself for a final confirmation of Jasper's whereabouts.

"When you couldn't get hold of Rose, what did you do?" I asked again.

"We told Grey," Jasmine said.

"You told Grey what?"

"That you were coming for Jasper," Declan said. "That we couldn't stop you."

"That we would come with you," Jasmine said.

"That you'd tear it all down," Declan said. "That we'd help you."

They fell silent. I shifted up, swinging my legs off the couch. Jasmine pressed her forehead onto my thigh. I settled my hand on the back of her head.

"And then?" I asked.

Jasmine passed me her phone. Her text app was open to a conversation with Grey. I read the last few lines.

>*I can't get hold of Rose either. When did she say she was going?*

An hour ago.

>*I've contacted Violet. We'll go to the manor ourselves. Dad. Be careful.*

>*Of course, pumpkin. We'll get to the bottom of this. Love you.*

Then, by the times indicated in the app, thirty minutes had passed.

Dad?

Dad?

Dad?

Before I could look up or respond, Declan thrust his phone in my face. Two text messages appeared on his screen. The first was also from Grey.

>*I keep forgetting to tell you how proud I am of you. Take care of the girls.*

Always, Grey. Don't underestimate Jasper.

I looked at Jasmine, who had lifted her head and was watching me with a fierce sadness. I shook my head in disbelief, looking over at Declan. "You sent them after Jasper. You waited until I was asleep, then you contacted them behind my back."

"It's their goddamn job, Wisteria," Declan snarled. "Even if it's almost thirteen years too late."

"You asked me to find out where he was," Jasmine protested, talking on top of her brother.

I stood up. And by the time I made it to my feet, I was absolutely livid. I'd had it under control. Yes, it would have gotten messy once I'd come face-to-face with my uncle, but we'd have the element of surprise and Kett to back us up, and…

The full ramifications of the missing elders hit me like a sledgehammer to the chest.

I spun to face the only two people I loved in this world, trying to moderate my tone with that affection in mind. "Did you tell them he was out of the wheelchair? Did you tell them about the birth dates?"

They glanced at each other.

"Did you tell them about the names on the contract? How they're legally binding? Each and every one, before Kett crossed them off?"

"What does that have to do with anything?" Jasmine asked. "We were just trying to rescue the kids...and not lose you in the process. Protect you as you always protected us."

I pressed my hands to my face, attempting to hold myself together. "So..." I whispered. "Now we're facing all the elders."

"They're never going to stand with him," Declan said. "They might be assholes, but we just told them we have evidence and witnesses of kidnapping, and—"

"Declan." Jasmine cut her brother off sharply. "Listen for once." She slowly straightened from her crouch, keeping her gaze glued to me. "What are you saying? With the birth-dates? And the contract? You've put something together we haven't."

"If he can bind the elders and everyone else magically on a piece of paper, then he can control them in person, using the estate magic," I said. "And the kids? He's trying to recreate the power of three so he can stand against us when we eventually come for him."

Declan shook his head. "That's impossible so quickly. That took years of conditioning..." He trailed off. "Dawn's kidnapping."

"Yes," I said, pleased that my voice sounded steadier than I felt. "He was expecting to be caught. Eventually. The accident was going to call attention. He just needed time. Time to reclaim the estate magic. And time to bond the children to him and each other."

I looked at Jasmine and Declan in turn. They stared back at me, dismay etched across both their faces.

"But he won't use natural bonds this time," I whispered. "Declan's right. That would take too long."

Jasmine pressed the back of her hand across her mouth. Declan closed his eyes, pained.

"And…" I faltered, needing to vocalize all my fears at once, simply to get them out in the open. "If… when he kills me, then Kett will be forced to remake him. And he'll have the coven and immortality."

I stepped close enough to thread my fingers through Jasmine's. Then I reached up and cupped Declan's face. His stubble caressed my palm.

"Running away was never an option," I said.

"We're with you." Declan's voice was husky with emotion.

"Always," Jasmine murmured.

"I know. I'm sorry. And I know."

I let my hands fall to my sides, hoping almost helplessly that wasn't the last time I was going to touch either of them ever again. "Keep trying to contact the elders," I said to Jasmine. "Hopefully I'm wrong." I retrieved my bag and headed for the bathroom.

She nodded, already texting on her phone.

"Where's Kett?"

"Out for a snack," she said without irony. "Also, I think Copper took the SUV, so I'd guess he's replacing it."

I nodded, then I looked at Declan. "I hope you're ready. We're going to need you to get into the manor."

"I doubt it," he said. "I think he'll let us walk right in."

"But not out?"

"That would be the idea."

"Good thing the estate likes us better than it likes him."

Declan snorted. "Right. I'll get the vampire up to speed. Do you think he'll be with us?"

"To storm the stronghold of one of the most powerful witch covens in the world? Yes. I imagine he thinks it's taken us far too long to get to this point."

In the bathroom, I made myself presentable. I couldn't face Jasper looking less than perfect and poised. My ability to maintain composure under pressure was one of the only things I did better than him.

Other than love.

Unfortunately, composure alone wasn't going to get me through the coming battle. And love? Well, love might not survive the war either.

Not wanting to leave the jet too far behind, Kett had insisted that we fly directly into Litchfield. Copper had, in fact, taken the SUV, forcing the vampire to source another before we could leave. Maybe that would cure Kett of the habit of leaving his vehicles unlocked.

As close as we already were to the Connecticut border, the flight to the Fairchild airfield pretty much consisted of taking off, then immediately landing again. Not enough time for us to really prepare, but also not enough time for any doubts to set in and unsettle our plans.

Declan, Jasmine, and I disembarked into the bright early-morning light without speaking. Kett lingered in the jet, still texting or emailing. We had radioed ahead, but were forced to wait for a vehicle to be brought around for us from one of the far hangars. We hadn't given enough notice and weren't expected, at least not by the airfield's regular crew.

But though Jasmine hadn't managed to establish contact with any of the elders, I was quite certain that Jasper had become aware of our arrival the second the jet touched down.

Declan immediately found a patch of grass and stripped off his boots and socks. He began powering up his blasting rod and spelling whatever stones and other items he had within reach. Jasmine was still fiddling with a number of devices she was constructing from small electronics she'd snatched—and promised to replace—from Dawn Fairchild's home.

I wandered toward the nearest hangar, needing to confirm for myself that the Fairchild jet was currently grounded. It was. Hearing a vehicle approaching, I started to turn back.

Then a glimmer of magic caught my attention.

I stepped into the shadow of the open building instead.

Lark appeared atop a steel desk tucked into the far corner of the hangar. She was wearing a white-and-navy-blue-striped sleeveless dress that looked suspiciously like the tea towels that normally resided in a drawer in my kitchen in Seattle. Not that they ever got used. Also, the brownie had a real talent for stretching a bit of fabric.

"Hello, Lark," I said, quickly crossing to her. Even standing on the desk, she was still a head shorter than me.

"I've been waiting for you, mistress," she said in her gravelly voice.

"Have you been to the manor?"

She shook her head. "I have been there. But he found a way to keep me out a little while ago. I'll be able to follow you back in."

"No," I said. Though I would have preferred to not give the brownie any direct orders, I knew that doing so was necessary to protect her from Jasper. "You aren't to follow, Lark. You've lost enough of your family to the Fairchilds."

She settled her clenched, overly large hands on her hips, jutting her chin out defiantly. "Are you going after the children?"

I hesitated. Though I knew I should lie in order to keep the brownie out of harm's way, I also needed to know what she knew. "Does he have them at the house?"

She nodded, regarding me unblinkingly with her large deep-brown eyes.

"Is that how he took the estate magic back? With a spell involving the children?"

She nodded again, sadly. "I tried to disturb the magic, to hold the estate. But once he figured out what I was doing, he figured out how to stop me."

"Are they … are they still alive? Did he kill them to tie the estate to him?"

Lark fingered the ruffled hem of her dress. "Not then, mistress. But I wasn't able to keep him away from the children when he came for them a few hours ago. Nor was I able to voluntarily leave the estate without losing hold of it, after he'd sensed my presence."

My heart squelched. Lark had been protecting the children this entire time. And I'd put professional duty over coming when she'd called for me. "I'm sorry, Lark."

The brownie pulled herself up to her full height, glowering at me. "You are not responsible for my actions, mistress. I choose whom to serve. Once I knew what he'd done, I chose to stay for the children."

"Okay, okay." I breathed deeply. I had known it was likely that Jasper was holding the children hostage on the estate—and possibly the Fairchild elders with them. That confirmation didn't change what we were going to have to do.

Lark leaned toward me. A crafty smile spread across her face. "The house doesn't like the interloper. It was happy when the children came, but not happy when they cried."

"The house?" I echoed incredulously. "The house doesn't like Jasper?" I had said as much to Declan about the estate, but I'd been attempting to be playful.

Lark settled back on her heels and crossed her arms with much satisfaction. "The house likes me. I keep the magic flowing. It heeds him because he's forced it to. But it is more. More than he thinks, more than he knows."

I stared at the brownie. "Will...the house help us rescue the children?"

Lark tilted her head thoughtfully. "Are you planning to take them away?"

"Well...they'll need to return to their families."

Lark frowned. "Don't mention that part."

"When I what? When I talk to the house?"

She nodded as if talking to a house, and to Fairchild Manor specifically, was something everyone was capable of.

"Does it...will it answer back?"

"Not how you mean, mistress. And you'll have to free it from his grasp. But it will help you if you ask."

"You mean the estate magic? Like with the vampires?"

Not answering me, Lark lifted up on her tiptoes, peering over my shoulder.

"Jasper is powerful," I said. "I won't be able to take control from him if he's on the grounds."

"I'll do what I can," Lark said. Then she disappeared.

"Lark! No!"

"I thought you were talking to someone." Declan's gruff voice came from behind me. "The brownie?"

I turned to him, nodding and already weary with the thought of the task ahead of us.

"The car is here." He held out his hand to me.

I crossed to him, accepting his hand. "I'm sorry about Copper," I whispered.

"It wasn't a thing," he said. "It just seemed..."

"Easy?"

"Normal."

I laughed sadly.

"What did the brownie say? Has he got the kids? Can she enter the property?"

"Yes. No. And the house likes her."

He snorted. "Well, let's see if we can woo it back to our side." He lifted my hand, pressing a kiss to the center of my palm.

A warm shiver ran through me.

Declan met my gaze as he said, "We'll promise it the birth of our firstborn."

"Don't be nasty, Bubba," I whispered.

"I'm not, Betty-Sue," he said gruffly. "I'm just not giving up."

He squeezed my hand. Then he tucked it into his elbow and led me out of the hangar.

They were waiting for us. Though I had expected to find all the Fairchild elders at the manor, I hadn't really expected them to stand against us. Not willingly, at least.

We had parked at the curb when we arrived, rather than continuing up the driveway through the open gate—an entrance that normally stood closed and warded against entry.

As I stepped onto the sidewalk, already feeling the pull of the estate magic despite the fact that I was holding my personal shields as tightly as I could, I cast my thoughts back over all the proper things I should have done. The steps I should have taken, including calling in a Convocation task force. But I couldn't stop thinking about how if I hadn't been so quick to follow proper protocol when Lark had asked for my help, I would have given up on the investigation and come to her—and found the missing children before I'd even known they were missing.

Though if I had, there was a good chance that Jasmine and I would have unwittingly fallen to Jasper without Declan and Kett.

Just as there was a good chance we were all about to fall to him, even forewarned.

But even though we were out of practice, I was fairly certain Jasper couldn't stand against the power of three. He had crafted us into a weapon. And no matter what black magic he'd performed over the last few days, I knew he hadn't had enough time to do to the children what he'd done to us.

Unless he'd killed them, then harnessed their collective life force. Then none of us stood a chance of standing against Jasper. Except maybe Kett, if the contract hadn't been set with such well-defined parameters.

Declan, Jasmine, and I stood shoulder to shoulder, surveying the extensive grounds of Fairchild Manor in the morning light. Kett, wearing the baseball-hat-and-sunglasses combo he favored on sunny days, prowled the edge of the six-foot-high stone wall encircling the estate's two hundred and eighty acres. Rolling lawns led toward the ten-thousand-square-foot English country manor. The various types of deciduous trees that sparsely forested the bulk of the grounds were a riot of new leaves rustling in the light breeze.

I couldn't see anything nefarious on the surface of the estate. But then, I never could. I reached my senses toward the outer wards that ran along the edge of the property. The magic responded to me almost eagerly.

"Here we go again," I murmured. "The wards are open."

"Why risk having us tear them down?" Declan said grimly. "That would make it more difficult to keep us contained on the other side."

"He won't be keeping us," I said. "He never could."

Kett reappeared beside Jasmine on my left.

She flinched, then laughingly growled. "Don't love the look on you, vampire."

The executioner arched an eyebrow over the top edge of his black-rimmed sunglasses.

"At least switch to brown frames," my best friend said. "It would suit your coloring better."

"We'll go shopping later," Kett said.

"Oh," Jasmine gushed, putting on a high-pitched, singsong tone. "And buy me anything I want?"

"I thought the offer implied."

"In Paris?"

"I was thinking Milan."

Jasmine chortled.

I took a deep breath, knowing that the banter was Jasmine's way of coping. And that Kett indulging my best friend was part of his playful anticipation of the chaos to come.

I stepped through the wards, crossing by the twelve-foot-high gateposts and sticking to the driveway. Jasmine and Declan followed me without hesitation. The protective magic slipped through and around us—and then it snagged on Kett and attempted to eject him from the grounds.

I reached back to the vampire, even as he was wrapping his arm around my shoulders. I took another step. The warding pushed back against us.

On my left, Jasmine grabbed Kett's other hand as Declan grabbed a fistful of the vampire's sweater.

We took another step.

Kett made a slight noise that might have been frustration, but might also have been pain.

I kicked off my shoes, feeling the power of the estate churning underneath my feet. "Let us pass," I whispered, deliberately taking another step.

The magic eased at once, until it had dropped to an almost-playful simmering underneath my feet. Almost as if it had simply been testing my resolve.

"Jesus," Declan muttered.

Kett loosened his hold on me.

Jasmine spread her hands before her, acting as though she was touching the magic floating in the air. "I thought Jasper severed the bond."

"He did," I said.

Lark appeared on the driveway a few feet ahead of us, glancing back with a look of intense satisfaction. Brownies were notoriously possessive.

I sighed. "But the estate likes us better."

"Who wouldn't?" Jasmine asked archly.

Lark disappeared, presumably having shown herself only so I'd know she was with us in some capacity. If she was anything like Bluebell, the children would be her first priority. Which was good.

"Don't count on it," I said, slipping on my shoes and continuing to walk up the drive toward the manor. "If Jasper didn't actually want us here, we couldn't have crossed through at all."

Three luxury sedans—all in shades of gray—were parked before the front entrance of the mansion. It was an easy guess that they were Rose's, Grey and Dahlia's, and my parents' vehicles. In that order, indicating that they most likely arrived and confronted Jasper separately, which was just rash and stupid all around. But then, the Fairchilds were known to attack first and cover up the evidence later. Except for Jasper. And me.

Well, not including the attack I was currently mounting.

"I'll check the grounds," Kett said.

"No," I said. "Stay with us, please. Jasper will know you're on the estate already."

"We're a stronger force together," Declan said.

"If we're separated, he can pick us off one at a time." Jasmine glanced at Declan over my shoulders.

We knew Jasper's tactics, unfortunately. Intimately.

Kett nodded.

Swathed in cream silk and linen, Dahlia stepped out from beyond the open doors of the manor. Her arms were slightly spread to both sides, and her blue witch magic simmered in her eyes.

I cracked open my personal shields, scanning the front of the mansion. Dahlia was connected to a web of magic stretching out all over the manor, presumably tapping into the secondary wards that shielded the main house specifically.

Two large pockets of magic simmered on either side of the stairs, no doubt shielding two more of our parents.

Though we were obviously walking into a trap specifically designed for us, we continued to slowly approach the front doors.

Grey, dressed in beige corduroy slacks and a white shirt with the sleeves uncharacteristically rolled up, wandered out of the house. He stood within the magic his wife was wielding, just behind and to the side of Dahlia. He looked exhausted, standing quietly with his hands stuffed in his pockets.

"Time to turn back, kids," he said.

Ignoring him, I glanced to Declan. "A display of our intentions will work better than words with this crowd."

He grinned manically. "How about I just clear our path?"

"Wisteria," Dahlia snapped. "Now is not the time for a temper tantrum."

I paused, leaving a good twenty feet between us and the vehicles arrayed across the end of the driveway. Declan crouched down beside me, holding a flat metal disk in his palm.

I reached out to the estate magic, gathering it around us like a comforting blanket, and creating a shield between us and the elders on the front stoop.

"Jesus," Grey muttered.

I wasn't certain if he was reacting to my pull on the estate magic or the fact that we were prepared to stand against them.

"Weaknesses?" Kett asked.

"Dahlia is the strongest with ward magic," Jasmine said briskly. "Grey will rely on basic witch spells, such as distraction or confusion spells, but he's particularly skilled at stealth. Though he's already given up that advantage."

Declan tossed the disk, throwing it as he would a Frisbee. It spun straight underneath the nose of the middle sedan.

"Violet is more than proficient in poisons," Jasmine continued. "And don't assume she doesn't have anything that can take you down. You better believe she'll be armed for vampire."

"Not this vampire," Kett said coolly.

Declan snorted.

The nose of the car suddenly compressed, slamming down onto the disk. Its front tires exploded. Then, with a burst of magic, the front of the car lifted, upending and crashing down on the car behind it.

Glass shattered and metal buckled—but nothing penetrated the shield I held effortlessly before us. Dahlia's warding was completely unaffected as well—though that was as expected, given that challenging it hadn't been Declan's intention.

The path before us into the house was now clear, other than the wards.

Dahlia curled her lip into a snarl aimed at Declan. "I'm going to enjoy giving you the spanking you've deserved your entire life, you ingrate."

She thrust her hand toward us, fingers clawed. The house wards she'd tapped into moved as an extension of her hand. And with that force, she tried to grab Declan.

Her magic hit my shield, actually driving me back a couple of feet.

"Dahlia!" Someone who sounded a lot like my father gasped. So that confirmed at least one of the two shielded presences on either side of the stairs.

"We don't have time to play," I said. Bending my shoulder into my shield to hold Dahlia at bay, I gathered the estate magic into my right fist. Then I punched forward, aiming for her as if she were standing only a foot away from me.

The force of my blow shoved the ward magic she was holding toward her. Her head snapped back and she gasped. A trickle of blood ran from her nose.

Dahlia touched her face, glancing down at her bloody fingers with disbelief. Grey stepped up, touching her shoulder. She twisted away from him, spreading her fingers and appearing to reinforce the ward magic.

"And what about Slate?" Kett said, quietly prompting Jasmine to continue detailing the specializations of the Fairchild elders. Specifically requesting background on the magic my father wielded.

As if summoned by his question, a beam of blue light sliced through the pocket of magic to the right of the stairs, revealing my father, Slate, just as my mother, Violet, appeared to the left.

"That," Jasmine said grimly.

My father's magical blade spun toward me—similar in size to a throwing knife, but much, much sharper than honed metal. In a perfectly timed, well-practiced maneuver, the energy blade cut through the protective magic I held, moments before my mother unleashed a writhing mass of malicious magic.

Jasmine and Declan spun away. I snapped my forearms to the sides, instinctively calling forth an intensified barrier of magic, then stepping forward to knock my father's knife away and catch the bulk of my mother's spell across the shield.

Jasmine and Declan hit back in the same moment.

My cousin flicked one of the devices she'd built on the plane toward the lamppost at the base of the stairs near Violet. It latched into place. Then magic exploded out from all the mansion's exterior lights, arcing across Dahlia's shields as blue streaks of electricity. My mother stumbled, more annoyed than harmed.

Jasmine's tech powers weren't quite so benign when she was on Fairchild land and near enough to draw electricity from the house.

At the same time, Declan tossed a series of stones toward my father. A volley of blue-tinted lightning strikes exploded across the wards, momentarily obscuring Slate from my sight.

My intensified shield dissipated. Out of practice, but fortified by the steady trickle of estate magic that I could access, I was able to call the shield forth instinctively—but I couldn't hold it for long.

I pulled another layer of magic from the endless pool rolling underneath my feet, repairing the hole my father had sliced through my shield. Reminding myself of the tenor of Slate's magic, I added another layer of protection with my father's power in the forefront of my mind.

Declan's and Jasmine's magic cleared before us, revealing Violet, Slate, Dahlia, and Grey standing arrayed across the front stairs. They were unharmed, but looking ruffled.

Jasmine and Declan stepped up to either side of me. Kett was tucked in behind my right shoulder.

"They're pulling their punches," I murmured.

"We're not any good to Jasper dead," Declan said. "Not until he kills us himself."

"No one is killing anyone," Grey said, attempting to be reasonable. "There have just been some…crossed wires." But he frowned as if he didn't quite believe himself. As if he was simply parroting something he'd been told. Jasper wasn't a reader like Nevada, or capable of ensnaring someone's mind as Kett could. But perhaps his control of the coven magic allowed him to plant suggestions in the others in a more insidious fashion than I'd thought.

"Get me through Dahlia's shields," Kett said.

"Yes," Jasmine crowed. "Release the vampire!"

I glanced over at her questioningly.

"What? Release the kraken? Come on! You know that movie."

"Wisteria isn't remotely powerful enough to get through any shield I hold." Dahlia was boasting, despite the fact that she didn't sound particularly sure of herself. But a Fairchild never backed off goading others over their power in the middle of a fight.

"You're right," I said pleasantly. "Not by myself. At least not without killing you." I lifted my palm before me. "So why don't we give you a glimpse of what Jasper created? A glimpse of the power of three?"

All our parents glanced at each other, disconcerted. Then, without a word and without taking their eyes off me, they each started building offensive spells.

Declan placed an innocuous-looking, smooth, flat stone on the palm of my hand. It buzzed with his magic.

Jasmine raised her hand, looking over my shoulder at Kett. "Would you prick my finger?"

The vampire reached around my shoulder, carefully slicing his thumb across the pad of Jasmine's forefinger. Blood bloomed from the wound.

She pressed her finger to Declan's stone, adding her own magic—along with the blood tie she held with her mother, Dahlia—to its spell.

I raised the stone to my mouth, whispering, "Dahlia," so that my breath and magic flowed across it.

"Dodge this, Mommy," Jasmine singsonged.

On cue, Declan grabbed the stone and flicked it directly at Dahlia. She reacted instantly, clapping her hands together and commanding the ward magic to absorb the spell we had created.

Except I had given this spell her name, which was possible for me only because Jasmine had tied it to her mother through blood. Combining the power of three was what we'd been trained for, what we'd been conditioned to do, since we were nine years old. It was magic that Jasper must have imagined he would use one day to fell his mightiest foes—until we turned it against him.

The spell exploded, shredding the wards Dahlia held. The magic of the manor shuddered, as if in pain. Dahlia fell, instantly insensible as her connection to the house wards was severed.

Slate and Violet immediately stepped into our path in the midst of throwing spells. But with a single thought, I reached out to the estate magic and opened the ground underneath their feet, swallowing them up to their shoulders.

I didn't spare them a second glance or thought. They were as inconsequential in this moment as they had chosen to be when they hadn't protected us from Jasper the first time.

Moving as one entity, Declan, Jasmine, and I stepped past them without pause, climbing the stairs to where Grey was standing over Dahlia.

"That's enough," he said, actually pointing a finger at me as if I were a naughty child.

The vampire latched onto Grey's neck and took him down without a sound.

Leaving our parents to Kett's brand of mercy, which I had no doubt included quelling them through blood loss but not killing them, we continued into the house unimpeded. Side by side, we crossed through the marble entranceway, beyond the massive marble-carved staircase to the second floor, and back to the kitchen where the door to the basement stood open.

Because there wasn't anywhere else Jasper would be.

Chapter Eleven

The below-ground level of Fairchild Manor wasn't at all like a typical basement, utilized for storage or even as a recreation room. Even though electrical wiring and plumbing ran throughout the mostly open, twelve-foot-high raftered ceiling, the dirt-floor basement had only one purpose—the casting of magic.

The main section of the basement was situated below the kitchen, dining room, and front parlor of the manor. But years and years of magical excavation had created a web of antechambers that extended far underneath the front lawns of the estate.

With their rough ceilings held up only by occasional wide beams and haphazardly placed posts, these dirt caves had once been filled with magical items, spells in progress, and even botched castings that had to be contained and walled off. But without even checking, I was quite certain that most of the basement would currently be bare. Lark and her family had stripped the estate of all 'dark magic' last January, following a directive I'd unintentionally given them. And it was highly unlikely that Jasper had managed to replace even a hundredth of what would have taken the

Fairchilds centuries to accumulate and pass down from generation to generation.

That sanitizing, unfortunately, didn't mean that the basement didn't contain years of memories for Jasmine, Declan, and me. Including the last time we'd confronted Jasper in a bid for our personal freedom. Even though we hadn't known that was what we were fighting for at the time.

Declan and I had simply tried to stop Jasper from harming Jasmine, perhaps even killing her. We had ended up breaking our uncle, confining him to a wheelchair, and splintering the coven. Or at least the younger generation of the coven. But now we were back, as rash as all the Fairchilds that had come before us—except we were fueled by morality rather than the desire to accumulate power.

But I knew that the darkest part of my soul would whisper fiercely if I paid it any heed—reminding me that vengeance was the fuel that propelled our righteousness.

I traversed the open wooden-tread stairs, one at a time. I was leading, with Jasmine, then Declan bringing up the rear. I didn't bother fretting about being grabbed from between the steps, as I had every time I'd descended into the basement as a child. I could feel Jasper's magic ahead of me, even before I'd set foot on the first stair.

Though the basement was wired with electric lights, Jasper had chosen to line the stairs and walls with white candles, except for the large circle he'd called forth in the very center of the main room. For that, he used four elemental candles—the same colored candles I carried always in my bag. I had learned just about everything I knew about manipulating magic from my uncle. As we all had.

I stepped off the bottom stair, removing my bag from my shoulder and placing it carefully against the wall. I wasn't going to need it or anything it contained for the coming confrontation. There would be no time to call forth protection circles—or at least not carefully planned and placed ones.

Jasmine and Declan paused behind me on the last two stairs. The three of us took a moment to absorb the scene that Jasper had set for us.

My uncle was standing on the northern edge of his circle, before the green candle for earth. He and I shared that natural affinity. The circle that arced out around and behind him shimmered with magic and appeared empty. But I knew that he wouldn't have constructed such a large circle if it wasn't meant to hold something.

Jasper held his hands loosely clasped before him, smiling at us. He wore pale-blue jeans and a white T-shirt. His feet were bare and his cuffs were slightly rolled up, exposing his ankles. He appeared to have no difficulty standing. But then, I'd broken his back, not his legs. Magic stirred sleepily all around him, ruffling his wispy blond hair.

I transferred my attention momentarily to the only other person I could see or sense in the basement.

Rose.

My aunt was kneeling, positioned at an angle to Jasper but outside of his circle. Her pale-pink skirt was pooled prettily all around her, almost as if she'd arranged it that way. Or someone had shoved her down, abruptly and forcefully enough that she couldn't get back up.

My aunt looked easily ten years older than she had in January. Her skin was sickly even in the soft glow of the candles. She caught sight of us, twisting her hands in a gesture so similar to the day she'd handed us back to Jasper that a terrible, wrenching pain shot through my chest. Jasmine, Declan, and I had come to our aunt under the guise of saving a rabbit, though we'd really been seeking refuge for ourselves. I had never forgiven her for letting Jasper take us back to the manor. I'd never forgiven her for everything that had happened afterward. Rose had been given that moment to rescue us, and she hadn't even tried.

Still, I met her desperately hopeful gaze across the candlelit chamber and somehow knew it wasn't her first visit to the basement. In that moment of connection, I saw her for the first time as an adult, understanding her actions as an adult might.

The healer of the Fairchild coven had been just as trapped as we three. Perhaps more so.

"Rose," I whispered.

"Wisteria," she cried. Then she pressed her hand to her chest, trying to moderate her reaction. She tried to smile. "I'm so sorry. Please, don't—"

Jasper looked at her sharply. And for a brief moment, I could actually see a cord of darkly twisted magic connecting them.

Rose clamped her mouth shut. But not of her own volition.

Jasper's control over my aunt wasn't simply a manipulation of the coven magic, as it seemed to be with our parents. He had actually bound her with some sort of dark power.

Declan muttered something nasty behind me. He was putting the puzzle pieces together as quickly as I was.

Returning my gaze to Jasper, I took off my shoes again, one at a time, feeling the estate magic undulate beneath my bare feet.

Jasper frowned, most likely in response to feeling the estate and the house respond to my presence. Our presence.

I took a single step forward, giving Jasmine and Declan space behind me. I could hear them removing their own footwear.

"What have you done, Jasper?" I finally asked, though I knew deep in my soul that talking wasn't going to get me anywhere. "To Rose? To get out of the wheelchair?"

"Well, you forced my hand. Didn't you, my sweet?"

I stepped farther into the room, slowly moving toward the center opposite my uncle, but keeping a good twenty feet away from him.

Jasper's gaze flicked to Jasmine on my left and Declan on my right as they kept pace with me.

"You should have had him cross you off the contract," my uncle said.

"You started leeching from Rose long before I knew about any contract," I said mildly, eyeing the connection I could see twisting between Jasper and Rose. I could try to sever it, but I had nothing with which to cut through magic. I'd never learned to manifest knives as my father could. And I couldn't carry a sharp-edged artifact because I would eventually erode its magic.

"Come, children. Take your places at my side," Jasper said, as if already annoyed at the casual conversation. "Together, we'll be unstoppable. As we were always meant to be."

"No one is stopping us from doing whatever we want, Jasper," I said. "Except you. Whatever boundaries you wish to surmount, we will not be crossing them with you."

Jasper eyed me. "I can simply take what I want, Wisteria," he said. "Move you where I will, when I will it."

"If that were true," Declan said, "you would have done it a long time ago. No, Jasper. You might have been able to call forth enough coven magic to have bound us to the Conclave contract, but you can't move against the three of us." He shifted his feet on the dirt floor, deliberately picking one foot up at a time and placing it back down. "You don't even wholly command the estate magic. We still share some of the connection."

"An oversight I will correct immediately," Jasper said, sounding utterly unruffled.

Jasmine tilted her head thoughtfully. "I don't think so. Word on the street is that the house likes Wisteria better than you."

Jasper pinned me with his washed-out blue gaze. "I'll take care of that troublesome brownie as well."

Jasmine barked out a laugh.

Declan and I looked at her.

"What?" she said. "You know *Scooby-Doo*."

"There were brownies in *Scooby-Doo*?"

"No...I...never mind," Jasmine said. "Let's just get back to vanquishing the evil overlord. We skipped breakfast. I'm getting hungry."

Kett suddenly appeared before us. He was standing in front of me but slightly to the side, so as to not block my view of Jasper. My uncle eyed the vampire without any obvious reaction. He would have known Kett was on the estate and inside the house even before he appeared.

"The elders?" I asked.

"Subdued."

"But alive, right?" Jasmine asked nervously.

"Kettil," Jasper said. "I had hoped you'd stay out of this."

"You brought the situation to my attention when you had Yale kidnap witch children."

Jasper waved offishly. "He's an outsider whose transgression cannot be connected back to the Conclave."

"The Convocation will not see it that way."

Jasper smiled charmingly. "The Convocation will see what I show them."

"Wisteria collected a reconstruction that ties you to the murder of Dawn Fairchild's parents, and to her kidnapping."

"Wisteria..." Jasper snapped, his composure momentarily slipping. "Wisteria will soon be brought into line."

He shook his head. "Enough. Vampire, none of this would have been necessary had you just made the correct decision more quickly."

"That would have only delayed it," I said. "It was always going to come to this. Us against you. It's what you created us to do."

"No," my uncle said. "That's what you created. But no matter. I will fix it." He nodded to Kett. "And then we can discuss my remaking."

"Oh, please," Jasmine said. "You don't think that Kett would—"

"This is witch business," Jasper formally intoned, interrupting her. "Fairchild business. Your welcome here is rescinded."

Magic slammed against Kett. The vampire leaned his shoulder into the onslaught, but his feet slid back in the dirt.

Reacting to the vampire's natural resistance, or perhaps the resistance he'd gained through drinking my blood, the energy intensified, whipping around and between us.

I reached into the tornado, willing the estate magic to heed me. But it didn't. It couldn't disobey a direct command from Jasper.

Kett turned, reaching back for me. His eyes were flooded with the red of his magic, but vampire magic wasn't going to counter witch magic in witch territory.

Our fingers brushed.

Then Kett was ripped from my grasp and dragged up the stairs. Ejected from the estate, as I had ejected Yale in January.

The whirlwind of magic ebbed, dissipating. Though oddly, I could still feel it as a light film on my hands, face, and forearms.

Jasper brushed his hands together with great satisfaction. "Now, where were we? Oh, yes." He stretched his arms out to the sides. Magic rippled throughout his circle.

The shimmer shifted, revealing three children. Ruby, Jack, and Dawn were lying spread-eagle in the dirt, seemingly insensible. They'd been deliberately arranged, their heads facing toward the center of the circle and their outstretched limbs not quite touching.

Rose made a pained noise.

Without any more boasting or grandstanding, Jasper stepped back into the circle, so that he stood between the children's heads.

It was just the three of us against him now. And he wielded the combined power of the Fairchild coven, in addition to whatever spell he was powering with magic being leeched from the children.

The time for talking was done. We three were going to have to be enough.

"Declan," I said. "I'll need you to crack his shields. Then I'll take them down."

Declan nodded. He lifted his left hand and three small stones began spiraling just above his open palm. He already had his blasting rod in his right hand. The runes etched along its length pulsed with power.

Jasper closed his eyes, rolling his head back. He gathered the magic that hovered almost tangibly in the circle toward him, preparing some spell.

I pivoted, pacing around Jasmine and Declan and laying magic in my wake as I did so. "Jasmine," I said, keeping my gaze on Jasper. "Grab Rose and get her into this circle. Or out of the basement altogether, if you can."

"I'm not babysitting—"

"She's tied to Jasper somehow," I said, cutting off whatever rant she was about to launch. "Can you see it? You're going to need to cut through the magic. Have you got something?"

Jasmine snapped her mouth closed, squinting in Rose's direction. Then she started digging through her satchel. "I'll rig something."

I nodded, pausing in my circling to step back between them. I pulled layer upon layer of magic from the earth, quickly constructing a protection circle in a process similar to how I created my oyster-shell cubes.

Jasper slapped his hands together.

The three of us froze, steeling ourselves for whatever he was about to hit us with. But instead of casting, our uncle simply opened his eyes, which were now glowing a fierce blue. "Violet," he whispered. "Dahlia. Grey. Slate."

Magic boomed through his circle.

"What the hell?" Declan muttered.

"Summoning spell." I felt slightly light-headed in response to the power that my uncle commanded so effortlessly.

My mother appeared just outside of Jasper's circle, to the far right. She swayed on her feet, then collapsed to her knees.

I knew the feeling. Pearl Godfrey had once transported me from Vancouver to London, and it had taken me a week to feel like I was no longer inside out. Of course, Pearl had needed my explicit permission in order to move me at all. Jasper had simply whispered, and my mother appeared.

Declan swore nastily. "With just their first names?"

Dahlia appeared. Jasmine's mother landed directly on her back. She appeared to be still unconscious as a result of our breaking her wards.

"Go," I said to Jasmine. "Now. He's gathering them for a reason."

"To bind us," Declan muttered.

Grey and Slate appeared at the same time, each beside his wife. The basement air was heavy with magic. Almost suffocating. Grey kept his footing, but he looked as though he could use a blood transfusion. Which, depending on how much Kett had taken in order to subdue him, was probably accurate.

Slate bent over and threw up.

Stepping out from the protection circle I'd cast for Jasmine and Rose, I gathered all the magic I could hold toward me, fueling my bracelet. There was so much power in the air that I didn't even need to tap into the estate and the house.

Jasmine dashed across the basement for Rose.

Declan tossed a series of his spelled stones toward Jasper's circle.

Violet covered her face and shrieked as Declan's magic exploded above her. Grey threw himself over Dahlia.

I thrust all the magic I'd gathered toward the circle in a messy, haphazard push, counting on whatever cracks Declan had made to be enough to get me through Jasper's shields.

Then Jasmine slammed against an invisible wall about a foot from Rose. She stumbled, falling soundlessly onto the dirt with blood pouring from her nose.

Declan's magic rained down over all the elders' heads. The candlelit air between us and Jasper cleared.

Magic rippled across my uncle's circle. It appeared pristine, undamaged.

Jasmine made it to her feet, scrambling back toward us. Declan stepped out of my protection circle, grabbing her and dragging her back.

I didn't take my gaze off Jasper. Or step back into the circle.

My uncle smirked at me. "You're out of practice, my sweet Wisteria."

My stomach soured, and I struggled to keep my creeping fear from my face.

"Get up, my siblings," Jasper said. "Up, up. On your feet. It's time to unify the coven. It's time to bring the children back into the fold."

My mother gained her feet, glaring at her brother. "This wasn't what we discussed, Jasper."

He waved a hand in my direction. "You'll need to take that up with your daughter." Magic rolled through his words as he spoke. "Now...take your place..."

Violet flinched. And for a brief moment, I watched her struggle to shake off the compulsion Jasper had just hit her with. Then she pivoted, stepping forward and pausing as if awaiting more instructions.

She pinned her gaze on me, gritting her teeth. Sorrow and regret flitted across her face.

My heart pinched, but I brushed the emotion away. Her concern was too late. Too little.

"Everyone else," Jasper said. "Come, come. The vampire is rather dutifully trying to break through the outer wards. I don't need to be waging a war on two fronts."

Rose started weeping.

"Damn you, Jasper," Grey snarled. He attempted to help Dahlia, barely conscious now, to her feet. "You can't make us fight our own children."

"I don't need you to fight, Grey. I just need you to contribute your magic and your blood ties. I'll do the rest."

And triggered by Grey's words, I understood suddenly what I needed to do. It all became crystal clear.

It was rash and it was dangerous. But only for me. I turned my back on Jasper, catching the start of his confused look as I did so.

If, on some level, our parents did still care for us—enough to pull their punches when we faced off at the front door, enough to curse and rail against Jasper's manipulation of the coven bonds—then perhaps I could unify that tenuous connection for just long enough to break Jasper's hold on them.

Reaching for Jasmine, I whispered so only she and Declan could hear me. "He can't make them kill us. They can break the compulsion. Together, they're strong enough. They just need the right push."

Jasmine frowned, but she took my hand unquestioningly. I turned to face the elders again.

Slate stepped into place beside my mother without being commanded to do so by Jasper. "Don't make this worse than it needs to be, Wisteria," my father pleaded. "This isn't worth dying for."

"You were saying?" Declan asked wryly.

Ignoring my father, I wrapped my other hand around Declan's.

"Screw you, Jasper." Dahlia finally found her voice, though she was still leaning heavily on Grey's shoulder.

I closed my eyes, reaching out with my magic and through Jasmine's and Declan's power, ignoring everything else.

"What are you doing?" Declan asked.

I didn't answer as residual magic stirred around us. Layers upon layers. Years and years of spells. Years and years of my, Jasmine, and Declan's collective childhood imprinted in the darkness, seared into the dirt underneath our feet.

Whispers rose at my bidding, brushing against me. Caressing me.

"What are you doing?" Jasmine cried.

I opened my eyes. The magic I'd called forth danced around us in vibrant streaks of blue.

Momentarily distracted by my change in tactics, Jasper was frowning at me.

I looked at my parents. They were frightened, worried. "I should have dragged you down here twelve, thirteen years ago. I should have shown you. Shown you what is worth dying for."

"No ... " Jasmine whispered.

I wasn't sure whether it was compassion for our parents or fear for me that made my cousin speak, but I had already called the reconstruction spell forward. Without my candles, without any boundaries. Magic poured out of me, fueling all the residual in my immediate surroundings.

"Get the kids," I said. "Take our parents out of play. I'll keep Jasper busy."

"What the hell does that mean?" Declan snarled.

"Declan, please. Just get the children out of here."

I didn't wait for his response. The magic wouldn't let me hold it back any longer. I dropped Declan's and Jasmine's hands, lifting my palms toward Jasper, toward the elders. Toward the past, where it was ready to spring forth all around me. I opened myself up to it. I poured myself into it.

Reconstruction after reconstruction came into being all around us. Echoes of our childhood. Echoes of the three of us from ages nine to sixteen. Echoes of everything Jasper had ever made us do, everything he'd ever done to us.

Including him holding a knife to Jasmine's neck, on an altar that had reappeared in the middle of the room right in front of our parents.

Jasmine made a terrible pained noise, but I didn't stop. I allowed all the terrible moments of abuse to manifest. I watched Declan and me charging in, fighting Jasper. Pulling Jasmine from the altar.

Dahlia cried out. My father shouted something. But I couldn't listen. I wouldn't soften or apologize.

"Get ready," I whispered, heedless of the tears streaming down my face.

Jasmine placed her hand on my back at the same time as Declan placed his on my shoulder.

"Stop this at once," Jasper snapped, gathering his own magic toward him so that it pooled in his hands. "You'll only burn yourself out, Wisteria. Reconstructions are utterly benign."

"But the power of three isn't benign, is it, Uncle?" I shouted over him, raising my arms to encompass the dozens upon dozens of reconstructions I'd called forth. Dozens of Declans, Jasmines, and Wisterias. Dozens of images of Jasper. Layers and layers of residual magic.

Declan whirled his blasting rod in his right hand.

Jasmine reached out to the ceiling, toward the electrical wiring.

Power twisted back and forth between us, shared magic building around and through us in a tightly wound coil. The estate magic responded, surging beneath our feet.

I kept my gaze glued to Jasper. "This is what you wanted, isn't it?" Then I pressed forward with our combined magic, wordlessly commanding the residual that I'd called forth.

The reconstructions stopped moving, stopped repeating.

"We never needed you, though." With a deliberate swipe of my hand, all the echoes of Jasper disappeared. With another push of intention, all the echoes of Declan, Jasmine, and Wisteria shifted. They stood shoulder to shoulder, arrayed before us like soldiers.

I shouldn't have been able to manipulate the residual in such a way. But Jasper had made us. Had combined us into something more powerful than any one witch should be.

"Oh my God..." Violet said.

Jasper snarled, raising his hands toward us. They pulsed with dark-blue energy.

Jasmine reached out with her magic and tore the electrical wires from the ceiling.

Then, as one, we attacked.

Declan hurled his blasting rod like a club toward Jasper. Jasmine slammed the live wires against the circle, hitting multiple points all at once. And I marched the reconstructions over our parents.

Magic exploded through the basement.

The foundations of the house shook.

Wood splintered.

The air sizzled.

Our parents scattered, throwing themselves to the sides.

And Jasper's circle cracked.

Before the magic cleared, I ran straight for Jasper with Jasmine on my left and Declan on my right. The reconstructions of ourselves, the echoes of our childhood, ran with us.

One of the girls trapped in the circle with Jasper started screaming, then the other. The children had woken. But I blocked out the sound. I had one job. Jasper. I had to let Jasmine and Declan see to everything else.

An orb of magic flew toward me, most likely whatever spell Jasper had been preparing. As I sidestepped it, Declan actually punched whatever Jasper had thrown out of the air.

More magic exploded. Our parents were suddenly scrambling around us, shouting. Slate stepped into my path, but before I could assess if he was acting as friend or foe, Jasmine hit him with something that took him down and left him convulsing.

My reconstructions poured into Jasper's circle through the crack that Declan and Jasmine had made. Still running, I slammed my right palm and all the magic I'd gathered in my bracelet into the damaged circle.

Magic boomed throughout the basement, knocking everyone but Jasper and me to the ground.

"Impressive," Jasper said, smiling proudly. He was holding the knife he'd used to kill Bluebell. When he caught me looking at it, his smile widened.

Though I couldn't see them, I could feel Jasmine and Declan gaining their feet behind me. The children had scrambled together for protection near the white candle on the eastern edge of the circle, wrapping their arms around each other but not making a sound. The two older kids, Jack and Ruby, had Dawn sandwiched between them.

My reconstructions filled every other inch of the space, creating a path between my uncle and me. They were waiting for instructions.

I smiled at the children. Then I stepped into the broken circle.

Jasper laughed. "Mistake number one, Wisteria."

Magic churned as the circle sealed closed behind and around me. Jasper had resurrected the boundary, hoping to cut me off from Declan and Jasmine.

I raised my fists. Magic boiled in my right hand and all around my bracelet. "Actually, Uncle," I said coolly. "It's all going exactly as planned."

He frowned.

"You've forgotten," I said. "The estate remembers. And the house likes me better."

Lark appeared behind Jasper, moving through his hastily restored circle without apparent effort. I didn't know whether she could do so because she was tied to me, or because Jasper hadn't thought to ward himself against brownie magic. She moved toward the children, pressing her finger to her lips to caution them to remain quiet. Then she fished a blade from her pocket and sliced into the circle, just above the white candle.

Jasper spun toward her. I punched him in the kidneys. Well, where his kidneys would have been if he hadn't been shielded.

He whirled to face me, livid as he slashed his knife across where my neck should have been. Except I'd danced back.

Lark finished cutting a hole in the circle. Declan appeared on the other side of the opening, silently coaxing Dawn to crawl out toward him.

Jasper slashed the blade at me a second time, drawing my attention back to him. He hit the shield I was trying to hold between us, knocking me sideways. I spun, falling to one knee.

I called the reconstructions to me, gathering them all around me while I shook off Jasper's blow. They were so infused with my magic that I had practically given them mass.

Jasper slashed fruitlessly at the echoes, at every Declan, every Jasmine, every Wisteria. Panting with the effort, he then backed off, pausing to gather more magic.

On the other side of the barrier, Declan passed Dawn to Grey, then kneeled back down, reaching for Ruby. I risked a glance over my shoulder, looking for Jasmine and finding her and Violet helping Rose up the stairs.

I pulled my attention back to Jasper as I slowly made it to my feet.

"Wisteria Elizabeth Marie Fairchild," Jasper intoned. "Come to me."

Jasper's compulsion hit me hard, driving me back against the edge of the circle and pinning me there. The spell ripped through my shield, digging into my skin.

My vision became muddy. The reconstructions pressed against me, incapable of helping.

Jasper laughed, stepping closer.

Somewhere beyond the circle, Jasmine screamed my name.

"Jasmine..." I gasped my cousin's name. Then I pinned my gaze to my uncle's. "You can't have me, Jasper. I already belong to someone else. Two someones. You made it so."

The magic released me, and I fell forward onto my hands and knees. The reconstructions pressed against me, trying to help me get up.

Jasper snarled. But instead of pressing his advantage, he spun around, stalking back to where Jack was trying to crawl through the hole in the circle.

I tried to scream a warning to the boy, but still fighting the residual of the compulsion spell, I couldn't manage more than a shrill shriek.

Declan appeared on the other side of the circle, grabbing Jack's arms just as Jasper grabbed his leg. Jasper thrust his hand forward, slamming some sort of spell through the hole in the circle. It hit Declan in the chest, and he tumbled out of my sight.

Jasper dragged Jack back from the hole into the center of the circle. The boy silently fought him every inch of the way, battering Jasper's shields with wild magic as he clawed at the dirt.

I gained my feet again, already gathering my shredded shields.

Jasper flipped the boy onto his back, holding him pinned in place with the magic he wielded so effortlessly. He raised his knife over Jack's chest. Then he looked at me.

"Let's see you shake this off."

Lark appeared between him and the boy.

I lunged forward, pummeling Jasper with the reconstructions. But even as I did, I knew I was going to be too late.

The knife arced forward, then down.

Jack wrapped his hand around Jasper's bare ankle, hitting him with some sort of wildly conjured spell. It barely touched my uncle, but it slowed him.

Gathering the ragged edges of my magic around me in the strongest shield I could conjure, I threw myself between Jasper and Lark.

Jasper's knife hit my shield.

The brownie grabbed the boy, dragging him away.

The blade sliced through all the magic I held against it. Jasper's washed-out blue eyes widened, his anger transforming into surprise. His shoulders shifted, as if he might be trying to take the edge off his blow.

The knife caught me just underneath the rib cage, then buried itself to the hilt in my flesh.

Jasper gasped.

I looked down at the blade protruding out of me. "You always were too powerful," I mumbled.

"Wisteria..." my uncle whispered in disbelief.

Pain exploded through my torso, radiating through my chest and stomach, then down my legs. The magic that the blade carried was more deadly than the wound itself.

I stumbled back. The reconstructions pressed against me, holding me upright.

"Wisteria!" Jasper cried, reaching for me.

"No!" I slapped him back with a desperate pulse of magic. "You don't get to touch me." I reached down and wrapped my hand around the hilt of the knife.

"Don't touch that, Wisteria!" Panic laced Jasper's command as he reached out to the circle and tore the barrier down. "Rose! Rose!"

I could smell smoke suddenly. Something was on fire. Heedless, I pulled out the knife.

"No!" Jasper lunged for me.

The reconstructions welled up around us, momentarily holding him at bay.

I held the knife aloft, blood dripping from the blade. My blood. I could feel the magic contained within it. So much underutilized power.

"This wasn't... this can't be... " Jasper was muttering, pressing against the reconstructions.

"I'm dying," I said calmly. "I can feel my magic shifting. And I know how that feels because of you, Jasper. Because of when you killed Bluebell."

"Listen to me carefully, Wisteria," my uncle said, ignoring me. "Gather the magic of the estate around you. Don't move, don't expend any more energy. I'll summon Rose."

"It's going to be okay, Jasper. Because I'm going to take you with me. And then Jasmine and Declan will be free." I laughed harshly. "Free of both of us."

The reconstructions flew at Jasper, dissolving against the shields he held around him in a glittering display. He stumbled back, but they were just a distraction. I could never broach his shields with just the echoes of magic.

I reached for and claimed the power of my own life essence. I gathered it, readying one word, packing all the magic I could into a single name.

"Jasper... " I whispered.

Magic was ripped from me, tearing through my uncle's shield and breaking his back a second time.

He screamed as he crumpled to the ground.

I stumbled toward him, falling, the knife still in my hand. I dragged myself up his body until I could lock eyes with him.

"Goodbye, Uncle," I whispered.

He gurgled something in pain.

Then I slit his throat. Blood streamed out of him, spraying across my hands and forearms.

I pushed back from him as I tried to stand, but I made it only to my knees. I lost hold of the knife. Magic twisted through me, claiming my own death.

And it hurt. It burned.

No. It was the basement that was ablaze.

I looked across the chamber, seeing Declan, Jasmine, and Jack still at the base of the stairs. Except there weren't any stairs that I could see. The walls and much of the ceiling were on fire. No sort of protection, magical or otherwise, had ever been applied to the old wooden beams and posts, the open rafters. The basement floor was dry dirt, no hint of moisture in the air. Nothing would contain the blaze.

Declan was trying to clear a path through the burning rubble that had swallowed the stairwell. Jasmine had turned back, looking for me. She spotted me kneeling next to Jasper.

Him dead. And me dying.

I smiled at her. It was all I could do.

She screamed, trying to shove Jack into Declan's arms so she could run to me.

I frowned, all my thoughts made distant by the pain searing through me. Jasmine and Declan...they were going to die down here...with me and Jasper.

That hadn't been the plan.

I pressed my hands into the blood still pouring from my uncle, effortlessly harnessing his life essence.

"Wisteria!" Jasmine screamed again, trying now to run through the fire that had swiftly shifted to rage between us. Declan grabbed her before she could hurt herself. Jack's face was streaked with tears and soot.

"I love you..." I said. Then, with Jasper's magic pooled in my hands, I visualized picking Jasmine, Declan, and Jack up and placing them gently down in the orchard, right beside the rabbit hutch we'd built so many years ago. Right where I knew they'd be safe.

The magic obeyed me without question, gathering around them.

Jasmine screamed. "No!"

"I love you," I whispered again.

They disappeared.

I had only the fire for company now. But that didn't matter, because I was done. I had given up. I'd given in. I slipped forward across Jasper without even bothering to stop my fall.

And death was warm...comfortable...peaceful...

I reached for the darkness eagerly waiting for my soul, ready to greet me as an old friend.

Chapter Twelve

I was still dying. It was taking too long, but there was nothing to do about it. Annoyingly, I kept floating in and out of consciousness, aware of the manor as it collapsed around me. I couldn't move. I didn't want to move.

Even if some miracle were to occur, I didn't want to be broken like Jasper. I didn't want to be a burden to Jasmine and Declan.

The heat of the fire was intense. The blaze had to be sucking all the oxygen out of the basement, so if the magic coursing through me didn't end me, I expected I would suffocate. Hopefully before the flames got to me.

Something shifted to my right.

No… not something.

Someone.

Rose.

I wasn't certain how my aunt had gotten into the basement—then I remembered that Jasper had tried to summon her. He must have been successful.

She was crawling toward me, laying her hand on my shoulder. "Wisteria."

"You need to go." I wasn't certain I'd spoken out loud. I wasn't certain I was capable of speech, of moving my mouth to form words.

But even if she heard my warning, instead of heeding it, instead of leaving, Rose pulled me into her lap.

I screamed with the pain of being moved. Then I blacked out once more.

I became aware again. Rose was singing a lullaby she used to sing to Jasmine, Declan, and me when she thought the three of us were asleep and couldn't hear her. I'd forgotten that.

Those moments of tenderness had been buried underneath all the terrible memories I'd called forth in the basement to fight Jasper. All the moments I'd forced myself to forget.

Rose's magic, weak as it was, danced across my torso. She was trying to heal the stab wound. But it wasn't the wound that was slowly killing me.

"Rose..." I croaked. "Rose. Don't." I'd expended too much magic. I'd known I was doing so when I reconstructed all the basement's residual energy at once, fueling the echoes of our childhood with my own magic. With the power of three. Then I had used my own life essence to take down Jasper. Even with the estate magic still roiling around us, Rose wasn't strong enough to heal me.

"They'll need you now, Wisteria," my aunt said. "You'll have to hold them together."

The house was still burning. The flames had formed a neat ring of fire around us, maybe ten feet away. It was as if something was holding it back. The edges of Jasper's circle? I could see my uncle sprawled out next to me, his face turned away. His white T-shirt was soaked in his own blood.

Dead by my hand. Murdered. And I couldn't bring myself to feel sorry about it.

I wasn't sure how much time had passed since that moment. Maybe only minutes.

I tried to push Rose away but I couldn't lift my arms. She was stroking my hair, whispering words between the tune she was humming.

"I always wanted you to be mine. My child, not just my niece."

She leaned over, her white-streaked hair falling in a tangle all around my face. Her eyes shone bright blue with her witch magic.

"I'm sorry," I whispered. My throat was so dry I could barely get the words out. "I should have known he was holding you. I should have come sooner."

"You don't say sorry to me, Wisteria Elizabeth Marie Fairchild. I love you. I love you, my niece, my baby. I didn't bring you into this world, but I can hold you here."

She pressed a light kiss to my forehead, and her magic rushed through me. My fingers twitched, then my legs.

My aunt had stopped humming, stopped moving.

"Rose? Rose?"

Her magic ebbed away, the final strains of it seeping into my skin.

"Rose!"

I managed to move, to shift her off me. She slumped to the side.

Then something above us cracked, and a main beam of the roof snapped, swinging down directly over us.

I fruitlessly flung myself across Rose. The air shifted around us. But the blow I'd been expecting across my shoulders didn't fall.

I looked up.

Kett was holding one end of the beam. His hands were ablaze. Dining room furniture was raining down across the basement, china and glass shattering within the ring of flames that still held around us.

"Move, Wisteria," Kett said.

"Rose—"

"Dead. Move. Now."

I rolled away. Kett let the beam drop, sweeping me up in his arms at the same time.

I clung to him.

The inferno raged around us. Kett pivoted, looking for an exit. I couldn't figure out how he'd gotten into the basement—but by the burns slowly healing on his face and shoulders, he had come through the fire.

For me.

"You got through the wards," I said.

"They fell."

I nodded. "I killed Jasper."

"I noticed. But I'm slightly more concerned about getting you through the fire right now."

The heat of the blaze was already scorching my skin. Kett slowly pivoted again.

"I killed Jasper," I murmured. And as I did so, I realized that the estate magic was now wholly mine to command. Well, Declan, Jasmine, and me. Hope flooded through my chest. "Maybe…"

"Yes?" Kett asked patiently.

"Put me down. I need my feet on the ground…in the dirt."

He set me down, but I couldn't stand on my own. So he grasped my forearms, holding me upright.

I reached for the magic still roiling underneath my feet. I reached for the magic of the house. It came to my call—thin, but I could feel it. I could also feel Lark's magic in the mix, as if she was trying to help. Perhaps she was the one holding the flames at bay.

And with no real understanding of how I did so, I reached out and smothered the fire with the estate magic, pressing the flames down to be absorbed into the dirt floor and the foundations of the house. The magic sucked the billowing smoke away from the beams and rafters, leaving them charred and smoldering hot. But I had doused the inferno completely.

Kett laughed huskily. He lifted my wrist, pressing a kiss only an inch away from my bracelet.

I wrapped my hands around his face. "Jasper's dead," I repeated for the third time.

"I look forward to spending the remainder of eternity with you, Wisteria." Kett's tone was intimate but formal.

"Well, I'm not sure you have a choice now."

"There is always a choice. I simply choose to remain, rather than return to ash."

"You won't be able to call me 'little witch' anymore."

He laughed. "There will be other terms of endearment. But might I suggest we discuss them somewhere where the roof isn't caving in on us?"

"Agreed."

Kett swept me into his arms again, moving carefully through the smoldering remains of the basement. We were heading toward where I thought the kitchen stairs were supposed to be.

"The stairs are gone," I murmured.

"No matter," he said. "I can feel fresh air from this direction. And I am capable of climbing."

As we moved through the basement, the magic embedded throughout it appeared to be still holding the burned beams in place. Though for how much longer, I wasn't certain.

I could see light ahead of us but little else. Kett moved easily, smoothly. His sight was apparently much better than mine.

Faint voices filtered down to us, calling back to one another. Perhaps Declan and Jasmine had seen the fire snuffed out and were searching the main floor, trying to find another way down into the basement?

I opened my mouth to let them know we were coming to them. To caution them against—

Something massive collapsed ahead of us. More light flooded through the ceiling.

I heard Jasmine scream. A second section of floor gave way.

Then...nothing.

Kett moved forward so swiftly that the dirt walls blurred around us. He set me down before I even knew where we were.

I stumbled, realizing I was staring at a pile of gray-streaked white marble on the compacted dirt floor.

Marble?

"Kett?" The vampire was gone.

Blinking in the suddenly bright light, I stumbled around the white stones, realizing that the still-settling rubble was from the hand-carved entranceway stairs, now one floor lower than they should have been.

The pile before me shifted. I scrambled away, pressing myself against the dirt wall. The stones moved once more as Kett emerged. He was shrouded with white dust—and carrying Declan and Jasmine in a bundle of limp limbs.

I stifled a scream as I lunged forward, fruitlessly trying to help Kett hold their weight as he lowered them to the ground.

They must have raced into the house when the fire vanished, not realizing how badly it had weakened the foundations. Then their weight had collapsed what appeared to be part of the entranceway, and the marble stairwell with it.

Declan immediately rolled to his side, coughing.

But still cradled in Kett's arms, Jasmine wasn't moving. Her hair had fallen across her face.

I reached for her, but Kett shook his head sharply at me. He settled into a crouch, gently keeping Jasmine tucked against him.

I paused, my hands still outstretched toward my cousin, terror flooding through my entire body.

Kett was holding himself too still. His gaze on me was too steady, too…sad.

"Jasmine?" I whispered. I crawled forward without touching her.

Declan stopped coughing, heaving himself upright until he was kneeling beside me. "Thank God. The vampire found you," he said. "We were looking for…" His gaze fell on his sister, growing concerned. "Jasmine shoved me to the side, then the floor…caved in…"

"Please," I whispered, brushing the hair from Jasmine's face. But I wasn't sure who I was pleading with. "Please."

"Please, what?" Jasmine spoke without moving or opening her eyes. Blood trickled down from a hidden wound I'd uncovered at her hairline.

Joy flooded my system. I pressed my hand over my mouth to stop myself from crying out.

But Kett continued to hold himself so terribly still. Looking at me with such steady regard.

"Let's get out of here." Declan stumbled as he rose, but he made it to his feet.

"We shouldn't move her," Kett said.

"What?" Declan paused, turning back.

"Why?" I asked. But I could already see the answer in every chisel-edged feature of his face.

"The vampire likes holding me," Jasmine chortled quietly. Then she started coughing up blood.

"Shit!" Declan cried. "Where's Rose?"

I tugged my sleeve down over my hand, carefully wiping the blood from Jasmine's chin.

"I don't feel so hot," she murmured.

"Goddamn it," Declan said. "Where the hell is Rose?"

"Dead," I said. The words felt empty, dragged out from deep within my soul. "Rose is dead."

Jasmine opened her eyes, pinning me with her bright-blue gaze. "Betty-Sue," she said. "He's dead, isn't he? We're free?"

"Yes," I said, starting to sob. "We're free."

She reached up shakily, touching my face, then looking at the tears she'd collected on her fingertips. "I'm dying, aren't I?"

I glanced up at Kett.

He nodded.

The vampire didn't want to move Jasmine, and we didn't have a healer.

"Yes," I whispered.

"What?" Declan shouted.

"Bleeding internally," Kett said, not looking away from me.

"Maybe the magic of the estate..." I reached for the energy I had just wielded to put out the fire. But it felt thin, distant.

"Hold my hand," Jasmine said. "If I'm going to die, I'll do it holding your hand, Betty-Sue."

I grabbed her hand, sobbing raggedly. Completely and utterly powerless to save her.

Declan knelt next to me, pressing his hand to Jasmine's head. "This is insane," he said thickly. "We have to do something. There must be something within our power ... "

Then a harsh realization hit me. A terrible realization. Followed by a flood of desperate hope.

It wasn't within my power or Declan's to heal Jasmine, but ...

I lifted my gaze to meet the silvered eyes watching me. "Kett ... "

"No," he said, not even letting me finish the thought. "She's too badly injured. Magic is tied to blood—"

"And most of hers is still inside her." My voice was stronger, my mind racing as I quickly tallied all the reasons I was going to pose the question that he was trying to stop me from asking.

"Blood that is not flowing correctly, Wisteria," he said patiently.

"Jasper is dead," I said.

"Yes."

"Leaving me as the sole name on the contract."

"Yes."

"What the hell are you talking about?" Declan asked.

"Remaking me," Jasmine murmured. Her intense gaze was glued to me. Witch magic burned within her eyes.

"It's not even a question," Kett said.

"It's out of the question!" Declan roared as he shot to his feet.

Ignoring him, I placed my hands on either side of Kett's face, unintentionally smearing Jasmine's blood across his pale skin.

"Please," I whispered. I leaned over Jasmine slung across his lap, pressing light kisses to his immoveable lips as I spoke. "Please. We can have forever together in the next lifetime."

"And if I kill her?" he asked darkly. "You won't be able to bear looking at me."

"I don't have to see you to love you…" My voice broke. "But I can't live without Jasmine. Even if you turn me against my will to fulfill the contract, I'll be a shell. Empty. I can't exist in a world without Jasmine. Please. Please. Give her a chance to be the person you need. To be the family you want. Please, Kett. For me. For our future. For our forever. Take Jasmine."

"This is insane," Declan muttered behind me, pacing.

I kept my gaze riveted to Kett.

"She won't be your Jasmine," he said coldly. "You'll love a memory either way."

"Maybe…" Jasmine whispered. "But maybe I'll prove you wrong." She lifted her hand, placing it over mine on Kett's cheek. "Let's be monsters in the dark together."

Kett laughed harshly.

Jasmine's hand slipped away from mine. "I want to be the storm," she whispered. "But I'll settle for the next sunrise."

A terrible groan of pain was ripped from Declan.

A flood of tears washed away my vision.

Kett wrapped his hand around the back of my neck, pulling me forward and kissing me tenderly. "Promise me."

"Anything," I said, gasping for breath through my sobbing. "Anything you want."

"I'll take the next lifetime," he said. "Stay alive until I come for you."

"It's yours."

"Get the contract," he said. "From my bag. If we're going to circumvent its binding, I'd like to do so without sacrificing myself in the process. Quickly, Wisteria. Quickly."

Blinded by my tears, I dug into the invisible bag that I knew Kett wore at his hip. My fingers brushed paper.

"You need to scratch out Jasper's name and sign it in his stead," Kett said.

"I don't have a pen," I cried, unfolding the contract and dropping all the pages of parchment except the last. "And I'm not the coven leader."

"It doesn't matter," Kett said patiently. "Jasmine can countersign for herself." He looked down at her. "Is this what you want?"

She nodded, her face almost tranquil. Peaceful. She was struggling to keep her eyes open.

My sobs became ragged, torn out of me with a terrible pain. The worst pain I'd ever felt. Worse than being stabbed. Worse than dying.

"Thumbprints," Kett said sharply. "Thumbprints will have to do. Wisteria. Now."

He pressed his thumb against mine, drawing my blood with a sharp pinch.

I pressed my thumb over top of Jasper's signature at the bottom of the page. Then I carefully lifted Jasmine's hand, smearing her thumb in the blood dripping from her temple. I rested the contract and her hand on her chest.

"I can't do it for you, Betty-Lou," I said. "I'm sorry. I'm sorry. You have to do it yourself."

She nodded, the movement no more than a tired dip of her chin. But she managed to turn her hand, pressing her bloody thumbprint to the contract.

I leaned forward, breathing my magic across the parchment. "Jasmine Belinda Jane Fairchild accepts the terms of the contract with Kettil the elder and executioner of the Conclave. Witnessed by her coven mate, Wisteria Fairchild."

The magic embedded in the parchment heeded me. It shifted across our blood, rendering our thumbprints into our signatures.

Kett brushed his fingers across my face, touching my neck where he'd bitten me for the first and only time. "Go now."

He dropped his hand from my neck, but I couldn't move. I couldn't bring myself to leave.

"Go, Wisteria." Kett's eyes blazed with the red of his magic. His nearly two-inch-long fangs appeared. "Go."

Declan grabbed me from behind, dragging me away.

I lost hold of Kett. I lost hold of Jasmine. "Betty-Lou!" I cried, incapable of doing anything else.

Jasmine smiled at me. "I love you, Betty-Sue ... and Bubba." Then she turned her trusting gaze up toward the fanged monster within whose arms she was about to die.

"Declan," Kett called. "Collapse the entrance. Whatever happens, whether either of us survives, we'll need to be sheltered through the next sunrise."

Declan grunted in response as he hoisted me in his arms. Then he slung me over his shoulder so that he could climb up and over the remains of the collapsed marble staircase.

I craned my neck, wanting to watch for the moment Kett struck ... for the moment he drained whatever blood still stirred in Jasmine's veins. But Declan pulled me out of sight before I saw my cousin ... my love ... my heart ... die.

Declan set me onto my feet just beyond the front stairs to the main entrance of the manor. Then he turned back and carefully collapsed what remained of the front entrance.

From the corner of my eye, I caught a glimpse of the burned-out windows on the main floor, the charred siding, and the bubbled paint, but I couldn't bring myself to turn around and watch Declan work. To see more of the destruction we had wrought.

The remaining elders of the Fairchild coven, the three children Jasper had kidnapped, and Lark were arrayed on the grass at the edge of the drive. The brownie had positioned herself between the children and our parents. A shimmer of magic danced around her like some sort of protective shield.

"What are you doing?" Dahlia cried out. She stumbled a few steps forward before falling onto the grass. "Where's Jasmine?"

Grey knelt beside his wife, holding her gently. But his gaze was glued to me.

Declan stepped up beside me, brushing his fingers against my hand. I could still feel the magic he'd used sparking off him.

Then Jasmine died.

The magical bonds that Jasper had so painfully crafted between us—the bonds that we had turned against him, twice—snapped. The power of three dissolved.

Pain shot through my chest, ripping my heart asunder. I fell to my knees, screaming.

I was only vaguely aware of Declan doing the same beside me.

Then the pain faded, leaving just a wash of numbness and an ache deep within my bones.

"Jasmine's dead," I whispered, staring down at the pavement between my hands. "Jasmine's dead."

Dahlia shrieked. Grey bowed his head, sobbing. I was aware of the other elders talking, asking questions, but everything was distant.

My hand found Declan's shoulder. Using his strength, I made it to my feet, but he remained kneeling beside me. I wasn't certain why I'd bothered standing, though. I had nowhere to go, nothing I could do.

My mother and father stepped up to my left. Grey half-carried, half-dragged Dahlia to join them.

I didn't understand what they were doing. Attacking us? After all that had happened?

But then Declan rose and took my hand. Violet took my other hand. Forming us into a rough circle.

Unbidden, the magic of the estate rose up, channeling through all of us. Echoing and reinforcing our own personal power and energy, traveling from witch to witch through our joined hands.

Jack slipped between Declan and me. Following some instinct, he pressed his hands to our hips. And I felt the coven magic accept the boy into the loop the others had called forth.

Then to settle that magic—to heal it—the elders, Declan, and Jack unanimously anointed me the head of the Fairchild coven.

And though my heart was a deadened husk, I accepted.

I had already done enough damage by walking away the first time.

Chapter Thirteen

Later, I remembered asking Declan to take the children and me to Rose's. But I didn't remember climbing into a vehicle, or how or when we reached Fairchild Park.

I stood in the darkened ballroom where I had once danced with a vampire, even though there'd been no music. I gazed out at the grounds. I couldn't see the moon, but I knew that the roses contained within their white picket fences would begin to bloom soon.

Afterward, they would fade. Without my Aunt Rose's touch, her gardens would dwindle, until only a brittle skeleton of their former vibrancy remained.

The house around and above me was quiet, everyone asleep within.

I didn't sleep.

Though I wasn't awake.

"You're doing that thing again," Declan said quietly. "Holding your magic too tightly."

I looked away from the paned-glass window, not wholly aware of how I'd come to be curled on the chaise in Rose's office.

Declan was leaning in the doorway. He was wearing his leather jacket as if he was going out.

"How many days has it been?" I asked.

He grimaced, then ran his hand across his face as if doing so would hold all his emotion at bay. "Five."

"The front door of the manor was open," I murmured, returning my gaze to the window and hazily recalling another conversation I'd had with Declan. But whether we'd spoken yesterday or three days before, I didn't know. "When you checked."

"Yes—"

"If she survived, she would have texted by now."

"You don't know—"

"I do. I do know."

"The vampire would have contacted us."

I sighed, laying my head back on the chaise. "He wouldn't."

Declan made a pained noise.

I closed my eyes, denying my need to reach out to him and welcoming the numbness that weighed down my chest. It had cleared momentarily at the sound of Declan's voice, but now I let it take me once again.

"I'll only be gone a few hours," Declan said. "I'm taking Dawn to her grandparents."

I didn't answer. The house would miss the girl's presence ... no, that was a different house ...

"Wisteria?"

I nodded, dutifully offering Declan a smile. "Thank you."

He looked momentarily pained, as if I had knifed him in the chest. Or slit his throat…except doing so to Jasper had appeared to alleviate his suffering…

Declan wasn't standing in the doorway anymore. And I wasn't sure how long he'd been gone.

A simple buffet was laid out in the dining room, most likely courtesy of Lark. The brownie moved through the house like a ghost, her presence felt but unseen. At least by me.

Jack was already seated, watching me as I entered. The other seats around the dark wooden table were empty.

"Good morning," I said.

The boy bobbed his dark head. His deep-blue eyes were wide, watching me as if I might attack him. He was eating cereal, though there were scrambled eggs with cheese, sausages, and pancakes being kept warm on the sideboard.

I fixed a plate, carefully covering the silver chafing dishes, then turned to the table to switch it out for Jack's cereal. The boy looked at me, startled, but he didn't protest. I set his cereal off to the side, within reach if he wanted it. Then I moved the syrup closer to him.

I turned back to the sideboard, pouring myself a steaming cup of coffee from the silver carafe. Jack curled his arm around his plate possessively, shoving scrambled eggs into his mouth.

Declan had eaten like that when he'd first arrived at Fairchild Manor.

A tight spot of pain bloomed in my chest, cutting through my numbed senses. I tried to push it away, but it remained lodged there. I took a sip of coffee. It was too hot to drink, taking a layer of skin off the roof of my mouth. I swallowed my gasp of pain, not wanting to startle Jack any more than I already had.

I turned back to the table. Then, remembering that I was to sit at Jasper's place at the head of it now, I corrected my course dutifully.

Jack had already cleared more than half his plate.

I sipped my coffee, more carefully the second time.

"Declan took Ruby home," Jack said.

"That's good." I was completely aware of how wooden I sounded, but I wasn't certain how to warm my voice. "Her mother ... Coral, and her uncle, Jon, will be happy to see Ruby."

Jack chewed through the last of his sausages.

I sipped my coffee, the burn on the roof of my mouth easing further.

"I have nowhere to go," Jack said quietly, speaking to his empty plate.

"Why would you need to go anywhere?"

He looked up at me and smiled.

The pinch of pain in my heart faded. I smiled back.

Jack was halfway through his second plate and a story I wasn't really following about a basketball game when Grey arrived. My uncle was wearing a light-gray suit, a dark-blue tie, and a white dress shirt. He was also carrying a briefcase, as if he were going to work. And perhaps that was what I was now—to him, to the Fairchild coven. Work. Something to manage, to control.

Jack stopped talking midsentence, dropping his arms into his lap.

"Good morning," Grey said, helping himself to coffee behind me. His words and presence were coated in a false cheeriness and familiarity that cut through the sense of comfort Jack's chatter had created. "Declan texted to say he's—"

"Are you finished your breakfast?" I asked Jack.

He nodded, not meeting my eye. I pushed my chair back, turning to nod politely at Grey. He was staring at me and his coffee had overflowed. He'd added too much cream, still holding the silver creamer over the china mug. Perhaps he was baffled by my cold rebuff, but I didn't have it in me to coddle him, or to deal with whatever was in the briefcase.

"Library?" I asked Jack. Not waiting for an answer or for the boy to follow, I crossed through into the grand entranceway that stood at the heart of the house.

"Did she eat anything?" Grey asked behind me.

I stepped into the library, not hearing Jack's answer.

As I slowly wandered through the library, I was vaguely aware of Grey following me with his coffee and briefcase, and of Jack somewhere behind him. The white-painted shutters were closed to protect the room from direct sun, but I found the dim light comforting.

I ran my fingers along the books in the floor-to-ceiling bookshelves nearest Rose's office, plunking one from the middle and turning it over in my hand to read the cover. *The Talisman* by Stephen King and Peter Straub.

That seemed oddly appropriate. Jack skirted around Grey, who had paused to sip his overly creamed coffee a few steps away. The boy eyed me with a strange mixture of bravado and shyness.

I handed him the book, turning into the office without a word.

Jack followed, curling up in the corner chaise by the window, already bending his head over the book.

Behind me, Grey cleared his throat. I looked away from Jack.

"King? Isn't that a little mature for him?"

"I read it at his age," I said coolly.

Grey didn't answer, gazing at the boy.

"I'm not Jasper, Grey," I said.

That statement shook Jasmine's father out of whatever had been going on in his mind. "Of course not. I...I've drawn up compensation packages, including the trust for Ruby and Dawn, as you requested. Though, honestly, I'm not sure anything is expected—"

"I'm sure you've done well," I said, having no idea what he was talking about or when I'd asked him for anything.

Grey nodded, crossing to place his briefcase on the desk. He reached for a pretty coaster speckled with tiny rosebuds that sat next to the burgundy velvet blotter. Placing his coffee on the coaster, he opened his briefcase and pulled out three intimidatingly thick file folders.

Any energy I'd gained from the coffee and conversation with Jack was immediately drained out of me. "Would you outline the details for me? I'm not certain I have the...energy for reading the entire thing."

"Already done," he said gruffly. "The first page is always a summary of whatever is contained within each folder."

He set the files in the center of the blotter, apparently thinking I should sit down behind the desk to read them.

I awkwardly stepped around the desk, pulling the high-backed, deep-brown leather chair out. But I couldn't bring myself to sit. It felt awkward... wrong. I placed my right hand on the files instead, hoping Grey would leave me in peace if I was polite. "Thank you."

My uncle lowered his voice, leaning slightly toward me. "We haven't found any relatives for Jack."

"He's staying."

"With you?"

"If he wishes."

"Will you be... fostering him? Adopting?"

"Did you draw up formal paperwork when Jasper took Declan off the streets of New Orleans?"

Grey clenched his jaw. "That is... I'm Declan's biological father—"

"But Jasper wasn't."

Grey's lips thinned. He looked away from me. His face was haggard, paler than normal, and with dark circles etched underneath his eyes. Perhaps I should have noticed his state earlier and softened my attitude accordingly, but for some reason, his grief only sharpened my anger.

Because what good was his grief for Jasmine now?

"Would you like to tell me it isn't any of my business?" I asked edgily.

"Everything is your business, Wisteria. Now." He ground the words between clenched teeth.

"When Declan returns, you can take up any more business with him." I settled into the desk chair finally, but only because I was tired of standing. "And he can bring it to me."

Grey looked aghast. "You don't wish... I'm the coven's business advisor and legal counsel."

"But you don't appear to want to be my advisor, Grey. Would you rather Violet or Dahlia was sitting here?"

"No." He turned his light-blue gaze to meet mine. "I would rather have Rose alive and well."

"And I'd rather be having breakfast with Jasmine."

Grey reeled back in response, but he held my gaze despite the obvious pain I'd stoked. Perhaps I'd allowed my anger to sharpen my words more than I should have, but I couldn't bring myself to retract the statement. Doing so would have felt like a betrayal of my love for Jasmine. Even dead, I would defend her to my last breath.

Grey nodded stiffly, looking away from me to gather his thoughts. Then he reached across the desk to open the top file. "I'll need the financial and property documents signed first. You need to be in control of the money before I can execute any settlement packages. Fortunately, Rose willed her part of the estate directly to you, including this property, with some cash set aside for Declan." Then he hesitated, rubbing his hand across his forehead.

Rose would have set money aside for Jasmine as well. But Grey couldn't bring himself to say it.

I stared down at the page before me, seeing nothing of the words typed across it.

Grey cleared his throat. "Jasper willed his entire estate to you as well, though the coven stripped him of most of his property."

"Thirteen years ago," I said wryly.

He grimaced, then nodded. "If you have any questions, please let me know. There are funeral...a memorial arrangement for Rose to be discussed."

"Not for Jasmine?"

"We were thinking of...hoping for a private ceremony. Contractors need to be brought in to shore up the house before we can conduct a proper search..."

I nodded, pushing the thought away to be dealt with later. I hadn't mentioned the deal I'd forged with Kett while Jasmine was dying, not knowing whether or not the vampire had succeeded in remaking my cousin. Not knowing if the coven would accept her if she had survived.

And either way, there would be no body to find. Kett wouldn't have left Jasmine behind.

Rose and Jasper would need to be exhumed, though. Unless I just had the house bulldozed over them ...

"And you'll need to meet with the Convocation," Grey said, pulling me from my dark thoughts.

"A few times, I imagine," I said wryly. "Though Declan must have already taken care of most of it, regarding the children?"

"No. For the seat. You do intend to occupy it?"

I frowned. I hadn't thought about that. I was fairly certain that doing so would make me the youngest member of the Convocation, maybe by decades.

"Perhaps ... " Grey started to speak, then trailed off.

"Since you apparently want to be my advisor ... "—I waved my hand across the files on Rose's desk—"... speak your mind."

"Perhaps you'd have a conversation with Dahlia?"

"About joining the Convocation? She'd be interested?"

He tilted his head thoughtfully. "Not today. And not tomorrow."

"But being occupied is a good thing."

Grey pinned me with his gaze, and for the first time I could see some of Declan's features in his jaw and cheekbones. "Being needed. Being useful."

"The Fairchild seat on the Convocation should be occupied by someone prepared to speak for the entire coven. Not just the members she chooses to acknowledge."

Grey nodded. "Hence the conversation you need to have."

"Shall I order her to be kind to Declan?"

"I believe kindness might be difficult to demand...but we..." He swallowed harshly. "We elders are all aware that we almost lost all three of you, and we couldn't...we couldn't..." His voice cracked. He turned away, pacing across the width of the office.

"Jasper was very powerful," I whispered, but I wasn't certain whether I was speaking to myself or to Grey. Either way, it didn't exonerate any of us.

He nodded without looking at me.

Jack turned a page of his book, then mumbled something to himself. His tone was tense, excited. I didn't remember the story in enough detail to guess at what had intrigued him so much.

Grey shifted his shoulders, perhaps steeling himself to continue dealing with me.

I knew I was being cold—even unfeeling, and to the point of being cruel. But I just couldn't seem to get a handle on myself. And the more days that passed, the more I welcomed the numbness.

I reached for the first file folder, pulling it closer and scanning the overview page clipped at the front.

Grey crossed around the desk to stand beside me. As I read, he quietly clarified anything I hesitated over.

I grew quickly tired of signing my name. But I'd made my choices, and I was caught within the consequences. Walking away wasn't really an option.

I wasn't certain it ever had been.

I found my Dior briefcase and navy blue trench coat hanging in my closet. Both were pristine, retrieved and cleaned by Lark from the destruction of the manor, but I wasn't

going to need either for the quick trip I had planned into Seattle. I could have hired someone to pack up my apartment
and ship my things to Rose's, but I hadn't left the property
in three weeks.

I checked my case, pulling out the candles and the
extra reconstruction cubes. I wouldn't need either of them.

Then I brushed against something gritty at the bottom
of the bag.

I pulled my hand out. My fingers were covered in ash.

My legs gave out. I sat down hard in the center of the
walk-in closet, dumping the contents of the bag onto the
floor.

The ash I'd encountered fell out in a cohesive clump.
It hadn't touched my wallet. No trace of it coated my lip
gloss or my phone.

I stirred my fingers within it, feeling the residual
magic—and knowing that if I called a reconstruction forth,
I'd be able to see the ash reforming into the contract with
the Conclave.

But had it turned to ash because the contract was now
fulfilled? Or because it had been nullified? What if Kett and
Jasmine were now nothing but ash themselves underneath
the marble stairs of Fairchild Manor?

A sob ripped through me, then forced itself out. I
choked down a second wave of pain, clenching my jaw
against the onslaught of grief.

Then I shakily stood up, leaving the bag and its contents for Lark to tidy once more.

Declan climbed onto the jet, storming through the galley as
if he was claiming his territory. I was already belted into the

middle seat, and had been about to inquire why we hadn't taken off yet. The steward shut the door behind Declan, and the plane lurched into motion.

"Were you going to mention you were leaving?" Declan growled. He threw himself into a seat in front of me, then swiveled it to face me.

I frowned, certain that I had actually done so before leaving Rose's house. I glanced back at the hangar as the jet turned onto the runway, seeing Declan's Jeep parked to one side.

"Where's Jack?" I asked.

"He has Lark. That was good enough for us at his age."

Declan was watching me too closely, scanning my face over and over again. I didn't know what he was looking for. I didn't know what he was hoping to find. So I turned away, looking out the other window as the jet gained momentum. I should have called the steward and asked to have our takeoff canceled, delaying my trip long enough to get Jack. Except I just couldn't push past the numbness and make the decision to act.

Declan slumped back in his seat with a sigh. "I asked him if he wanted to come or if he wanted to stay with Grey and Dahlia. He chose to stay."

"With Grey and Dahlia?" I said sharply. "Because they raised you and Jasmine so well?"

Declan leaned forward, eyeing me closely again. "Why would that be a concern? If you're only going for three days? That's what you had Grey book the plane for, isn't it? Or were you planning to alter your flight plan after takeoff?"

I looked away from him. Again. I was just so tired. It hurt to talk. To think. To form thoughts into sentences.

The jet took off, soaring into the clear blue sky. Once it leveled off, Declan thrust himself out of his seat, pacing the aisle back and forth.

"I'm sorry," I whispered. "I just don't have it in me to soothe you right now, Declan."

That stopped his restless movement. "Soothe me? Soothe me?" He reached out, allowing his hand to hover before me. "You need to let us soothe you, Wisteria."

I shook my head. "The contract turned to ash," I whispered.

Declan withdrew his hand, sitting down. His gaze was steady on me. "That's why Ember couldn't find any copies in the vaults of Sherwood and Pine," he murmured. "Like you said, yes? It must be part of the magic. Damn xeno-phobic vampires."

I nodded, though I couldn't remember the witch law-yer offering up that detail, or me relaying the information to Declan.

"Have you texted him?" he asked.

I frowned, suddenly uncertain as to where I'd left my phone. Uncertain whether or not it had even been charged. Something about that was stupid...because Jasmine might have texted. Kett might have texted. I reached to undo my seatbelt, ready to race up to the cabin and demand that the pilot turn the jet around.

But then I remembered that Jasmine had Declan's number. She would have texted her brother if she hadn't heard back from me. I let my hands fall to my sides.

Declan sighed raggedly.

Silence stretched between us.

"I'm not running away," I finally said.

"I don't care if you're running, Wisteria," he said. "You have every right to run. I'm just coming with you if you go."

My heart pinched. And for one terrible, breathless mo-ment, I found myself wishing I could take him up on the offer. Then the pinch of pain, and the glimmer of hope that had come with it, faded until I was numb again.

We didn't speak much more for the remainder of the five-and-a-half-hour flight.

A large jasmine plant was perched in the kitchen window of my apartment, speckled with white flowers. I stopped dead in my tracks, staring at it dumbly. Declan was still in the entranceway, collecting the mail that had accumulated while I'd been gone.

The apartment was sparkling clean, of course, thanks to Lark. But I didn't keep plants. I didn't spend enough time in any one place to grow them.

I stepped forward, raising a shaky hand to pluck a thick white card out from between the leaves of the plant. A sweet aroma wafted toward me as I disturbed the flowers.

Jasmine's B-cubed tattoo was meticulously drawn onto the two-inch-by-three-inch card. The word *Forever* was written underneath. The handwriting was heavy, severely denting the paper. Almost as if she wasn't certain of her strength anymore.

Jasmine.

Jasmine's handwriting.

Jasmine's tattoo, immortalizing our childhood fantasy of being Betty-Sue, Betty-Lou, and Bubba. Of being together with our perfect house and garden…

I stumbled away from the kitchen, crossing blindly through the living room into my second bedroom.

"Wisteria?" Declan called after me, concerned.

I stopped in the doorway, scanning the room. The Murphy bed was folded up, my Pilates apparatus tucked against the wall.

And Jasmine's boxes were gone.

Declan pressed up behind me, scanning the room over my head.

I swayed into him, choking out a sob. "She's alive. Declan, she's alive." I spun, pressing the card into his hands.

He stared at it for a long moment, rubbing his thumb across the image of the tattoo. Then he lifted his tear-filled gaze to meet mine. "Well," he said wryly. "She's not dead."

I laughed, just to force myself not to cry. I reached up, pressing my hands to his face, feeling his warmth, seeing glints of his magic in his golden-hazel eyes.

He stared down at me, as if he couldn't look anywhere else.

Joy flooded through my chest. Lifting up on my toes, I wrapped my arms around Declan's shoulders, knowing he'd been waiting for weeks, even months for me to do so.

He kissed me, brushing his lips across mine tenderly.

"Declan," I whispered.

"I missed you," he said.

"I'm here."

"Don't leave me again. I couldn't bear it."

"I won't."

"Let me give you a life," he said, his voice cracking with barely contained emotion. "I know I can't offer you what he did..."

"Who? Kett?"

"You've been mourning him, haven't you?"

I laughed quietly. "No. How could I mourn the eternal? Kett hasn't left me. I was just so, so afraid that Jasmine had."

"I don't mind sharing your heart with the both of them. I know you're booked for the next lifetime, but I'll take this one. Will you share it with me?"

"It was always yours."

Declan and I made it into my bedroom, already half unclothed. We stayed in bed for hours, remembering each other, learning who we were and what we wanted as adults. Then the sky darkened and murmured thoughts of food began to intrude.

Stretched out across Declan's warm chest, his rough fingers stroking long passes down my back, my gaze settled on Jasmine's card. Despite our rush to be intimately connected, to celebrate Jasmine's existence by cementing the bond between us, I had carefully placed the hand-drawn tattoo on the bedside table. The white of the card stock caught in the moonlight flooding in through the windows.

The *Forever* inscription was a promise Jasmine could now keep. A promise she would keep.

Lying there, completely satisfied but oddly awake, I realized that I'd taken a step toward a future unfettered by the past, or by any obligations inflicted upon me by outside forces.

Whether or not I would head the Fairchild coven. Whether or not I'd choose to stay in Seattle. It was my future, defined only by myself and with Declan. The echoes of the past would fade away, replaced by the new moments of magic we'd create.

We three. Beyond death. *Forever*.

Acknowledgements

With thanks to:

My story & line editor
Scott Fitzgerald Gray

My proofreader
Pauline Nolet

My beta readers
Terry Daigle, Angela Flannery, Gael Fleming,
Desi Hartzel, and Heather Lewis.

**For their continual encouragement,
feedback, & general advice**
Megan Gayeski–for the Chicago weather report
John and Louise Croall–for finding niggling errors
SFWA
The Office

Meghan Ciana Doidge is an award-winning writer based out of Salt Spring Island, British Columbia, Canada. She has a penchant for bloody love stories, superheroes, and the supernatural. She also has a thing for chocolate, potatoes, and cashmere yarn.

NOVELS
After the Virus
Spirit Binder
Time Walker
Cupcakes, Trinkets, and Other Deadly Magic (Dowser 1)
Trinkets, Treasures, and Other Bloody Magic (Dowser 2)
Treasures, Demons, and Other Black Magic (Dowser 3)
I See Me (Oracle 1)
Shadows, Maps, and Other Ancient Magic (Dowser 4)
Maps, Artifacts, and Other Arcane Magic (Dowser 5)
I See You (Oracle 2)
Artifacts, Dragons, and Other Lethal Magic (Dowser 6)
I See Us (Oracle 3)
Catching Echoes (Reconstructionist 1)
Tangled Echoes (Reconstructionist 2)
Unleashed Echoes (Reconstructionist 3)

NOVELLAS/SHORTS
Love Lies Bleeding
The Graveyard Kiss (Reconstructionist 0.5)
Dawn Bytes (Reconstructionist 1.5)
An Uncut Key (Reconstructionist 2.5)

For recipes, giveaways, news, and glimpses of upcoming stories, please connect with Meghan on her:
Personal blog, www.madebymeghan.ca
Twitter, @mcdoidge
Facebook, Meghan Ciana Doidge
Email, info@madebymeghan.ca

Please also consider leaving an honest review at your point of sale outlet.

OTHER BOOKS BY MEGHAN CIANA DOIDGE

WWW.MADEBYMEGHAN.CA